THE PARTI

MRS. NICHOLAS VAYNE, *widow of oil magnate, who loves jades and Chinese houses*
EUGENE VAYNE, *her not always admirable son*
FAITH VAYNE, *nee Kingston, wife of Eugene*
LYDIA KROLL, *Mrs Vayne's married daughter, who reads tea leaves*
JASPER KROLL, *Lydia's husband*
JETHRO COGGIN, *Mrs Vayne's secretary*
GOBLIN, *a descendant of aristocratic ancestors*
MICHAEL FRY, *the Vayne chauffeur*
WING, WENG and WONG, *Chinese servants*
EIICHI KAWABE, *Japanese gardener*
KERRY O'CONNOR, *who lived to tell the inside story of the Sino-Japanese war*
DR. LIAO PO-CHING, *a visitor from Peking*
MADAME WU, *a lady of much mystery*
PEARL BLOSSOM, *the lady's maid*
F. C. LEE, *dealer in Oriental art objects*
CHARLES LEE, *his son*
CORAL FRY, *related to one of the above*
MR. and MRS. MYRON HAWKINS, *formerly of Frowning Plains*
ADRIENNE LAUNAY, *an old acquaintance of Westborough's*
CAPTAIN M. P. COLLINS *and Sergeant James Webber, Homicide Bureau, City of Los Angeles Police Department*
CAPTAIN ALBERT CRANSTON, *Bureau of Investigation, Sheriff's Department, Los Angeles County, and*
THEOCRITUS LUCIUS WESTBOROUGH, *authority on Roman history*

Reader Take Warning: Eskins, Rawley, Anderson, Olie, Yee Feh-lu and the district attorney are positively non-guilty.

The Vayne estate exists only in fancy, but why should I attempt to conceal from my readers that there is a city called Los Angeles? There are also cities called Peking and Tientsin, and what happened to the latter on the afternoon of July 29, 1937, is, regrettably, history. I have mentioned Ch'ien Lung and K'ang Hsi, Manchu emperors, and there was in the eighteenth century a King Bodawpaya of Burma. Other characters are fictitious, and the nonexistent beings herein depicted do solely in the writer's imagination kill, hate, steal, get drunk, make love or perform their sundry other acts. If the name of an actual person is used it is due to bad luck and coincidence. Shall we get on with the story?

C.B.C.

In the Theocritus Lucius Westborough canon:

The Fifth Tumbler, 1936
The Death Angel, 1936
Blind Drifts, 1937
The Purple Parrot, 1937
The Man from Tibet, 1938
The Whispering Ear, 1938
Murder Gone Minoan, 1939
(English title: *Clue to the Labyrinth*)
Dragon's Cave, 1940
Poison Jasmine, 1940
Green Shiver, 1941

Green Shiver

by Clyde B. Clason
Introduction by Tom & Enid Schantz

Rue Morgue Press
Lyons / Boulder

Green Shiver
0-915230-97-6
978-0-915230-97-6
was first published in 1941.

New material in this edition
Copyright © 2006 by
The Rue Morgue Press

Printed by
Johnson Printing

About Clyde B. Clason

CLYDE B. CLASON'S career as a mystery writer took up only five of his 84 years, but in the short span between 1936 and 1941 he produced ten long and very complicated detective novels, all published by the prestigious Doubleday, Doran Crime Club, featuring the elderly historian Professor Theocritus Lucius Westborough.

Born in Denver in 1903, Clason spent many years in Chicago, the setting for several of his novels, includinghis most famous work, *The Man from Tibet*, before moving to York, Pennsylvania, where he died in 1987. During his early years in Chicago Clason worked as an advertising copywriter and a trade magazine editor, producing books on architecture, period furniture and one book on writing, *How To Write Stories that Sell*. Clason stopped selling mysteries on the eve of World War II, although he published several other books, including *Ark of Venus* (1955), a science fiction novel, and *I am Lucifer* (1960), the confessions of the devil as told to Clason. He also produced several nonfiction works dealing with astronomy as well as *The Delights of the Slide Rule* (1964), his last published book-length work.

Clason left the crime fiction genre never to return, primarily because the postwar mystery fiction world was dominated by what he called the sex and violence school popularized by writers such as Mickey Spillane. He believed that readers—or at least publishers—were no longer interested in his thoughtful and leisurely tales of detection. Indeed, he went so far as to ignore his copyright renewals, figuring that no one would ever be interested in reprinting his books. Yet, long after they went out of print his books remained popular with readers and have always fetched premium prices in the antiquarian book trade, though those prices were partly inflated because the jacket art was the work of the noted artist Boris Artzybasheff. And modern critics, though taking the occasional potshot at his sometimes florid prose (more evident in his earliest books), still commend him on his research and ability to construct convincing locked room puzzles.

Indeed, seven of Clason's ten Westborough mysteries feature locked rooms or impossible crimes. Along with John Dickson Carr and Clayton Rawson, Clason was a leading exponent of this very popular subgenre, with locked room mystery connoisseur Robert C.S. Adey referring to the Westborough canon as being among "the more memorable" entries in this narrow field. Adey had special praise for *The Man from Tibet*, calling it a "well-written. . . above average golden-age novel" that was "genuinely interesting, and well researched," and citing its "highly original and practical locked-room murder method."

Other contemporary critics also looked upon this short-lived series with approval. Howard Haycraft, the genre's first major historian, predicted that Clason was on the brink of becoming a mainstay of readers, while two-time Edgar-winning critic James Sandoe listed *The Man from Tibet* in his *Readers' Guide to Crime*, a 1946 compilation of required titles for libraries, noting that this, as well as other Westborough titles, appeared frequently on the lists submitted to him by other critics for inclusion in his guide. Modern critics like Bill Pronzini and Jon L. Breen have also offered kind retrospective reviews of Clason's work, although they disagreed on the merits of at least one of his books, with Pronzini praising *Blind Drifts* (1937) for its "particularly neat and satisfying variation on (the locked-room) theme," while Breen said "the plot is farfetched and overelaborate, and the killer stands out rather obviously." Both critics, however, were impressed with Clason's research in this book in describing the operation of a Colorado gold mine. Breen was far more enthusiastic about *The Man from Tibet*, listing it as one of the 25 best amateur detective books in Max Allan Collins' 2000 *History of Mystery*.

Research was obviously a passion with Clason, who certainly felt the need to provide his readers with an accurate portrait of Tibet, a country whose borders were closed to foreigners and whose religion, a form of Buddhism, was then little-known in this country. Purists might have objected to the amount of space Clason devoted to educating his readers but they can't fault the skill with which he works the fruits of his research into the narrative. Such scholarship is evident in other titles as well, including *Murder Gone Minoan* (1939), in which Clason recreates an ancient civilization on an island off the California coast, or *Green Shiver* (1941), his last mystery, in which the reader learns a great deal about Chinese jade and culture.

Murder Gone Minoan also showcases the author's love of literary quotations. Westborough (and others) throw a bit from Shakespeare or Browning or Homer into their conversations whenever given the chance. Yet, these lines are far from mere window dressing and the reader would be well advised not to ignore this seemingly inconsequential banter. Very little of what Clason incorporates into his books is without motive. This was the age of "fair play" detection and Clason was a master of the form, planting clues and hints for the reader on practically every page.

Clason's narrative skills were not inconsiderable, although modern readers might wish that his characters could deliver their lines with more "he saids" or "she askeds" than with such Tom Swifty's as "he choked" or "he opined." On the other hand, it's somewhat refreshing to read a mystery in which ejaculations refer only to exclamations of speech.

Like other mystery writers of the day, Clason was not above inserting a little romance into his stories. In the crime novels of that era—Georgette Heyer's mysteries spring immediately to mind—such romantic entanglements were actually useful in helping the reader sort out potential murder suspects. If you could figure out which two young people would eventually find their star-crossed way to each other, you could automatically eliminate two suspects from your list. A wise reader of *Green Shiver* would do well to sort out such relationships. On the other hand, Westborough, like many other central characters of the period, seems if not asexual, at least beyond or above such temptations.

Unlike many other mystery novels of the time, Clason's books are remarkably free of racial prejudice, at least on the part of the ever-rational Westborough, who on more than one occasion gently rebukes his companions for expressing racist sentiments. In *The Man from Tibet* he even manages to find a kind word or two (their foreign policy notwithstanding) to say about the Japanese, who were at the time plundering most of their neighbors in a dress rehearsal for World War II. However, Clason recognized that anti-Japanese sentiment was rampant among most Americans of the late 1930s. Westborough's best friend, Lt. Mack, has little use for "Japs" and when the two visit a Chicago Japanese restaurant for lunch, Clason subtly mentions that the place is nearly empty. Anti-Japanese sentiment is even more evident in *Green Shiver*, published in the year that would end with the sneak attack on Pearl Harbor. Yet, even given that climate, Westborough himself (unlike other characters) refrains from making any racial or ethnic slurs, while still painting a vivid portrait of a time when American Chinese are going to great lengths to insure that they are not mistaken for Japanese Americans.

Too often modern critics excuse writers of the 1930s, such as Agatha Christie or Dorothy L. Sayers, for fostering racial prejudice or anti-Semitic views, by jokingly dismissing complaints about such lapses as runaway political correctness. What these apologists forget is that while it may be acceptable and even necessary for an author to show that such views were commonplace at the time (as Clason does), the authorial expression of such views is never acceptable. Take for example, Bruce Hamilton's 1930 English mystery, *To Be Hanged* (much praised by those two great snobs of crime fiction, Jacques Barzun and Wendell Hertig Taylor), in which a very minor—and very disagreeable—character is offhandedly described in the narrative as a "little Jew." It is to Clason's great credit that he was able, in the words of Ruth Rendell, to fulfill "the duty of the artist in rising above the petty prejudices of the day."

Like other fair-play mysteries of the day, Clason's books tend to end very abruptly once the murderer is revealed. Yet, even some of his biggest fans, like Pronzini, suggest that his books could have been improved by some judicious editing to cut their length from 80,000 words to 65,000. On the other hand, 80,000 or more words was the rule rather than the exception in the mysteries of Clason's era. It was not until World War II, when paper restrictions prompted publishers to use lighter paper and to cram more words on a page, that the length of a typical mystery was reduced to 60,000 words. This will fill 192 pages, the number needed to make up six 32-page signatures, a very economical size book to produce. This has remained the standard until quite recently, and it wasn't so long ago that Dodd, Mead cut—without explanation or editing to make sense—a major character from a Wendy Hornsby mystery just to ensure that the book did not exceed 192 pages.

Today, however, publishers are once again looking for bigger books, especially with "breakout" or bestselling authors, and a number of books in the crime fiction field have suffered from this verbal bloating. P.D. James, for example, started out writing tightly crafted gems, but most of her books after *An Unsuitable Job for a Woman* (1972) bog down in endless details about the contents of suitcases or in long pieces of melancholy introspection by her leading characters.

Clyde B. Clason may have occasionally waxed poetic over the Southern California landscape or Asian culture, but he stayed away from the kind of pretentious drivel that pads many modern mysteries. Indeed, it's his asides into Tibetan customs, or Chinese jade, or the working of a gold mine, as well as his unobtrusive social commentary, that make his books as appealing to today's readers as they were to those of the pre-World War II era, even if his plots, characters and prose are decidedly old-fashioned. However abbrreviated his writing career may have been, he still left behind a remarkable body of work.

Tom & Enid Schantz
Lyons, Colorado
Autumn 2003
Revised August 2006

CONTENTS

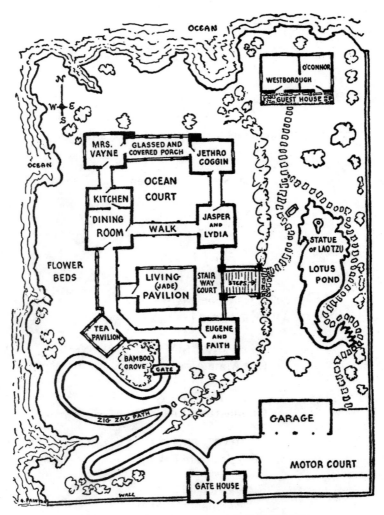

GROUND PLAN OF VAYNE ESTATE

PART ONE: INTRODUCTIONS IN A CHINESE COURTYARD

THE CAULDRON was already bubbling. Toil and trouble were even then being brewed in a witches' crucible, but of that elderly Mr. Westborough knew nothing when, on a Monday morning, he first entered Jocasta Vayne's remarkable vermilion gate.

His pilgrimage to the Screen of Heaven began with disarming normality. Standing in the road where his host had deposited him, Westborough paused briefly to reconnoiter. The hesitation was characteristic of the mild little scholar, who seldom crossed a threshold with the assurance to which his white hairs and accomplishments entitled him. He noted (it was one of his habits to observe carefully) that the gray stone wall towered at least three feet higher than the seven-foot father of Confucius; that the gatehouse was a two-story structure of indigo tiles, gilded beam ends and an uptilted roof; that the gate's ponderous vermilion leaves were adorned by black lacquer circular characters. These he recognized as the Chinese symbols for luck and longevity and reflected that on neither score did he personally have grounds for complaint.

The gate stood slightly ajar. Sauntering through the massive portal, Westborough found himself in a short tunnel. A narrow table was jammed tightly against one wall, and beside this sat a black-haired Chinese in a white house coat.

"You want to go in? Two dollar, please."

"A reasonable charge." Westborough fumbled for his billfold.

"Help homeless Chinese, Missy Vayne say."

"I am very glad, indeed, to contribute to so worthy a cause."

The gatekeeper answered, "Missy Vayne say lite name in book."

The book rested on the table by the gatekeeper's chair. It resembled an old-fashioned hotel register. Doubtless, Westborough mused as he examined it, the early morning hour explained why he had been preceded by only one visitor, a Kerry O'Connor, who represented himself as stopping at the Biltrich Hotel in Los Angeles. The historian unscrewed the cap of his fountain pen. The Irish name was tantalizingly familiar, but he was, for the moment at least, unable to name the circumstances under which he had previously heard it. This troubled him: failure to recall is one of the slight signs which herald approaching senility. Dear, dear, dear! He did hope his dotage was many years in the future yet. His handwriting being naturally cramped, he contrived to squeeze "Theocritus L. Westborough, Chicago; c/o J. Launay, Palmas Peninsula, Calif.," into a single line.

"Take left-side path, see jade. Savvy?"

"Savvy perfectly," Westborough replied. Emerging from the porte-cochere, if one might properly apply that term to the passageway, he beheld one of those enchantingly intricate Chinese gardens. A magnificent specimen it was, with pond and hill, pavilions and groves. A railed footpath branched from the auto drive. That it was a winding path goes without saying. It traced a zigzag line to the cluster of blue-roofed buildings on the hilltop.

The slopes were gentle. The morning sun had not yet attained an unduly calorific vigor. The sea air was saltily stimulating. In short the walk promised to be one of unalloyed pleasure. Fuchsias bloomed in tiny bells of white and rose, violet and scarlet. Behind the first curve was a wishing well, guarded by a placid bronze Buddha. Westborough remembered the delightful Chinese dictum that every bend in a garden walk must disclose a fresh surprise. The next turn revealed a life-size crane painted in natural colors. Presently he was in a bamboo grove; the bamboos were thin and sparse, conforming to another gardening dictum of the Middle Kingdom. His memory, secretly working on the assignment in the quiet way of memories, startled him by belatedly producing the information he had asked of it.

Kerry O'Connor was the young war correspondent who had written *Bombs and Bayonets*. Could it be possible? What rare pleasure! Westborough's elation quickly vanished. There were probably other Kerry O'Connors, and this, life being as disappointing as it is, was probably one of them. Ambling beneath the peaked roof of a doorless gateway, he entered into a Chinese courtyard.

It was an odd residence for the Occident: a group of single-room, one-story pavilions connected by covered walks. Each little house had walls of glazed blue-gray bricks and Prussian-blue roof tiles. All of the eaves turned gracefully upward, in accordance with a Chinese belief of unknown antiquity that evil spirits are deflected thereby. All the beams supporting the roofs extended through the outer walls, and all beam ends were ornately decorated. Except for minor details, such as glass windows in place of rice paper, the compound might have been whisked miraculously from Peking.

The separate edifices were grouped around open courts in true Celestial tradition. A sign's painted arrow directed the visitor to a large central pavilion. Westborough took a few steps forward. Through the open door was revealed a breathtaking rainbow of jade.

There were so many greens that the vegetable world was soon exhausted of names: lettuce, moss, apple, grass, spinach, olive … There were greens laced with white in the exquisite blendings the Chinese term "pine-on-snow." There were glistening snow-white jadeites and cloudy "mutton-fat" nephrites. There were mauves and purples from Burma; yellows, pinks and reds from Turkestan. And there were orchid, rose, lavender, varied browns, pale to deep grays, baby blue, sky blue, turquoise, indigo and inky black. How matchless is jade, the heavenly substance! With what consummate artistry had the natural stone been transformed!

Crowded together upon tables and cabinets were rouge pots, sweetmeat boxes, incense burners, vases, flower baskets, earrings, pendants, bracelets, snuff bottles in assorted shapes and sizes and butterfly hairpins. Westborough, at his first inspection, had eyes for only a few of the many pieces. An architecturally complete pagoda under a foot high. A Taoist longevity mountain. A jade boat, black as the plumage of a black swan, which had cabin and mast and sails and oarsmen.

Writing implements were represented by brushes, boxes for ink slabs, a small desk screen to conceal the scribe's face while he worked, polished spheres the size of walnuts to keep Chinese fingers supple for the exacting art of calligraphy. The visitor paused beside a tablet with which a proud courtier had once covered his mouth lest his ignoble breath offend the nostrils of the Son of Heaven. He turned to regard a bouquet of all-jade narcissuses blooming in a white jade bowl. But all of these articles, though some were miracles of patient labor, were secondary to the celebrated "Screen of Heaven."

It had been designed for an emperor, the tall, haggard K'ang Hsi, whose sacred edict proclaimed that while it was a small matter to starve it was a great one to lose one's virtue. Its height was six feet. The wooden framework supported a mosaic depicting the Jade Palace of the Jade Emperor on the Jade Mountain by the Jade Lake near which grows the Jade Tree of Immortality. The buildings with their curling roofs, the streams, bridges and the long-robed men and women who sauntered upon the terraces were all formed by colored insets of jade. The monetary value was incalculable.

"Please do not touch the pieces on display,: someone was caution in a queer, hoarse whisper. Westborough, whose besetting sin was curiosity, immediately turned his head.

The speaker was a tall, middle-aged man with nose glasses and a rabbit face. He was addressing a tall young man, who was just replacing an object on a cabinet.

"Sorry," the latter apologized. "Do you mind telling where this particular number came from?"

"It was included among the pieces which Mrs. Vayne brought back with her from China."

"Mrs. Vayne? Then it can't be the same. And yet ..."

The young man was broad at the shoulders, narrow at the waist. His hair was of the shade described by such adjectives as auburn, carroty and brick red. There were freckles under his tan, and his eyes were gray green. If his name were not an Irish one he should have been heartily ashamed.

Westborough wondered if he were Kerry O'Connor, *the* Kerry O'Connor, and if a meeting could be arranged in the absence of a mutual acquaintance to perform the rites of introduction. The elderly historian sometimes carried modesty to Confucian extremes.

"And yet the lady's crown *is* broken." The young man's forehead had knitted in a puzzled manner. "May I speak to Mrs. Vayne, please?"

Rabbit-Face replied, "You may state your business to me. I am Mrs. Vayne's secretary."

"Where did Mrs. Vayne pick up the queen with the broken crown?"

"Not a queen. A Taoist goddess."

"Whatever she is, where did Mrs. Vayne buy her?"

"Do you mean Mrs. Nicholas Vayne?"

"She owns all this junk, doesn't she?"

"Mrs. Nicholas Vayne is the owner of the collection," the secretary corrected pompously.

"Then I want to talk to her."

"I do not believe she is receiving visitors today."

"What's she giving this show for if she doesn't want to see people?" the younger man snapped in exasperation. "I'm Kerry O'Connor. Tell her that. I wrote a book called *Bombs and Bayonets*. Maybe she's heard of it. Some people even seem to have read it—not that I can furnish affidavits."

He was *the* Kerry O'Connor after all, Westborough cogitated. The time, however, did not appear to be a propitious one for a stranger to introduce himself.

"I'm sorry, Mr. O'Connor, but I cannot tell her at present. I am not able to leave the pavilion."

"It's done with the legs." (It was quite evident that the rabbit-faced man was no cripple.) "Try it, anyway. A little practice and you may be able to walk all right."

"I cannot leave the pavilion unwatched."

O'Connor laughed. "I won't take the whole collection."

"It would be gross negligence for me to leave." The secretary seemed to be suffering from some kind of vocal impediment which forced him always to whisper.

"Tsk, tsk, tsk! Try calling her on the telephone."

"I'm sorry, there is no telephone."

"No telephone in the house?"

"None in this particular pavilion."

Shrugging, O'Connor acknowledged defeat. "You win, Mr.—"

"Coggin," the other supplied.

"Coggin, is it? A good name. Will you deliver a note from me to Mrs. Vayne?"

"Certainly, Mr. O'Connor."

"Thanks, Mr. Coggin."

Taking a card from his pocket case, the redhead began to write. Westborough transferred his attention to a jade tree, an excellent example of the high standard of craftsmanship attained by the Sons of Han. Leaves of moss-green jade were wired to colored metal branches while the fruits were formed of polished marbles of carnelian, amber and amethyst. A remarkable piece of work!

Only half of his mind was regarding it, however. The other half continued to wonder whether it would be advisable to attempt to strike up an acquaintanceship with Mr. O'Connor. Probably not. One of Westborough's frail, thin hands meditatively stroked his small chin. It was unlikely that Mr. O'Connor was in the mood to converse with a man old enough to be his grandfather. Confucius had an observation to apply: "In manhood doing nothing worthy and living on to useless old age: this is to be a pest."

Raising his eyes from the jade tree, Westborough became aware of the attractive young woman in a green tweed suit who was standing on the threshold. She was of medium height, rather slender, with a very fair skin and soft light brown hair. Seeing her, Kerry O'Connor stopped his writing.

He stood marble still, and so did she. For an instant it seemed as if a high-voltage current, arcing the gap between man and woman, had struck them both into lifeless immobility. Then O'Connor marched forward.

"Faith!" he said, and the Irish expletive was eloquent. "Let's get out of here."

She followed him through the door as helplessly as a somnambulist. Her face was stunned, dazed, apathetic. Westborough was unable to find the exact shade of expression in words.

II

She gazed silently at the flower beds which sloped the brief distance to the edge of the cliff fronting the Pacific, a hundred or so feet below. She had the same gentle dignity as of old. The same delicate poise of the head, the same little trick of cupping her left hand about the softly rounded chin. Kerry O'Connor became conscious of the beat of his heart.

Not since the Shanghai disaster of August '37 had that normally well-behaved organ set the blood racing through his veins with such wild abandon. "I'm a fool," he said. (Or a romantic Irishman, which came to the same thing.) "I could have written, having your father's address if not your own, but I didn't. Pride's silly, Faith, but we're made the way we are. Since——"

He saw that several people were just entering under the roofed gate to the compound: a man and woman who looked like retired Main Streeters and a gray-haired Chinese in a frock coat. "Might as well be at the World's Fair," O'Connor grumbled. A breeze from the sea ruffled the light brown hair about her temples. "Damn it!" he exploded impetuously. "It doesn't cost anything to be polite. You might at least say you're glad to see me."

She didn't answer—obviously because the Gopher Prairie-ites had already reached them. "Even if you're not," he added in an undertone. The elderly Chinese smiled in cheerful friendliness as he passed. "*Chi ko fan mo?*" O'Connor asked him. He bowed silent acknowledgment of the greeting and disappeared within the pavilion where the jade was being shown.

"Take me where we can talk in private," O'Connor ordered. His companion moved listlessly to the left. "You're like a banshee," he observed. "A woman of the hills. There's one in the O'Connor family—saw her myself once."

She wasn't frowning, and that encouraged him to continue.

"She has blue eyes like yours and wears a green dress the color of that suit you've got on. And she wrings her hands and looks mournful. Faith, just the way you're looking now."

She returned no comment. Pausing before one of the little pavilions, she turned the doorknob. Inside he saw a cozy little room with sliding windows on three sides. The bamboo shades were rolled three quarters up, exposing gorgeous views of ocean, flower beds and a bamboo grove. The furniture was lacquered: vermilion and gold designs over a bright-green ground. As she waited for him by the entrance her face suddenly altered its expression. Fear, he saw, had abruptly superimposed itself.

"I won't bite you," he said, glancing casually toward a cabinet on which rested an electric hot plate and a polished brass kettle. "Nice little place here. What's it called?"

"The tea pavilion," she answered in a soft, weak voice. Those three words, it struck him, were the first of any kind she had addressed to him since their meeting among the jades. She was cringing against the wall, helpless as a fly in a spider web, too terrified even to run away. And, watching the shame of cowardice, he endeavored to conceal his contempt.

"You needn't be afraid of me, Faith. What's done is done. Why I should have wanted to find out what became of you I don't know. It was the article in yesterday's paper about the Vayne jades that decided me, I suppose. Pushed me over the boundary line, you might say. In there"—he jerked his thumb toward the larger pavilion—"I ran straight into the little Taoist lady with the broken crown. What's her name? Let's hear you give it in Chinese?"

"P'i-hsia Yüan-chün," she replied, forcing herself to smile.

"Still got the right singsong," he said approvingly. "Tone's good as ever. You were better at Mandarin than I was. Didn't your father, the professor, start teaching it to you at five on the theory that an intelligent child can absorb two languages as easily as one?"

"Yes, he did!" she exclaimed wonderingly. "How did you know?"

"I've treasured up every little scrap of information you ever gave me."

"*I* gave you?"

"At the siding—the second one, I think—where they shunted us to clear the tracks for the Peiping troop trains. Or maybe it was on the station platform." He paused reminiscently. "Lord, I can see it now! It was heaped with boxes and barrels and crates and gasoline tins, and the Japs had stacked a regular dam of sandbags and old railroad ties around them all. There were machine guns on the station roof, just in case, and dumpy, dark-faced soldiers lounged on their rifles. But they didn't try to stop us so we walked on through the town."

"A little mud-walled Chinese village," she added in reverie.

"Groups of natives loitered in the streets, not daring to come close to the station, but squinting toward the soldiers with hate-filled eyes."

"And the little clay-plastered houses—the same brown as the ground. Then the green waving grain."

"We should have turned back at the end of the village. But we had all the time in the world on our hands and nothing much to do with it. So we went on. I carried your suitcase. Good thing, wasn't it, that you wouldn't leave it on the train?"

"Suitcase!" she cried in excitement. "Why, there's one in mine! And a river. It seems like the Pei Ho."

"It was the Pei Ho."

"Does yours," she asked anxiously, "have a bridge in it too?"

"Bridge? Of course. Faith, I lived a dozen eternities while we were sprinting across it."

"That's it! That's just what happened."

"There was lots of wild shooting going on. One of the bullets went through the suitcase and did for P'i-hsia's crown. That bothered you more than anything else. As soon as I had pulled you down the embankment on the other side where we were out of the firing zone you insisted on opening it up to look at the damage. You had more nerve in those days," he could not resist adding.

"I've seen it all," she exclaimed breathlessly. "Just the same way, over and over. But you? Oh, it doesn't seem possible that—" Her voice wavered to an inconclusive stop.

"That what?"

"That two people can—can—" She faltered again.

"Can what?"

"Except Peter Ibbetson and the Duchess of Towers. But Peter and Mary weren't real, while we—"

"That's better, mavourneen," he laughed. "Maybe you didn't mean to do it. Maybe there was an accident of some kind. Maybe you really are glad I'm here." She drew back at once from his groping arms.

"We're not dreaming now, Mr. Ibbetson," she said, thrusting him away.

"I get the rough idea." He stared lugubriously at the brass kettle. "L'amour, c'est fini! I concede that our dream has ended."

"Wasn't it just a dream?" she asked.

"Naturally," he retorted in his bitterness. "It never happened at all if that's the way you want it." His disappointment deepened when he saw how quickly relief manifested itself on her strained face.

"No, it didn't. How could it have happened?"

"How indeed?"

"Tell me, Mr.—" She paused uncertainly.

"It's still O'Connor," he supplied irately. "It's going a little far, Faith, to pretend you've forgotten my name."

"O'Connor?" she repeated. "Oh, that explains it. You're Irish."

"My parents were Irish," he corrected. "I'm an American citizen."

"But they taught you to speak."

"Possibly. Didn't yours?"

"Isn't that why you keep saying 'faith' all the time?"

"And is it objecting you are?"

"There!" she cried triumphantly. "That's what I mean. That's very Irish."

"Every once in a while I do seem to slip into the brogue," he acknowledged, laughing. "Sure, and why not, me foine lady? Do you want to know what I've been doing all this time? After Tientsin I got a new job—one with the biggest syndicate in the U.S. My show ran till the short-legged ones took Canton. Hankow fell in the same month, and the central government moved on to Chungking. Then the war bogged down in a stalemate, and I got a yen for home. I sailed in December of '38. The Japs went through my luggage something like eighty times, but I'm clever. Some day when I'm in a bragging mood I'll tell you how I smuggled through a pack of two hundred war photos. It's a good story, but I couldn't give the secret away in *Bombs and Bayonets*."

"Your book?" she asked.

"My own. Have you, by chance—but of course you haven't."

"I'm sorry," she apologized—and she did look sorry. "I don't like to read books about war."

"Ostrich! There's nothing left in the world but war. As a matter of fact, though, I'd had enough of it myself. So I turned down a chance to cover the European fracas. Instead I signed with a lecture bureau and was even, God punish me for a sinner, sufficiently weak-minded to dicker with Hollywood. That's the reason I'm in L.A. now. And here you are still working for Mrs. Vayne."

"No-o," she replied hesitantly. "I-I'm married. I married Eugene Vayne."

"So that's how the land lies!" He shouldn't have been angry, but he was. "Allow me to congratulate you. 'Tis a clever stroke of business you've done, Mrs. Eugene Vayne. Marrying a jade collection!"

"I didn't! I—"

"Allow me to contradict, please. You didn't marry for love. A woman such as you cannot love any man. 'Tis one of the Hill People that you are, with the heart left out of you. 'Tis—" Abruptly he realized that his speech had gone Irish again.

That made him too furious for any words. He glared silently around the little room. At the lacquered chairs, table and tea cabinet. At the pair of stiff

Chinese portraits on glass, flanking the door. Outside at the flower beds, ocean, bamboo grove—his gaze stopped abruptly at one of the sliding windows.

When they came in, he remembered, it had been tightly closed, but now it was pushed open. Only an inch or so, just enough for an eavesdropper outside to listen to what they had been saying.

"Is your husband jealous?" he asked in a low voice. She shook her head in a sorrowful manner. "Wait here, please," he commanded. "Someone—if not your husband—seems to be pretty much interested in what we've been saying. I'll be back in a jiffy."

He ran down the hillside path to the bamboo grove. There wasn't anyone there now, but the window to the tea pavilion, he noted, could easily be reached by shinnying a few feet up one of the slender greenish-yellow stalks. There were freshly plucked bamboo leaves on the ground—any nincompoop could have deduced that they had been torn off inadvertently by a climber making a hurried descent. He retraced his steps to the top of the hill.

The tea pavilion was now empty. He wasn't in the least surprised.

III

"Second in interest only to the Screen of Heaven," Westborough recalled from the article in Sunday's newspaper, "the group of Chinese deities and mythological animals is probably the most complete collection of its kind to be found in the world." The figurines, of assorted colors and sizes, had been crowded onto a pair of Chinese redwood curio cabinets, one holding Buddhist, the other Taoist dignitaries.

It was the latter which Westborough found the most interesting. He was able to identify nearly all. The Three Stars of Fortune. The Eight Immortals. The God of Letters. The God of Wealth. Chang-O, the Moon Goddess. The Jade Girl, whose temple is on the sacred mountain of T'ai Shan. The Three Precious Ones: (1) P'an Ku, from whose carcass were formed heaven and earth (The vermin who had inhabited the vast body of this primeval giant afterward became the races of man—a slightly satirical conception.); (2) Lao Tzu seated sideways on the water buffalo upon which he had disappeared over five centuries before the birth of Christ; (3) The Jade Emperor, the Pure August One, the Grand Celestial Sovereign and Supreme Author of the Visible Heaven. The latter was indubitably a rare piece since, for reasons known only to disciples of the mystic Taoist religion, the Jade Emperor is seldom portrayed in jade. Westborough could not keep from speculating which of these was the fiery-haired Mr. O'Connor's "queen with the broken crown."

The problem was not difficult; there was, in fact, only one real candidate, the Jade Maiden, P'i-hsia, a beautiful statuette, ten or so inches high, carved from a limpid-gray stone veined with green (the blend most loved by the Chinese, who profess to see in these colors the picture of water bubbling over a mossy boulder). The little goddess was standing on a rocky pedestal on which was incised a Taoist symbol. Her ample kimono swept to her small feet; her hands were clasped in front upon a tablet, and the damaged crown was not unlike a bird cage atop the Oriental headdress. He saw that new visitors had entered the room.

There were three: a dignified Chinese in a long gray frock coat and a no-longer-young couple who were obviously man and wife. The man was plump and ruddy cheeked, and the wife was scrawny and garbed in—"decent black," she would probably call it. She cried out in horror at beholding the exposed navel of a fat Laughing Buddha.

"Myron, look at that disgusting idol! And they worship such hideous things."

"Heathen in his blindness bows down to wood and stone," blandly quoted the Chinese gentleman. Westborough's eyes twinkled behind his gold-rimmed bifocals.

"Humph!" sniffed the woman suspiciously. "Are you a Christian?"

"Follow faith of illustrious ancestors," the Chinese replied ambiguously and sauntered away to stand in rapt admiration before the Screen of Heaven.

The black-clad lady gave a second and louder sniff and focused her attention wholeheartedly upon the assortment of jade adornments for the female person. "Great climate out here!" proclaimed her husband to whom-ever would listen.

"Yes," Westborough hesitantly concurred.

"I'm from Nebraska. Maybe you hail from the East too?"

"Ordinarily I reside in Chicago."

"We've been living here ever since the first of January. Right in the heart of Hollywood. Great place. Green grass all winter long and palms, yes sir." The admirer of the Californian climate lowered his voice to a confidential undertone. "Just between us, mister, the wife made me drive her out here to look at this stuff. All the way from Hollywood too. The name's Hawkins."

"My name is Westborough." They shook hands.

"What do you do for a living?" Hawkins immediately wanted to know.

"At present nothing."

"Same fix I'm in. Not on relief yet, ha, ha! Looking around for a good investment. Used to have me a dairy in Frowning Plains."

"An excellent business, I presume."

"Made me a living and a mite more. Ever been in Frowning Plains?"

"I regret to say that I have not."

"Fastest growing town of its population group east of the Rockies. Fast, Chamber of commerce has the statistics to prove it. Figures don't lie, huh?" He chortled noisily. "Though liars sometimes figure. Well, well, well! Now that we paid two bucks to get in here (ever hear of anything so steep?) I suppose we might as well have a look at some of the junk. Is this bird a rooster or a pheasant?"

It was a spinach-green Feng with a tail of trailing arabesques.

"The phoenix," Westborough explained. "The bird sacred to the empress of China."

"Thought China was run by a guy named Cheyenne Ki-check."

"Only of recent years."

"Think the Japs'll ever lick 'em?" the ex-dairyman wanted to know.

"It is difficult to prophesy."

"I've got it doped out like this: the Japs may get away with it now, but not in the long run. China's too big a country for 'em, to my way of thinking."

"Perhaps you are right," Westborough murmured politely. The female Hawkins, who evidently saw no reason for listening to her mate's wisdom, marched off to the Screen of Heaven. Seeing her approach, the Chinese gentleman bowed courteously and walked away. He paused by a set of rich green imperial jade to address the rabbit-faced secretary.

"Pardon, please. May I intrude on good humor of your honorable self with one question?"

"With as many as you like. I'm here to answer visitors' questions."

"Owner of beautiful mansion has ring, bracelet, earrings and brooch of *fei ts'ui*. Does she also own necklace of same substance?"

"No, she does not. That set is the only jewel-jade in the collection."

"Thank you for courteous information."

Westborough had taken advantage of Myron Hawkins' momentary interest in a mutton-fat Fu-dog to edge slightly away from the logorrheic ex-citizen of Frowning Plains, Nebraska. The Chinese sauntered toward them. His grizzled hair was closely cropped; his olive face as smooth as if it had never known the caress of a razor. He was tall for his race—at least five feet ten. Doubtless he had descended from a family of North China.

"May I ask your exalted age?" Westborough inquired as they met.

" 'My ears are attentive to the truth.' " Bowing, the Oriental passed on to the Taoist cabinet.

"Sixty," the historian mentally interpreted.

The cryptic conversation proved too much for the curiosity of Myron Hawkins. "What sort of lodge do you fellows belong to?"

"Merely the scholars' fraternity of Kung Fu-tze—a name indifferently Latinized by Portuguese Jesuits into Confucius."

The other immediately chuckled as though a button had been pressed. "Ever hear this one? Confucius say ..." Westborough's attention soon wandered.

The Chinese had just picked up the statuette of the Jade Girl, and his hands were gently stroking the smooth, cool substance. "Please do not touch the articles in the collection," Coggin requested in his toneless whisper.

"Please forgive carelessness." The Son of Han immediately restored the statuette to its shelf on the redwood cabinet. "My race is best able through fingers to appreciate perfection of jade."

"I understand perfectly," Coggin replied.

"You are kind gentleman. May I ask ..." To Westborough's surprise he heard repeated almost the identical question which Kerry O'Connor had put not more than half an hour ago.

Coggin's answer, however, was this time a trifle more specific. "Mrs. Vayne brought it back with her from Peking."

"By Mrs. Vayne do you mean lady for whom you have honor to work?"

"No, that is Mrs. Nicholas Vayne. I meant Mrs. Eugene Vayne, who is her daughter-in-law."

"What, please, is history of piece before it came into possession of Mrs. Eugene Vayne?"

Coggin shrugged. "We know almost nothing about it, except that it's a reproduction of the Jade Maiden, P'i-hsia Yüan-chün. We can't even tell whether it's old or modern. Beautiful work of course, but they are doing fine work now in Peiping—Peking. It's hard to keep track of all the changes in the city's name."

"Northern Capital, Peking, became Northern Peace, Peiping, in Christian year 1928," the Chinese patiently explained. "Invaders restored former name of Northern Capital in year 1937. Peiping is again Peking."

Mrs. Hawkins, "jaded" at last, collared her loquacious mate and bore him from the pavilion. The little historian was free to follow the other conversation, which he did shamelessly.

"Is beautiful piece for sale?"

"Nothing in the Vayne collection is for sale," Coggin replied stiffly.

"Archer who misses target seeks cause of failure within himself," the Chinese declared reproachfully. "I am tactless person whose words offend."

Coggin smiled, mollified. "No, not in the least."

"Allow me, please, to explain present interest. In my youth I saw twin of this figure in possession of Taoist priest. It held ghost which worthy man had made prisoner so unhappy spirit might benefit from contact with jade, purest-known substance, symbol of virtues."

"Good heavens!" the secretary cried. "Do you really believe that?"

The Chinese nodded gravely.

PART TWO: LOST, STRAYED OR STOLEN

WESTBOROUGH had accepted with alacrity the urgently cordial invitation to spend a month on the Palmas Peninsula at the new home of old friends, Mr. and Mrs. John Launay.

There were at least three excellent reasons for accepting. The primary consideration, of course, was the opportunity to renew the threads of a brief but singularly pleasant friendship. Secondly, however, he was not sorry to provide his conscience with a satisfactory excuse for exchanging the snowy blizzards of a Chicago spring for the blue lupine and orange poppies which accompany the season in southern California. And finally, he was really at loose ends for an occupation. *Julian, the Pagan*, third in his biographies of Roman emperors, had been completed; the major European catastrophe had upset his plans to undertake an extended period of research in foreign libraries; and his avocation as a consulting criminologist was at a low ebb of activity. Since the perfume case of last July he had done nothing in that line, nor did it seem likely that another such affair would soon be called to his attention.

On Tuesday, at a time Chinese would designate as the Hour of the Snake and Americans call, exactly if more prosaically, 10:30 A.M., the elderly guest was breakfasting with his hostess. To be more accurate, she was breakfasting, he having partaken of the meal two hours before in the company of her husband, who had already left the house on business.

"At least you will have another cup of coffee," Adrienne coaxed. She was in an aquamarine negligee which blended most attractively with the copper tones of her hair. "One never can have too much coffee."

"I agree with you, my dear." Westborough smiled. "Very well, thank

23

you." He studied his reflection in the silver coffeepot with marked disfavor.

It wasn't much of a face by aesthetic standards—even for a man of seventy. The forehead, though broad and wide, was only the upper side of a triangle which terminated at a small, contemptibly pointed chin. Below sparse and silvery hair the faded blue eyes peeked owlishly from behind gold-rimmed bifocals. The neck was thin and scrawny. ... No, it wasn't much of a face.

"From what source came the wealth of the Vaynes?" he asked.

"Oil originally," replied the daughter of the deceased president of the Trevor Oil Company. "Mr. Vayne—Old Nick everyone used to call him—was in several deals with Father. He's dead now—Mr. Vayne."

"A family of amazing taste!" Westborough exclaimed. "A little bizarre, perhaps."

"That Chinese house?" Her laughter rippled easily. "Old Nick built it. He'd collected jades for years, and they say that you can't go in heavily for jade without everything Chinese getting you. Is that true?"

"It might very well be true," her guest deliberated. "The art of jade carving is not a mere ornamental refinement, but an indispensable accompaniment of the Flowery Kingdom's great civilization." He paused, recalling the scholarly Chinese who only yesterday had declared with solemn assurance that a human soul had been transferred to a jade statuette. "Pray tell me all about the Vaynes, my dear. There is a son, I believe?"

"A son and a daughter. Do have a piece of toast. They are an unusual family. To begin with, they all live under one roof—if you can call inhabiting a Chinese compound living under one roof—Eugene and his wife, Lydia and her husband. Mrs. Vayne is—well, bossy wouldn't be far wrong. And she has all the money. Every cent of the Vayne fortune was willed to her, and neither Eugene nor Lydia can get any more than she chooses to give them."

"You appear singularly well informed."

"Oh, it's all common gossip. And that's only the beginning." Adrienne lowered her voice to a mock whisper. "Eugene *drinks*."

"But no?" Westborough exclaimed, pretending to be shocked.

"He does. They say his mother put him in a sanatorium—alcoholism treatments, you know, but they didn't effect a permanent cure. He married a short time ago. Some girl that nobody had ever heard of. And Lydia and her husband are screw balls."

"Dear me," Westborough said mildly. "In what particular form does the—er—screwiness manifest itself?"

"The occult. Psychics and fortune-tellers and so on. Do you have any idea what makes people out here so crazy?"

"At the beginning of the decline of the Roman Empire, before Christianity had become fashionable, there was a similar interest displayed in equivalent practices of divination," the historian related. "The last two thousand years are, I regret to say, only a thin veneer over the elemental fears upon which primitive superstitions were founded. Any twentieth-century person may revert to type with astonishing ease."

"But we're reasoning human beings."

"I beg your pardon, but we are not. We are emotional human beings, which is something of a different category. As yet—"

He was interrupted by the mellow notes of the door chime.

"Gentleman to see Mr. Westborough, ma'am," reported the colored maid a few minutes later. Her face broke into a broad grin. "You all ain't been robbing no banks, have you? He says he's from the sheriff's office."

"The sheriff's office? Dear me! Perhaps it is Captain Cranston?"

"That's the name he gave me. Hope you all ain't gone and got yourself in a pecka trouble."

"That will do, Carrie," Adrienne said sharply.

"There is no cause for alarm. Captain Cranston and I are very good friends." Westborough's face clouded in perplexity. "But how could he have learned of my present whereabouts?"

The answer flashed into his mind as he walked toward the front hall.

II

"Might let a fellow know you're in his country," grumbled the head of the sheriff's bureau of investigation. "Too bad I can't see you unless I round you up on official business."

Westborough's eyes twinkled. "Am I one of your suspects?"

"You are at that. All of the general public who attended the Vayne jade exhibit yesterday are suspects. Your name appears on their register."

"I cannot deny it."

"What time were you there?" Cranston's manner was briskly business-like.

"Between the hours of nine and eleven."

"That checks." Cranston riffled the pages of a black-bound notebook. "Larceny," he said succinctly. "Case isn't so important, but Jocasta Vayne is. She lost a piece of jade. Value maybe a thousand or fifteen hundred dollars. Maybe not so much. I'm forestalling criticism by handling the thing personally."

"Do you care to give me additional details?" Westborough inquired.

"Sure, why not? Jocasta Vayne, as you probably know, decided to stage a benefit for Chinese refugees. Threw her house and grounds open at two dollars a head. Twenty visitors yesterday. The show was due to run a week so she'd have grossed something like three hundred. She could write a check for that and mind it no more than I mind spending fifteen cents, but that's not the way rich people figure. Tell me, did you see a redheaded fellow, about thirty or so, in the jade pavilion?"

"Dear me, yes!" Westborough exclaimed. "Surely that gentleman cannot be a serious suspect? He is Kerry O'Connor."

"I don't care if he's Errol Flynn. What did you see him do?"

"Nothing of grave importance. He lifted one of the figurines from its place. A gentleman who is, I believe, Mrs. Vayne's secretary, cautioned him not to touch any of the articles in the collection, and he put it down at once. That is almost all."

"Can you give me a description of the statuette that O'Connor handled?"

"I believe so. It was about ten inches high and carved from gray jade veined with green. The figure was that of the Jade Maiden, the Taoist goddess of T'ai Shan. She was standing on a rock on which was carved the symbol of the Hare-in-the-Moon-Pounding-the-Elixir-of-Life. She was holding a tablet, and a small piece of her crown had been broken off."

Cranston nodded. "That's the one all right. But Mrs. Vayne called her the Goddess of the Green Shiver."

"She has many names," Westborough said absently. "But it is my duty to tell you that Mr. O'Connor was not the only visitor who displayed interest in that particular statuette. I saw a Chinese gentleman—"

"Not guilty," Cranston interrupted peremptorily.

"But he was in the pavilion after Mr. O'Connor."

"Only partly true. He left the grounds in the forenoon—quarter to half an hour after O'Connor, according to what I could make out of the gatekeeper's pidgin. Coggin—Mrs. Vayne's secretary—remembers seeing the statuette later on in the afternoon."

"Then I do not see how either gentleman can be guilty of the theft."

"O'Connor came back. I'll give you the facts as I got them from Coggin. Mrs. Vayne's daughter-in-law came in about four o'clock to relieve him from standing guard over the jade, and he walked down the stairs on the east side of the hill and cut over to the gatehouse to check receipts with the gatekeeper, Wong. The old lady has three Chinamen working for her: names are Wing, Weng and Wong—if you can believe it. Wong said the 'led-haired man' had just signed his name in the book again and paid another two dollars for the privilege. Coggin was naturally a bit suspicious over that and hiked up the path to the pavilion. O'Connor was in there, standing around and doing nothing particular, and so were both Mrs. Vaynes and a bunch of society women. Coggin had a look at the statuette then, and it was there okay. He was planning on sticking around to watch O'Connor, he told me, but then old Mrs. Vayne collared him and made him come with her to show these society girl friends around the place. That left O'Connor alone in the room with young Mrs. Vayne."

"Would he not have experienced difficulty in carrying away so large an object?" Westborough pondered.

"He might have slipped it under his coat and held it there by keeping an arm close to his side."

"But could that possibly be done without attracting the attention of Mrs. Eugene Vayne?"

"I don't know." Cranston paused briefly. "There's something about that girl that puzzles me. She—" He broke off as Adrienne entered the hall.

Westborough performed the ceremony of introduction. "Wouldn't you two like to talk in John's study?" she asked. "He won't be back for hours."

"Thanks, no," Cranston replied. "I have to be on my way." He glanced at his onetime associate a little uncertainly. "If I brought you out to talk to Mrs. Vayne it might help me some. She knows the right people politically, and I want her to know that I'm being active. Can you ride out there with me now?"

"With pleasure," Westborough replied, reaching at once for his hat. In this simple fashion he officially entered that weird imbroglio mentioned in his notebook under a curious title:

CASE OF THE GREEN SHIVER.

III

Following the marine drive above the creamy stucco and red tiles of the homes fronting the iris-blue bay, Westborough marveled again at the marked resemblance of this section of southern California to the coast of the French Riviera. Turning inland, however, they crossed an invisible frontier and entered the treeless, semiarid hill regions of Italy.

Captain Cranston continued his narrative.

"O'Connor stayed ten minutes in the pavilion, Mrs. Eugene Vayne told me. Then he left the building and went out the gate for the second time about four-thirty. She locked the pavilion door at five. No one at all came in there after O'Connor left, she insists. But we've got to go slow. She didn't notice the statuette. She couldn't actually say whether it was there or not at the time she locked up."

Westborough lifted his eyes unto the hills. The dun mantle worn for ten months of every year had been doffed for a spring-green garment into which were woven the violet-blue threads of lupine, the warm golden-orange of myriads of poppies, the rose-purple of verbena, and the bright yellow of coreopsis.

"Is there no other possible suspect but Mr. O'Connor?" He wondered, even while he was asking the question, why he felt a surge of such ardent sympathy for a stranger. Or is any man really a stranger to one who has read his words in print?

"Figure that out from the facts. The pavilion was locked at five. No one went in until ten when old Mrs. Vayne went to get her jewel-jade—eighteen thousand dollars' worth—that she keeps in a wall safe in her bedroom. She relocked the pavilion. Again no one went near it until around 1 A.M. when Eugene Vayne came home. And he spent the rest of the night in there."

"But, dear me! Was not that rather a strange bedchamber?"

"I haven't talked to Eugene yet." Cranston braked for a sharp turn. "Anyway he *was* there, which makes the idea of a night theft improbable."

"When was the loss discovered?"

"Not till seven-thirty this morning. When Jocasta Vayne went to put her jewel-jade back on the table for the public to gawk at she took a quick look around to make sure that everything was in trim. Then she found out right away she'd lost something. Loss reported promptly and with one hell of a fuss. You'd think that having a million dollars' worth of the stuff around she wouldn't mind so much losing one little hunk. But the old girl couldn't take on any more about it if they'd cleaned her out of house and home. She called off the exhibition indefinitely, which won't please people who drive twenty to thirty miles from the city on account of her write-ups in the papers. And the first day's take of forty bucks won't buy many homes for the Chinese refugees, poor devils."

"May I ask a question? Is her jade ordinarily kept in the house itself or in a safety-deposit vault?"

"In the house," Cranston replied. "Fairly safe, I guess. A wire runs along the top of the wall. If it's touched—even by a finger—gongs ring in the gatehouse and garage to wake up her five servants."

"Five servants?" Westborough queried. "I thought that you said three."

"Three Chinese, I said. There's also a chauffeur—a white man—and a Japanese gardener, little mutt with a long name. We're almost there."

Though the flatter areas of the peninsula were under cultivation the uplands were tenaciously held by sage and creosote, yucca and cactus. Immediately across the highway from such a stretch of wasteland towered the ten-foot gray wall of the Vayne property. Since the estate sliced off the peninsula's extreme northwest tip, the wall bounded the south and east sides only. Westborough asked for Cranston's opinion of the sea defenses.

"Good," the officer returned at once. "Hundred-foot cliffs on both north and west. They might be scaled, given time and plenty of equipment, but where are you going to start from to do it? It would be a pretty ticklish job to land a boat in the middle of those rocks at the bottom."

"Indeed yes," Westborough agreed. His friend pressed the button of his horn to announce their arrival at the vermilion gate. It opened for them almost immediately, and they turned right to leave the car in the motor court behind the garage. They walked back along the short driveway to the railed footpath ascending the hillside. Three of Cranston's investigators were busily scouring the shrubbery.

"I don't expect them to find anything," their chief explained, "but there is a bare chance it was hidden here."

"May I inquire if all of the pavilions were searched?" Westborough asked.

A voluntary search had been made, he learned, of both family and servant quarters. Nothing had been found. Passing under the peaked roof of the doorless gate at the end of the path, they entered the first courtyard. Gilded dragons on the gable of the central pavilion threatened the approach of malignantly inclined spirits, and a row of porcelain household gods stood in a niche above the door to aid in giving encroaching evil ones a thoroughly bad time of it. There was no one inside.

"Sit down and be comfortable," Cranston suggested. "I'll go find Mrs. Vayne."

Most of the jade displayed yesterday in this room was gone, Westborough immediately noted. To be seen were only the Screen of Heaven, a vase or two, a jade chime and on the floor a spinach-green buffalo which was doubtless employed as a doorstop. All else had vanished like objects from a prestidigitator's cabinet. Westborough raised his eyes.

A Chinese attic ceiling. He recognized it at once though he had never before seen one like it in the United States. The lockers around the four sides of the room were covered with embroidered patterns on silk fabric, and their significance might easily escape one unfamiliar with the Oriental practice of storing household goods overhead. The locks and handles were at the very top, almost inconspicuous against the dark wood frames of the embroideries. The total cubic capacity, Westborough estimated, was sufficient to hold all the jades he had seen on the previous day. He looked downward again.

The room was a showplace in itself. Even divested of yesterday's treasures it held enough to occupy the attention for many minutes. The rug, woven from the thick wool of Mongolian sheep, had a rose-and-tan design of pagodas and willows against a ground of the shimmering blue for which Tientsin rugs have long been famous. The furniture was mostly polished mahogany and Canton ebony: Chinese in the simplicity of its graceful lines, decidedly un-Chinese in its comfortable upholstering. A pair of Japanese hara-kiri swords rested in carved ivory sheaths above a long low sofa against the south wall. The north wall was occupied in toto by an enormous lattice window, the east reserved as of yesterday for the incomparable Screen of Heaven. Westborough sprang at once to his feet as Captain Cranston reentered in the company of a woman.

She was tall, lean, white-haired, stern-lipped and severe in mien. Her hands, big for a woman, were strong and capable. It would be unkind to say that her protruding aquiline nose resembled the beak of a jabiru, but it was on that heavy order.

"Close the door," she ordered the officer curtly. "And pull down the shades, please. Does anyone know you are here, Mr. Westborough?"

"We saw only your gatekeeper, I believe."

"I'll talk to Wong myself and impress it upon him that he is not to mention your coming here this morning. I may have work for you."

"Dear me, but—"

"Captain Cranston told me about you and all that you accomplished for that Greek storekeeper, Paphlagloss." It was not, Westborough mused, exactly complimentary to allude to the mighty Minos of the department-store world as "that Greek storekeeper." But it was patent that Jocasta Vayne would do and say exactly what she pleased. Like the late Empress Dowager Tzu Hsi, she was a woman born to rule. He felt a little uncomfortable in her imperious presence.

"That involved a stolen statuette too," she stated.

"It began with one, yes. A most amazing article, a chryselephantine snake goddess from a civilization of four thousand years ago. But I cannot take credit for its recovery."

"Nevertheless, it was recovered. I have spoken to Captain Cranston about hiring you. He has no objection. I am prepared to compensate you liberally. Will you work for me?"

"But, dear me, I do not see what I can do."

"Please listen carefully. Captain Cranston is fairly sure that this man, O'Connor, is guilty. If he is clever enough to steal my Jade Lady under yesterday's conditions he is clever enough to hide it where an ordinary search won't find it. Do you agree?"

"Yes, perhaps," Westborough mumbled.

"O'Connor will have to be brought here and kept under observation."

" 'I can call spirits from the vasty deep,' said Glendower. 'Why so can I,' quoth Hotspur, 'or so can any man; but will they come when you do call for them?' "

Mrs. Nicholas Vayne was not impressed by the lines from *King Henry IV.*

"As soon as he accepts my invitation" (she did not say, "If he accepts") "I'll telephone you. It will be necessary, I presume, to tell you about the part you will play."

"It might be helpful," Westborough concurred.

"The guest house contains two rooms. I will arrange to have a small peephole bored through the door between them, so you can watch him when he's in his room."

"But is Mr. O'Connor likely to be so rash as to bring the statuette back here?"

"He may—rather than take a chance on leaving it in his hotel room. If he does leave it behind—" She exchanged a quick glance with Cranston. "That's not your affair, however. Your job will be at the guest house."

"Does the position have other assignments?"

"What you do is entirely up to you. I don't care how you work just so long as you can get back my Green Shiver. And if O'Connor's too clever for you—well, at least, he won't have grounds to sue me for a false arrest. Both you and O'Connor will take your meals in the dining pavilion with us; my secretary and I will be the only ones here who will know that either of you is an out-of-the-ordinary guest. As for compensation, well, what do you think?"

Westborough, who cared little for money, turned suddenly avaricious. "The laborer is worthy of his hire," he contended. "Shall we say five hundred dollars in the event of success?"

"The Green Shiver is only worth fifteen hundred," she objected.

"No more than that?"

"The carving is good, but it's not one of the best grades of jade. I couldn't possibly get a cent more than fifteen hundred, and I doubt if I could sell it for that. A third of the market value is way too much. Two hundred."

"I am sorry. I have other matters which require my attention."

"Well," she cogitated, "it does break up my mythological collection. All right then, five hundred. But only if you find it, mind you."

"Am I otherwise to work for nothing?"

"I'll pay you ten dollars a day to be deducted from the reward if you earn any reward."

"I could not," he haggled, "possibly work for less than fifteen." (Secretly he had made up his mind that all earnings from this source should be turned over to a fund for Chinese refugees.)

"It will cost you nothing to live here," she reminded him tartly.

"True. But I must consider my reputation."

"Well, I'll agree to fifteen for two or three days."

"Thank you. And now may I ask some questions? There is a chance, you recognize, that Mr. O'Connor is not guilty?"

"Who else could be?"

"A habitual criminal, perhaps a burglar by profession, might read in his newspaper of the costly jades to be exhibited and decide to take advantage of the opportunity."

She shuddered. "To think of the underworld coming right into my home! But it couldn't have happened."

"The possibility is slight, I confess. Nevertheless, it arouses interesting speculation. The Jade Lady of T'ai Shan is by no means the most valuable article of your magnificent collection."

"Far from it."

"Then why should our anonymous thief take that piece? Only one reason comes readily to mind. He knew no better. Obviously he is not a jade expert so he must have some other criterion than actual value for his guidance. Allow me to explain with a homely example before we finally dismiss this potential malefactor. Being in the market for a cake of soap, I am offered brands A, B, C and D. The wrappers of the four are equally attractive, and I know nothing of the essentials of soap quality. Assuming that I have formulated no previous buying habits, which of the quartet will I choose?"

"The one most advertised."

"Precisely. I visited your exhibit yesterday, Mrs. Vayne, because of advertising in the form of an article in a Sunday newspaper illustrated by a halftone reproduction of the Screen of Heaven. Could a picture of the Jade Lady have appeared similarly in another journal?"

"It could," she answered, "but it didn't. Jethro has clippings of all that we got in the way of publicity. The only picture used was the one you saw of the Screen of Heaven." She opened the door of a pearl-mounted cabinet. "We sent this set of a dozen photos to every local newspaper."

He found the Jade Lady on the third print he looked at, not by herself, but in a group of Taoist divinities arranged on the levels of the Chinese curio cabinet. Since the press had scorned her, however, it did not much matter whether she was there or not. It was fairly obvious, Westborough believed upon concluding his examination of the pictures, that one must either: (a) allow a third coincidence with regard to the Green Shiver (assuming that Kerry O'Connor and the Chinese gentleman already made two) or (b) abandon the theory of the outside criminal as logically untenable. And he had no particular liking for hypotheses founded upon an abundance of coincidences.

"These are excellently clear photographs," he observed, seeing that a remark was expected of him. She laughed acidly.

"They ought to be; the bill was high enough, goodness knows. I protested. Jethro and I—Jasper helped, too, because he wanted a set of prints for one of his silly articles—arranged all the pieces and backgrounds. The photographer didn't have to do a thing but fix the lights and make his exposures. His bill was outrageous."

Westborough murmured condolences and mentally surveyed the remaining possibilities before he spoke again. "I understand from Captain Cranston's account that this pavilion was locked last evening and was visited during the night only by you and your son."

"I came in about ten o'clock." She sat rigidly, her back an unbending line. "And Eugene slept here on the sofa, he says, from one o'clock on."

Recalling what he had learned from Adrienne Launay of Eugene Vayne's habits, Westborough decided that it would not be tactful to inquire the reason for selecting this rather unconventional sleeping place. "Who," he asked instead, "have keys to the pavilion's door?"

It turned out that the locks of the seven pavilions were identical so that the key to one was able to open all. "A sensible arrangement," he commented. "May I ask which of your servants have pavilion keys?"

"Wing, my number-one boy, and Weng, the cook," she answered in her harsh, deep-toned voice. "My servants have been with me for a number of years, Mr. Westborough. They can be no more suspected than Jethro Coggin or a member of my own family."

Westborough glanced toward the attic ceiling. "Am I correct in my surmise that your jade is ordinarily stored there?" He saw by her tightly compressed lips that he was. "Who has those keys?"

"Key," she corrected, distinctly displeased by the query. "A single key unlocks every compartment. I have one and Jethro had the only duplicate. That has nothing to do with the theft."

"Dear me, no. I am merely laying a background of general information. It might also be of some value" (it would at least assuage his curiosity) "to know how the Jade Lady was acquired for your collection."

"My daughter-in-law bought it in Peking in July 1937."

"July 1937! Why, that was the month the war began. Your daughter-in-law must have had rather a thrilling time."

"Yes. She doesn't like to talk about it, but she was in Tientsin during the Japanese bombing."

If the material in the harrowing *Bombs and Bayonets* were factual, as it purported to be, Kerry O'Connor had also been in Tientsin at the same time, Westborough pondered. He wondered if the young woman who had walked so suddenly away with the Irish journalist could be Mrs. Eugene

Vayne. The line of inquiry seemed to merit further investigation. "Did your daughter-in-law meet Mr. O'Connor in China?" he hazarded.

"No." The negative was unqualified, uncompromising. "She saw him for the first time on yesterday morning."

"H-m-m-m-m-m!" The historian deliberated.

"She never lies." The rasping voice became immediately edged. "I trust Faith implicitly."

"The Christian name is Faith?" Westborough asked. He recalled young O'Connor's startled outcry of, "Faith, let's get out of here!" The first word might have been merely an expletive. On the other hand … He saw that he was making a very poor impression on his new employer.

Captain Cranston came gratifyingly to the rescue. "I want to talk to your daughter-in-law again, Mrs. Vayne. And I also want to talk to your son Eugene. I'd like Westborough to be here to listen. Will you send them in one at a time, please?"

"I thought it was agreed that only Jethro and myself were to know about Mr. Westborough?" Her pale blue eyes were as frigid as an Alaskan glacier.

Cranston pointed to the Screen of Heaven. "He can sit behind that thing."

"That *thing*," Mrs. Vayne retorted witheringly, "is the most valuable screen in the world. My husband paid a quarter of a million dollars for it. I suppose it will do, though, if you think it's essential that Mr. Westborough stay here."

She walked grim lipped from the pavilion.

Cranston lifted a low Chinese stool and deposited it behind the tall screen. "I'm glad you decided to take this case," he remarked in an undertone. "It's doing me a big favor. When I was a kid I stumbled across a yarn about some old sailor who had to go through a narrow channel with a whirlpool on one side and a snaky thing with seven heads on the other. Get the idea?"

"Dimly."

"Call the whirlpool Jocasta Vayne. She has pull enough to cause me lots of trouble. If we don't find her pretty ornament she will too. You can take it from me that most rich women are hellions."

"And Scylla?" Westborough inquired.

"Silly?"

"The monster with the seven heads."

"You can call that the press. O'Connor is an ex-newspaperman, and members of that fraternity stick together. To arrest a fellow of his prominence on a charge like this with no more evidence than I have would be suicide. But I'm a public servant." The public servant sighed dolefully. "It didn't look like I had any out until Mrs. Vayne herself suggested you. She's a canny old girl—taking no chances on a suit for false accusation and damages to reputation. So you've been elected the goat!"

"I do not mind being sacrificed. As a matter of fact, I shall enjoy the excitement of another case. But I do not see—"

"Shh!" Cranston held up a warning hand. "Duck! One of them's coming now."

Westborough darted hastily into his quarter-of-a-million-dollar hiding place.

IV

"How old are you?" Cranston began bluntly.

"Twenty-five." Faith Vayne's soft voice had a pleasing quality.

Westborough regretted that it was impossible for him to catch even a glimpse of the young woman's face. He was, however, now fairly sure of her identity.

"Were you in China three years ago?"

"Nearly three. Mrs. Vayne commissioned me to buy jade figures for her mythological collection."

"Before you were married?"

"Yes."

"Was this missing statuette one of the pieces you purchased?"

"Yes. It came from the shop of Yee Feh-lu in Jade Street, Peiping." She pronounced the former name of the historic capital correctly, Bay-ping.

"Do you remember what you paid for it?"

"I found Mr. Yee's bill of sale afterward." That, Westborough mused from his vantage point behind the Screen of Heaven, was rather an odd thing to say. "Six hundred Chinese dollars—roughly two hundred dollars in our money as the exchange rates were then. It was a tremendous bargain."

"I don't know much about jade prices."

"I paid five hundred dollars, U.S., for a Kuan Yin of approximately the same size and grade of jade, and Kuan Yins are rather common."

"How did you become acquainted with Mrs. Vayne?"

"I met her at Buckley's."

"Buckley's at the Ambassador?"

"Yes. I worked there for about a year in the Chinese art department, and Mrs. Vayne was one of our best customers. We talked a lot together about jade, and—well, we became rather close friends."

"How did she happen to send you to China?"

"Perhaps because she knew I wanted to go there so badly. She has never admitted that, but it would be just like her."

"Did you go alone?"

"Yes."

"Weren't you rather young for such a trip?"

"Yes, I probably was. However, I could speak the language—the *kuo-yü*, that is, the national language of Northern China. I don't know any of the southern dialects."

"Who taught you Chinese?"

"My father, Professor Kingston. He is head of the department of Oriental languages at an Eastern university."

"Did you meet Mr. O'Connor in China?"

"I've already answered that. I didn't. I told you everything I know about him this morning."

"Just to make sure I've got it right," Cranston said smoothly, "I want you to tell me everything again. Will you do that?"

"Very well."

"Please begin with the first time you saw Mr. O'Connor. Where was it?"

"In this room. I was just coming in the door when I saw him—he was writing on a card, I think. I was about to speak to Jethro when he—Mr. O'Connor—looked up and saw me. He looked—stared at me." Her voice faltered. "This is frightfully hard to explain. I don't understand it at all."

"What happened?"

"Actually I don't know. I remember standing here by the door, and then it was as if a haze had lifted, and I realized that I was in the tea pavilion talking to a total stranger. I don't have any idea how I got there. I was frightened, I remember. I wanted to run away, but I didn't because I was also curious. Do you—this sounds silly, I'll admit—but do you think he could have hypnotized me?"

Cranston's tongue clicked skeptical dissent. "That isn't very likely, Mrs. Vayne."

"I know, I know. But how—"

Afterward Westborough was to reproach himself bitterly with obtuseness. The truth lay before him in those few minutes of Tuesday morning, and he failed to grasp even a hint of it.

"What did you and O'Connor talk about?" Cranston continued.

"Mostly about a dream. A nightmare that troubles me every so often. It was strange—he described it almost exactly. It was his dream, too, he said."

("An interesting psychological problem," Westborough meditated to himself. "Such dreams do occur, I understand, though they have been reported rarely. I must delve into the literature of collective dreams at some future date.")

Captain Cranston, however, evidently did not consider the subject worth the expenditure of any more time. Like the practical official he was, he plunged at once into the object of the investigation.

"Did he mention the missing statuette to you?"

"Yes."

"What did he say about it?"

"Let me see if I can remember. Oh yes. He said, 'I ran straight into the little Taoist lady with the broken crown. What's her name? Let's hear you give it in Chinese.' "

("Can this young lady be mendacious?" Westborough pondered.)

Captain Cranston obviously thought the same. "That doesn't make any sense."

"Nothing that he said sounded very sensible to me. Except when he was talking about himself."

"What did he tell you about himself?"

"Who he was, and what he'd done. I gathered, though he didn't actually say so, that he'd been a war correspondent. Then he mentioned writing *Bombs and Bayonets*. I had heard of that book, but I hadn't read it. He was—well, disappointed when I told him so. Right after that he became violent—almost incoherent."

"Would you say that he acted like a crazy person?"

"I—I don't know how a crazy person acts. But he talked very wildly. When I told him I was married he shouted that I didn't love my husband. Then he wanted to know if Gene were jealous. And finally he said in a whisper that there was someone listening to us and for me to wait till he got back. Then he rushed outside like a whirlwind. As soon as I saw he was going down the path I ran over to our own pavilion—Gene's and mine—and bolted the door. I was afraid he'd follow me, I'll admit. I never met anyone who behaved so strangely."

"Did you tell your husband?"

"No. Gene wasn't here then; he had gone to the races."

"What happened when O'Connor came back in the afternoon?"

"There were other people in the room with us at first—Mother Vayne and some of her friends. Later Jethro—Mr. Coggin—came in. They all went out together."

"Leaving you alone with O'Connor?"

"Yes, but no one knew. I hadn't told anybody about what had happened in the tea pavilion."

"What made you stay alone with the man you were so afraid of?"

"I was ashamed of myself for having run away. I didn't like to think that I really was a coward."

"So you stayed to test your nerve?"

"I guess that must be it."

"What was it he said then?"

"That he'd come to apologize. He wasn't violent that time. In fact he behaved quite normally."

"Do you think that he stole the jade statue?"

"I don't see how he could have. He was only in the pavilion for a little while, and I was watching him closely because I was afraid that there might be another outbreak. I don't believe I looked away from him for a single second, Captain Cranston."

V

"I leave jade to the women and Jasper. Have a cigar, Cranston."

Listening to Eugene Vayne's overassertive voice, Westborough conjured up the image of a small, chubby boy who, treated as a being of little consequence by his elders, had found it necessary to restore his shattered self-esteem by deliberate acts of naughtiness. "Anything else you want to know?"

"Understand you went to the races yesterday."

"That's right. I had to go somewhere. They were turning the place into a public menagerie."

"Win anything?"

"Hell no. I never win! Sure you don't want a cigar?"

"No, thanks. Where did you go after leaving the track?"

"What's this, a third degree? I dropped in and had dinner at a friend's apartment."

"Mind giving me the name and address?"

"Yes, I do mind. I don't like people prying into my personal affairs. What do you want to know for anyway?"

"In police work we have to make complete records." Cranston's voice was conciliatory. "What time did you get home?"

"How should I know?"

"Wong says it was about one o'clock when you woke him up."

"So it was one o'clock."

"We'll put it down as one. You spent the evening at the home of a friend—did you say in Los Angeles?"

"I didn't say. And I'm not saying."

"Arriving home at approximately 1 A.M.," Cranston continued as if he had not been interrupted. "Now tell me what you did after Wong had opened the gate."

"I left the car in the drive and walked up the path to the house. Damn crooked path! Then I opened the door of this pavilion and went inside."

"Why?"

"I did, that's all. And I laid down on the sofa and went to sleep."

"Why didn't you sleep in your own bedroom?"

"Because I didn't want to wake my wife. Is it any of your business where I go to bed, Cranston?"

"As a peace officer, yes. It's a serious offense in this state to drive a car while intoxicated."

"What the hell do you mean?"

"Vayne, it's obvious you came home drunk. You couldn't even put your car away. You staggered up the path to the house and opened the first door you came to. You were so plastered it didn't make a nickel's worth of difference to you where you spent the rest of the night. Isn't that right?"

"It's a lie. I spent a few hours on the sofa, but I wasn't tight. And you can't prove I was."

"If you were sober, Vayne, why didn't you go to your own bed?"

"Look here, Cranston, I—oh hell! I'd quarreled with Faith just before I left, and I didn't want to see her just then. Let it go at that, can't you?"

"Sleep soundly on the sofa?"

"Alcoholic stupor, eh? That's what you'd like to have me admit." Vayne laughed unpleasantly. "As a matter of fact, I slept very lightly. Make what you can out of that."

"The only thing I'm interested in at present is whether you were alone or not."

"I was alone all the time I was here."

"How long was that?"

"I don't know exactly. Three or four hours maybe."

"So you finally gave up the sofa as a bad job and went to your own bed?"

"Well, what of it?"

"Was it still dark when you left here?"

"Yes, I guess so."

"H'm. Vayne, you didn't happen to take away your mother's statuette, did you?"

"What the hell! That's a laugh, Cranston. Your flat feet went through our pavilion, didn't they? Turned the whole place upside down. Besides, what do I want a piece of jade for? The whole lot comes to Lydia and me some day."

"Which doesn't help much if you happen to need money now."

"Damn you!" Eugene Vayne yelled. "Mind your own Goddamn business!"

PART THREE: THE JADE GHOST

FAITH VAYNE was talking to Jethro Coggin. The sun had set an hour before, and four planets shone close together in the west. The white planet of Love was brilliant, the red planet of War insignificantly tiny. How unlike the world today, the secretary mused.

"Do you know how you look?" he asked in his characteristic hoarse whisper. "Like a saintly lady from a medieval tapestry."

"Only my dress," she returned, smiling. Below its hooded top the white folds fell like sculptured drapery almost to her sandals.

"You are going in Gene's Chrysler, I suppose?" His peculiar voice remained expressionless, but she sensed his anxiety.

"Yes, but it's all right. Gene hasn't yet—"

"Not yet," he broke in.

"I can drive home if it's necessary."

"Can you make him give you the wheel?" She didn't answer. After a time he added, "I often wonder why and how you stand it."

"Gene isn't really vicious." She spoke very quietly. "He's sweet sometimes. And I'm married to him, Jethro. I married him with my eyes open."

"Her Highness bullied you into it," he retorted. "Don't try to deny it. I know both her and you. You lack self-assertiveness. You insist on thinking the best of people. And you won't face unpleasant truths. Those are your three vices, Faith."

"Have I any virtues?" she asked.

"All the Christian ones. You turn the other cheek, for instance."

"Oh no," she demurred.

"Oh yes," he insisted. "I know you very well, you see, because—" With a determined effort he succeeded in changing the subject. "Have you heard the news? Two house guests are arriving, one tonight and the other in the morning. The first is a Mr. Westborough."

"I don't think I've ever met him." Her tone was casually unconcerned.

"You haven't. But you've met the other one. He's the author of *Bombs and Bayonets*."

"Oh!"

"I tried to talk Her Highness out of it," he continued uncomfortably. "It wasn't any use. We have made up our mind, she said."

"Jethro, why? She doesn't collect celebrities."

"I think she does. Why else telephone a stranger and invite him to change his hotel for your home?"

"She didn't do that?"

"She did exactly that."

"It isn't like her." She fell silent, nervously twisting her bracelet.

"Don't worry, Faith, please. You don't need to see him alone again. You don't need to see him at all except at meals. If he annoys you I'll pitch him out the gate myself."

Though he had tried to make her laugh he did not find her laughter flattering. It said—as Faith herself would never have said—that Jethro Coggin was forty-five, skinny, stoop shouldered, rabbit faced, nose glassed. That he was also the bullied slave of the imperious woman whom he spoke of so facetiously as Her Highness.

Faith quickly sobered.

"Jethro, I'd like your advice."

"So you want a father-confessor, eh? A nice, fat, comfortable Friar Laurence?"

"Hardly fat. Otherwise—well, you do give good advice, you know."

"Which no one ever takes," he observed in the whisper in which a vocal affliction forced him to talk. "All right, go ahead."

She had changed her mind however. "No, I can't. I can't seem to face it. You said I couldn't face things, didn't you?"

He looked at her sharply. "I was wrong; you can. You face them without whimpering—even without self-pity. Only a few people can do that, dear." He added the endearment under his breath.

"Real things, perhaps, but not—not phantoms. Not things that I know aren't real, that exist only—" She hesitated. "Do you believe in hypnotism, Jethro?"

"I suppose so," he rejoined, startled. "Why?"

"Do you think it's possible for a person to hypnotize somebody—oh, anybody—with a single look?"

"Offhand I'd say no. But I'm no authority on that. Why don't you ask Jasper?"

"I did. He says it is. But Jasper believes so many things."

He laughed. "Yes, you mustn't take Jasper's opinion too seriously. Is it the idea of his being here that troubles you?"

"Ye-es," she confessed. "Partly."

"It will only be for a few days. He can't harm you. You mustn't be afraid of him, Faith."

"I'm more afraid of myself," she said, shuddering. Under the globe in the porch roof he studied her face.

Misty blue eyes under delicate brows. Light brown hair. An intelligent forehead. Small nostrils. A sensitive, too-often-serious mouth. On the whole a gracious face. The face of a lady who has suffered.

"Do you wish to explain?" he whispered. "If you do—"

"I've never told you about—about my secret self, Jethro. I've never told anyone. Maybe it was wrong. Maybe I shouldn't have tried to keep it to myself. I think that I'm—no, I can't say it. But something happened to me in China that—"

"Fix this damned tie, please," Eugene Vayne growled, coming abruptly around the corner of the living pavilion.

His wife retied the bow neatly and competently. How quickly her manner had altered, Coggin reflected. She seemed now like a patient mother with an exceedingly obstreperous child. But Gene was thirty-five.

II

Westborough took up his residence on the Vayne grounds on Tuesday evening immediately before dinner. As he rounded the covered walk, a little breathless from his ascent of the hill, he saw three persons standing on the open porch which overlooked the western ocean: a man and woman in evening clothes and Mrs. Vayne's rabbit-faced secretary. The latter introduced himself and presented the others as Mr. and Mrs. Eugene Vayne.

Murmuring that he was happy to have the good fortune, etc., Westborough made an unobtrusive inspection of the married couple. Eugene was not prepossessing though the remains of youthful good looks still lingered on his sullen countenance. He was overweight and flabby, small eyed, shifty, obviously a man who had never learned the art of controlling his passions. Faith Vayne was in an altogether different category.

She puzzled the little historian extremely. The flowing, hooded gown made her seem taller than she was. Her actual height was about five feet six, he estimated. She had a quiet, almost archaic dignity and a skin fair as white jade. There was sincerity in her welcome, he thought, and yet ... He was not quite able to make up his mind about her.

The couple, he learned, were on the verge of departing for the evening. Their muted voices floated back to him while they were descending the hillside path. They appeared to be engaged in some minor domestic controversy.

"Gene dear, let's go in the Packard tonight. Your mother won't mind."

"Without Mike Fry?"

"No-o. But Mike could take us."

"I don't like him. I don't want to be in a car that Mike Fry's driving."

"But why, dear? That isn't sensible. Mike has never done anything to—"

"I'm driving tonight. That's final."

"Yes, dear," she answered faintly, and the discussion ended.

Coggin cleared his throat with an indignant cough. "The skeleton in this house isn't very well hidden," he said in his odd whisper. "Gene's taken some sort of antipathy to the chauffeur, a man as harmless as they come. It's senseless. Faith oughtn't to cater to it. She's taking her life in her hands every time she—" The whispering voice hushed quickly. "I'm talking out of turn, I'm afraid."

"I will not give you away," Westborough said reassuringly. "Moreover, I had previously been informed of Mr. Vayne's—shall we say predilection?"

"It's common gossip, isn't it?"

"I do not know how common it is."

"Mrs. Vayne has told me all about your—er—errand, Mr. Westborough. I am ready to cooperate in every possible way."

"Thank you, Mr. Coggin. It is gratifying to know that I may call upon you if necessary."

"We have a few minutes before dinner. Let's step into my office for a short talk."

A glassed and covered porch, with several sliding doors opening on a small terrace to the north, connected Mrs. Vayne's private pavilion with the much smaller one occupied by her secretary. There were no *chinoiseries* in the latter's domain. A big flat-topped desk, a filing cabinet, a studio couch and a typewriter made the bedroom look a great deal like the office he had called it.

"Sit down, won't you?" Coggin invited, pointing to a chair. "Sorry I can't offer you a drink. Mrs. Vayne allows no liquor of any kind on the premises."

"Understandable, I am sure."

"Unfortunately she can't keep Gene in a straitjacket. Though even that's been tried."

"Dear me! Is the condition so serious?"

The secretary nodded curtly. He was tall, bony—an angular man like Mr. Grewgious. "It doesn't concern us now, however."

"No, it does not," Westborough agreed, accepting the mild reprimand. Opening the top drawer of the desk, Coggin took out a pearl-handled 32-caliber revolver.

"O'Connor is much younger than you, Mr. Westborough," he said explanatorily. "He looks very powerful and seems to be somewhat inclined to violent outbursts. I suggest that you keep this handy."

"Dear me, no," the historian hastily demurred. "I will not need it, I feel sure. I cannot believe that Mr. O'Connor is as dangerous as you represent."

"He may be only half as dangerous," the other conceded. "But remember that the guest house is a good distance from any other building. Help couldn't reach you promptly. It might not be able to reach you in time." He extended the revolver, grip forward. "This will make it safer. Better take it."

"I would rather not."

"As you please then." Coggin replaced the firearm in the top desk drawer. "By the way, I'm sure I've seen your face somewhere before."

"I attended the jade exhibit yesterday."

"Of course. Stupid of me to forget it."

Westborough raised his eyes to the secretary's thin, pinched face. "A Chinese gentleman entered the pavilion while I was there. I presume that his name and address appear on your register?"

"The address is Peking. Just that. The name is Dr. Liao Po-ching. Spelled with a *p* and *ch* but pronounced Bo-jing, I understand. Do you see any excuse for the idiotic way Chinese sounds are represented in English?"

"Very little, I confess. Then it is not known where Dr. Liao is staying at the present time?"

"It shouldn't be hard to find out. You'll see him again tomorrow. He telephoned Mrs. Vayne this afternoon, and she immediately invited him to tea. It turns out that he is a lecturer of some prominence."

"A friend of Mrs. Vayne's?"

"So far as I know," Coggin replied soberly, "she has never seen him in her life."

III

That night Westborough had the pleasure of dining in one of the most rarely beautiful settings he had seen in all the seven decades of his life. The ceiling was tesselated. The walls were a pale yellow satin. To the west a gigantic moon window framed a huge circle of black sky and bright stars. On the east hung a choice Oriental tapestry. The chairs and table were of Chinese blackwood. The sideboard was a brass-mounted teak cabinet. The centerpiece was a costly pigeon-blood cloisonné bowl, ruby red as the term implied. He also had the additional pleasure of meeting Mr. and Mrs. Jasper Kroll.

Mrs. Vayne's daughter was straw-haired, plump and florid; no longer in the spring of youth and yet unable to qualify for the advanced summer of middle age. Her dress was an absinthe-green silk print which, to Westborough's astonished eyes, appeared to be coming apart in the middle. It took him some little time to realize that the large area of apparently nude abdomen was merely a strip of flesh-colored fabric in the midriff. Lydia Vayne Kroll chattered incessantly, stopping only at brief intervals to feed a surreptitious morsel to the coal-black Pekingese pug who curled languidly at her feet and was addressed by a varied assortment of such names as Black Goblin, Gobbie, Gobble, Goblet, Gobbo, Gobbins, Gobblekins and Mama's Treasure.

Mrs. Kroll had many topics of discussion. She informed the guest of her insomnia and how seldom it was alleviated by the hot milk which Jasper darling, a dutiful husband, always fixed nightly for her. When interest waned in this she mentioned someone called Madame Wu. It was the first time that Westborough had heard the name—one destined to blaze dazzlingly as a nova in the troubled sky of the Vayne family's affairs.

"Who is Madame Wu?" he ventured to inquire during a conversational lull.

Mrs. Kroll stared incredulously. "You mean to say you don't know? Why, she's the most wonderful psychic—actually initiated as a Taoist priestess, I understand. You must let her tell your fortune, Mr. Westborough. It's perfectly uncanny the way she is able to foresee the future. She could find your Green Shiver in half an hour, Mama. Really. All the movie people go to her."

Mrs. Vayne, regarding her daughter with the pity one reserves for a low-grade moron, reminded Westborough more than ever of China's once-famous empress dowager. She wore her jewel-jade—some of it—bracelet and earrings of brilliant kingfisher-green *fei ts'ui* as glassily translucent as emeralds and virtually as costly. To add to the Tzu Hsi analogy Mrs. Vayne's son-in-law seemed much like the hapless emperor whom the indomitable Manchu matriarch had made her imperial prisoner.

Jasper Kroll was a small, gray-haired elf of thirty-six, cheerily bright as Harold Skimpole and equally as impossible to take seriously. When his wife finally yielded the floor he chatted with considerable erudition on the possibility of making contacts with extra-dimensional beings. These, as defined by Mr. Kroll, were not necessarily the spirits of deceased persons but the elemental beings mentioned so plentifully in the mythology of all nations: banshees, gnomes, pixies, hobgoblins, sylphs, salamanders, imps, vampires, ghouls and demons. Such legendary creatures, he claimed, were not mere figments of the imagination but an effort to depict in the limited terms of man's experience the inhabitants of other universes. Mr. Kroll believed that there were many four-dimensional universes existing in a five-dimensional continuum and that they were stacked, one upon another, rather in the manner of flat sheets of paper. He also opined that the e.d.b.'s, as a study of comparative folklore showed, were in general of a highly malignant nature. Nevertheless, he declared, he would not let that deter him from his efforts to get in touch with them.

"But," Westborough argued, "how is one able to assure these demoniacal poltergeists of one's desire for a quiet social visit? As yet there is no telephone line to the fifth dimension."

"I am accustomed to facetiousness," Kroll replied, seemingly only half offended. "Thought is the medium, my dear fellow. You are lucky that your own disbelief guards you from the dangers. To believe in the existence of extra-dimensional beings—even to think about them for long—gives them power since thought is the means by which they travel. Thought is power. Someday it will be recognized that thought is the only true power."

"Dear, dear!" Westborough paused to digest this amazing hypothesis. "In that event I should certainly not think of extra-dimensional beings at all since thinking is so dangerous."

"Fortunately there's a shield." Unbuttoning his shirt, Kroll displayed a carved pendant on a chain. "Laugh if you wish, but I wear it always. White jade."

That, Westborough offered mildly, was rather an astounding idea. "Not when you learn what's behind it," Kroll immediately took issue. "The ancient Chinese knew a great deal about the occult—probably more than any other race of mankind. Except, possibly, the Hindus and Egyptians."

"We are overlooking the Tibetan grand masters," Westborough could not forbear adding.

"Study the Chinese beliefs," Kroll commanded, ignoring the levity. "Jade is universally recognized as the substance most imbued with the Yang principle. And what is Yang? It is sun, light, male and good—just as the contrary, Yin, is moon, dark, female and evil."

"Jasper is a genius," Mrs. Kroll said proudly. "Aren't you, darling?"

"Study Chinese history," the piping tenor of the genius continued. "White jade—the supreme purity—was reserved exclusively for the use of the emperor. We have a hint of this in Chuang Tzu: 'If white jade were unbroken who could make the regalia of courts?' Are you familiar with the sayings of Chuang Tzu, my dear fellow?"

Westborough nodded. "Only through the medium of Herbert Giles' beautiful translation, however," he conscientiously qualified.

"Jade—and particularly the white form—has been credited from earliest days with the ability to exorcise evil spirits. The ancient Chinese perceived the fact empirically. They did not know the scientific reason. No one knows it yet, but two hundred years ago no one knew anything of the laws governing electricity. I contend that there can exist other natural forces of which we are still ignorant—mental forces. It is my mission in life to be a pioneer in their exploration. I accept the dangers. I accept also the vilification."

Mrs. Kroll glanced adoringly at her pint-sized husband. Jethro Coggin coughed. Mrs. Vayne, like King Seuen on the pages of Mencius, "looked to the right and left and spoke of other matters."

IV

Early on Wednesday morning Westborough had his first encounter with the mad O'Connor. The little man was on the guest house veranda, contemplating in the dragon-shaped pond the tiny island on which stood a green-encrusted bronze of Lao Tzu. The broad green lotus pads floated serenely on the murky water, providing a Buddhist symbol for the edification of the great Taoist. Looking across to the garage, Westborough saw two men on the stone-paved path bordering the sinuous pond.

The first, laden with luggage, he recognized at once as the Vayne chauffeur. The second was as easily identified. The flaming-haired O'Connor did not look mad, the historian reflected as the two went into the guest house. Indeed quite the contrary.

The chauffeur emerged minus the luggage, tipped his cap and returned to the garage. O'Connor came out shortly afterward. "Hello," he said. "Nice morning."

"It is a perfect morning. My name is Westborough, and I believe that we are to share this little house for the next few days."

"I'm Kerry O'Connor, and 'tis a pleasure to meet you." He sat down on a porcelain garden stool though his legs were much too long to render that low perch at all comfortable. A broad-shouldered six footer, this young Irish-American, a man whose robust body had been tempered into a disciplined instrument to perform his will. "Have you been here long, Mr. Westborough?"

"Only since yesterday evening."

"Just a pair of freshmen, eh?" Wit lurked in the depths of the smiling gray-green eyes. "Smoke?"

"No, thank you."

O'Connor put away his cigarette case and meditatively regarded the bronze philosopher. "That scraggly bearded ancient," he said, "is an old acquaintance. 'The Tao that can be told is not the eternal Tao; the name which can be uttered is not the eternal name. The Nameless is the mother of Heaven and Earth ... the mystery of all mysteries.' "

" 'Tao is inactive, and yet it leaves nothing undone,' " Westborough took up the chant. " 'That without substance enters where there is no fissure. Thus it is that the weak overcome the strong, the soft overcome the hard. Without going out of doors one may know the Way of Heaven.' "

O'Connor whistled. "I gather, sir," he said respectfully, "that you have studied the Book of the Way and Virtue."

"I have peeked within its cover," Westborough owned modestly.

"You quoted just now from the Doctrine of Inaction. Is that your own philosophy?"

"To a certain extent."

"It's one hundred per cent wrong. Lao Tzu made a tremendous mistake. I can tell you that from my own hardboiled experience."

"Indeed, Mr. O'Connor?"

"The weak don't overcome the strong. The soft get pulverized by the hard. The deviltry that's in the world today will have to be put down—if it can be put down—with tanks, battleships and airplanes."

"Are you thinking of China, perhaps?"

"I was," O'Connor returned grimly. "I've seen things there ... enough to make a man sick. But China's just a small part of it now."

"You are warmly emotional, I perceive."

"The Celt in me." The other laughed. "I'll admit I hate what I hate: meanness, cowardice, all forms of bullying whether by individuals or by nations. What's your one line of activity, by the way?"

"I am a student of Roman history."

"A big field. But you look like the man for it. Westborough, Westborough ... I've heard your name somewhere. What have you written? Anything?"

"I have attempted three biographies: Trajan, Julian and Heliogabalus."

"Great! Haven't we met before?"

"I don't believe so." Not wishing Kerry O'Connor to associate him with Mrs. Vayne's jade exhibit, Westborough began to feel a trifle uneasy. True, they had been in the room together only a few minutes, during which the young man's attention had been rather fully occupied. Nevertheless ...

"Your face is familiar."

"Probably because it is a very common type."

"Anything but that," the redheaded war correspondent returned with Irish blarney. "It's the face of a—well, student of Roman history. Let me think now. Perhaps you were roped in on one of my lectures?"

"I am sorry to say that I did not enjoy the pleasure."

"Pleasure, my eye!" Rising from the porcelain garden stool, O'Connor stood facing the stairs on the east slope of the hill. Long and straight as the steps of Peking's blue-domed Temple of Heaven, they ascended from the lotus pond to a big gate studded with golden hobs. "What are the people behind that like?" the new visitor inquired.

Westborough thought it good tactics to pretend surprise. "Can it be possible that you are not acquainted with them?"

"One. At least I thought I was."

"That would be Mrs. Eugene Vayne, I presume," the historian hazarded.

"Oh, it would, would it? And what made you pick her?"

"A simple process of logic. She has been in China. So have you. China is large, but the space-time field may be narrowed appreciably. She was in Tientsin during the day of the Japanese bombing. I know from your own vividly written work that you were in the same city at the same time. Ergo—" He left the conclusion suspended.

"Ergo nothing! She won't— Well! Look up there, will you?"

The gold-embossed gate was slowly opening. Emerging at the head of the stairs, Faith Vayne began to descend a hillside banked densely with pittosporum. The sun spattered reckless high lights over the shiny dark green leaves and small white blossoms of the shrubbery; it cast a glowing nimbus around the young woman's soft brown tresses. The sun had old-fashioned technique as a painter, but there was no denying the charm of his effects.

"Lady who walks in light!" O'Connor ejaculated. "Don't move, please. Maybe she won't see us."

The hope was ill-founded. Faith Vayne did see them. She halted, froze for an instant into motionless rigidity, turned swiftly and fled back up the stairs.

"What the devil!" O'Connor grinned to hide his obvious discomfiture.

V

As she opened the door of the lacquered cabinet in the tea pavilion Mrs. Vayne asked, "Doctor Liao, do you prefer a green China blend or Darjeeling?"

"Darjeeling, if you please."

Mrs. Vayne swiftly measured eight rounded teaspoonfuls of shriveled black leaves—one spoonful per drinker, extra spoonful for the pot. A wisp of steam wafted ceilingward from the brass kettle's shining spout.

"Isn't this fun?" gurgled Lydia Kroll. "Just like one of those cute little Japanese tea cere—" She caught her mother's warning frown. "Why, what's wrong now?"

"I am ever so happy," Dr. Liao interposed tactfully. "Teapot and select group of friends—humble Chinese can ask no more. Do you also like tea, Mr. O'Connor?"

"Did you ever know an Irishman who didn't?" O'Connor retorted.

"I have known few Irish. English, yes; they are as fond of beverage as we. But Americans are not."

When the kettle reached the boisterous "third boil" Mrs. Vayne poured the scalding water over the leaves and consulted her watch to time the period of steeping. Faith Vayne arose to arrange the teacups. They were very beautiful: small handleless cups of white jade resting on leaf-shaped olive-green jadeite saucers. An emperor might have envied the possession of such cups and saucers. Perhaps an emperor—Ming or Manchu—had once owned them.

"Americans, I have learned, drink only coffee and cocktails," Dr. Liao continued.

"I see I'll be having to deliver one of my favorite orations," O'Connor said, grinning. "Tea in this country for some mysterious reason has come to be associated with old women, sissies, gossips and teetotalers (no pun intended). It's time somebody brought out the other side of the case. I happen to know that tea has been served for a long time at Notre Dame training tables. No sissies among football players! Most explorers—in the tropics or the Arctic—rely on good old tea to give them a lift when the going gets tough. They aren't sissies either. Nor are British troops. If tea is good enough for athletes, explorers and fighting men it ought to be good enough for Mr. Average American, don't you think? It is. It's among the noblest beverages humanity has discovered in something like three thousand years. And it's too good for the crooked little finger and gabble of gossip sessions. Someday I'm going to start a movement to take tea away from the ladies—most of them haven't even learned how to make it right." He glanced toward Mrs. Vayne. "My apologies to my hostess, who does know."

"Hear, hear!" cried Jasper Kroll, clapping his hands. Dr. Liao applauded also.

"Excellent speech, Mr. O'Connor. Will you allow me, please, to make few additions? One drinks to enjoy quiet company of friends. 'To forget world's noise,' as scholar of sixteenth century has said. Wine is drink of rejoicing, but tea is drink of philosophy. Do I make it clear, please? It is hard to dress Chinese thoughts in garb of English language."

Westborough took the floor. "You express yourself with remarkable fluency. I understand, Doctor Liao, that you give public lectures like Mr. O'Connor."

"Great Godfrey!" O'Connor whispered. "Don't insult the poor fellow by putting him in my class."

Dr. Liao bowed gravely. "It is not always on battlefield that one may best serve one's country. It is my mission to win public support in America for noble leader who fights heroically against invaders. Mr. O'Connor I have heard speak. I whisper; he fearlessly shouts. He is not a Chinese but he is with us because of warm heart and love of justice."

The tribute had the effect of causing Kerry O'Connor's rugged face to redden to approximately the shade of his hair. "I can't accept any credit," he mumbled uncomfortably. "I'm nothing but a kind of racketeer. I signed up with a lecture bureau only because it looked like an easy way to make money."

("Can it be possible," Westborough meditated, "that here is that noblest work of God, an honest man? And I have been commissioned to prove him a thief. Dear me.")

The younger Mrs. Vayne passed the handleless jade cups. The reddish liquid had something of the flavor of a warm, strong liqueur. It was a brew well worthy of the incomparable leaf which grows only on the seven-thousand-foot slopes of India's Darjeeling section. Dr. Liao took both sugar and cream.

That was a trifle puzzling. Chinese seldom use either. But then Chinese, as a rule, do not care for black tea, even for so lordly a beverage as the great Darjeeling. If so why had he not cast his vote for green tea? Perhaps he had chosen the leaf which he believed his hostess would prefer. In that event he was either an extremely courteous gentleman (not unlikely) or he was anxious that his wealthy hostess should be in pleasant humor. And if the latter—could it be possible that the object of his call was to ask some favor?

Westborough realized that he was building rather an elaborate structure of reasoning upon the basis of slight facts. He toppled it over and listened to the words of the visitor from Peking.

"In China only favored guest is offered jade cup or rice bowl. To eat in perfection of jade, as we say, means to enjoy blessing of immortality."

"Ah!" exclaimed Jasper Kroll, like a hunting dog who has caught a whiff of game. "Are you familiar with the Taoist traditions of jade?"

"I have studied them slightly."

Goblin's little black button of a nose sniffed perfunctorily at the wafer his mistress proffered to him. When he stood erect his rear end floated haughtily in the air, and his waving tail curled like a plume above his tiny body. Mrs. Vayne frowned resentfully at the scattering of cookie crumbs on the carpet.

"Do you know Madame Wu, Doctor Liao?" asked Mrs. Kroll.

"I regret I do not."

"My pet, how could he know Madame Wu? She was born in San Francisco, and he has traveled here from Peking."

"But he would like Madame Wu. Wouldn't he, Jasper?"

"I do not know, my pet. You were talking about the Taoist immortality traditions, I believe, Doctor Liao."

"Oh, he *would* like Madame Wu, Jasper. She knows all the Taoist secrets of fortune-telling. She's the most wonderful psychic, Doctor Liao. Everything she says comes true. I wish you could meet her. She's coming here tomorrow morning to find our stolen statuette."

"Lydia, please!"

"You promised, Mama. And I've already telephoned and made the appointment."

"Madame Wu sounds like lady I would be happy to know." Dr. Liao's oblique eyes were expressionless black pools. "May I please have telephone number and address?"

The address was 685 South Novella Street, Los Angeles. Westborough noted it mechanically, not dreaming how importantly it was to figure in the later, more tragic phase of the Green Shiver case.

"Has some article been stolen from you?" Dr. Liao inquired of his hostess.

"Yes." Mrs. Vayne looked frigidly at her daughter's straw-blonde head.

"May I express hope lost will be found?"

"Thank you."

"Is missing article of jade?"

"Yes, it *is* jade." Mrs. Vayne's flowing tea gown seemed suddenly to assume the starchy qualities of an Elizabethan ruff.

"Yesterday I had happiness of viewing magnificent collection."

"Day before yesterday," she corrected brusquely.

"Thank you. Time means too little to Chinese. In your country I learn to appreciate virtues of punctuality, but lesson is painful." Dr. Liao's smile had the magnetic charm so frequently encountered among the members of his long civilized race. "Looking upon beautiful objects, I am reminded of unhappy ancestor, physician to Ta Ch'ing emperor, who disgraced graced high office by making august emperor more sick with potion intended to cure. When stripped of coral button and peacock feather for crime miserable man must hang himself."

"But how could my jade remind you of that?" asked Mrs. Vayne.

"Presently it becomes clear. Suicide soul haunted room in which unlucky physician died, tempting living to perform same act of hanging. Taoist priest called in to exorcise dangerous ghost. Arts of adept Taoist forced wretched *p'o* soul to inhabit small statue of jade, kept hidden in monastery cellar. Tradition of my family that each oldest son must pay visit on entering state of manhood to pay respects to venerated ancestor. I am such oldest son. Long ago, at age when mind was bent on learning, I viewed jade abode of unhappy suicide. Have not seen same since until coming here."

"Among my things?" Mrs. Vayne cried. "That's impossible. How could your ancestor's statue leave its monastery?"

"I cannot explain on ground of fact but must resort to flight of fancy. Perhaps monk unworthy of high religious calling stole valuable jade to sell to Peking dealer. Perhaps, again, I am mistaken, and it is different statue. But that I soon can tell."

"How?"

"There exists secret mark, recognizable only by oldest sons of my family, by which carving may be identified. Day before yesterday I tried to look for it, but excellent gentleman, your secretary, prevented me from handling object. May such person as I ask of exalted lady, his hostess, so great a favor?"

"Of course. Unless it's the—"

"You are so kind. May I examine in private, please, for sake of respected ancestor?"

"Which statue is it, Doctor Liao?"

"Pardon, please, my stupidity. Statue of P'i-hsia Yüan-chün."

"That," Mrs. Vayne declared coldly, "*is* the one that was stolen."

Whatever emotions Dr. Liao may have felt did not appear on his bland countenance.

"Additional disgrace is brought to my family to have esteemed ancestor in hands of thieves. But perhaps thieves also may suffer. Suicide ancestor may escape from jade prison."

"Dear me!" Westborough exclaimed. "Do you think it's possible?"

"Evil always releases evil," Dr. Liao replied solemnly. "Freed soul may resume bad practice of tempting living to share fate. Perhaps thieves may soon take own lives."

The thing was perfectly incredible, but Westborough did not smile. Nor did anyone else in the room. Not even Jocasta Vayne, hard-bitten realist to the core. Jasper Kroll was the first to interrupt the brief moment of stunned silence.

"I accept ghosts, of course. All nations have believed in them, at all ages of mental development. Naturally consciousness persists after death. Why not? Scientists are beginning to recognize that the soul, so called, is merely a nonmaterial but living wave pattern, which may exist independently of the brain atoms. A soul, if you wish to call it that, may endure forever."

"I am inferior man who cannot grasp three corners of subject after first corner has been shown to him," was Dr. Liao's comment.

"Why shouldn't such a vibrational pattern be transferred to an inanimate object?" Kroll demanded in a rapid flow of words. "It can be. It frequently is. What's a haunted house but an example?"

"I am man," said the Chinese suavely, "who knows that he does not know. Thought without study is perilous, declared the great Kung. Perhaps, Mr. Kroll, we may meet at some future date when you will be so kind as to instruct me further?"

"I should like nothing better. Please stay with us for dinner tonight and you and I can talk afterward."

Dr. Liao glanced toward his hostess, who apparently had not heard her son-in-law's invitation. "Tonight, alas, I regret that I must lecture."

Westborough, in whom tea had induced a state of mental activity midway between stimulation and repose, listened to a jumble of fragments from simultaneous conversations:

"What a lot of leaves in your cup, Faith. You must let me tell your fortune. Turn the cup over and make a wish."

"Oh, that's too bad, but could you join us tomorrow night or the next?" (Mrs. Vayne still had not heard her son-in-law's invitation.)

"Turn the cup three times to the left and think very hard. It's your subconscious mind that forms the pictures."

"Long way to ask anyone to travel, I know."

"Don't take your thumb away, Faith. You'll have to mark the spot where you began since there isn't any handle."

"Perhaps, Mr. Kroll, you would be so kind as to dine at my hotel? If you do not mind so far a journey."

"This is near the handle—only there isn't any handle—so it refers to you personally. Would you say it looks like hemlock?"

"I was going to town anyway tomorrow to do some research work at the library. Where is your hotel?"

"It is hemlock. It stands for the shadow of your past, Faith. The shadow is going to interfere with your present, I think."

"Aubusson Hotel on Hollywood Boulevard. I have afternoon lecture in Pasadena, cannot return until late. Would eight o'clock be convenient hour, Mr. Kroll?"

"It's near the rim. The leaves near the rim stand for things that are going to happen to you soon."

"Eight o'clock is fine, thanks."

"A shark, Faith, see! It's near the rim too. A shark! That's a terrible sign. And this other is—why, it's a pistol!"

"Would you like Chinese dinner, Mr. Kroll? Excellent restaurant in hotel building will serve in my room."

"A pistol and a shark together! *Death!* Oh, my poor Faith!"

VI

A piece of white paper had been left on the dresser of Westborough's room in the guest house. It contained just twenty-eight typewritten words:

"Theocritus Lucius Westborough, you have been lucky so far, but there are matters in which it is dangerous to pry. Take care. There will be no second warning."

Westborough reflected that he had noticed a portable typewriter case that morning among his housemate's luggage. Walking to the east wall, he thoughtfully regarded a framed example of Chinese calligraphy. The vertical columns, he had been told, represented a poem by that "banished angel" of the T'ang dynasty who had written so feelingly on drinking alone with the moon and afterward lost his life leaping drunkenly to embrace his beloved's silvery image in the water. Below the rhythmically brushed characters of Li Po's verse had been bored the "peephole" which Mrs. Vayne had promised.

Westborough peered through the tiny round opening with marked distaste. His fellow guest, however, seemed to be absent. Clutching a small brass handle, he slid the wooden door panel a sufficient distance to permit him to squeeze into the next room. He found the typewriter case in a corner and carried it back to his own room. Closing the sliding door, he rehung the Li Po verse to cover the peephole.

Fortunately the square black case was not locked. Inserting a sheet of paper behind the platen of the machine, he hunt-and-pecked the twenty-eight-word threat. The original note he labeled with a lead pencil *A* and his own production he similarly marked *B*. Among his things was the big reading glass he had so often found useful in enlarging passages of small print. Under its magnification the separate letters of *A* and *B* appeared as alike as any objects produced by the same matrix.

Westborough nodded to himself. Again he took down the Li Po verse and looked through the peephole. Apparently it was safe to return the illegally borrowed typewriter. He deposited it in the corner where he had found it and was on the point of leaving the room when a partially opened drawer caught his attention.

"A firearm!" he gasped.

It was a 38-caliber revolver, he saw, and a peculiar-looking one. Stock, trigger, guard, hammer and cylinder were regulation size, but the stumpy two-inch barrel was grotesquely out of proportion. The construction offered one great advantage, however; the weapon, with an overall length of less than seven inches, would fit readily into a man's pocket or lady's handbag. A trifle gingerly he withdrew it from the drawer.

Though he had fired neither a pistol nor a revolver in his life, his friendship with Lieutenant Mack of Chicago, Captain Cranston and other police officials had taught him the essential facts of their construction. Moving the lever which swung the cylinder out to the side, he ejected the six cartridges simultaneously into his hand. He held them in his palm with satisfaction. He had drawn the tiger's teeth, he mused: large brass teeth with leaden fillings. The weapon was now harmless.

"Would you be minding returning those?" a voice asked icily from the veranda doorway.

Westborough jumped, startled. The redheaded O'Connor was six inches taller, something like twice as broad across chest and shoulders and some forty years younger. Without any question he held the balance of power. "I am sorry," the historian apologized, meekly surrendering the cartridges.

"Sorry you should be," O'Connor said sternly. "A man of your age!"

"I mean I am sorry I did not succeed."

"'Tis nerve you have anyway." The journalist reloaded the revolver and slipped it into his pocket. "Sit down," he ordered, his speech growing less Irish as his emotion waned, "and tell me what you're doing in my room."

"May I ask," Westborough countered, "why you brought that firearm here?"

"It's a habit of mine to carry this little fellow with me. He's seen me through one or two tough spots in China. And what business is it of yours? I'd like to know."

"Is it not true, Mr. O'Connor, that when you accepted Mrs. Vayne's invitation you experienced a presentiment of trouble?"

"Who's quizzing who, my friend? I don't have to account to you, but you do owe me an explanation, I'm thinking. Who put you up to this?"

"I am not at liberty to inform you."

"Good Godfrey, do you know what I could do to you?"

Westborough smiled gently. "Yes, Mr. O'Connor, I have no doubt that it is well within your power to inflict upon me a considerable degree of physical suffering. But there would be little glory in it. 'Mighty is he who conquers himself.' "

O'Connor's anger melted suddenly into hearty laughter. "A perfect example of the Doctrine of Inaction! And me saying only this morning that the Old Boy didn't know what he was talking about! I retract. The Old Boy did. Incidentally I mentioned, didn't I, that I hated all forms of bullying?"

The little man's mild blue eyes twinkled behind his bifocals. " 'The strong one who is content to be weak—he shall be the admiration of men.' "

"A private dick who quotes Lao Tzu and writes Roman history!" O'Connor marveled. "Or are you really Westborough the historian?"

"Yes, my identity is genuine."

"Isn't this sort of thievery rather a dirty business for a man like you to be mixed in?"

"I believe, contrary to the wisdom of Ecclesiasticus, it is possible to touch pitch without being defiled. Though I became, shall we say, a salaried minion it was not from desire to harm one whom I sincerely respected."

"Careful, old-timer, you're letting the soft soap dribble. You never saw me before today. You admitted it only this morning."

"I have read *Bombs and Bayonets*. A man's book is an extension of his personality. It is obvious, is it not, that a mean little soul is unable to think noble thoughts? Your own personality, Mr. O'Connor, is revealed as warm and generous. I should be proud to be numbered among your friends."

"A peculiar little man sneaks into my bedroom." O'Connor addressed some invisible entity in the air. "He goes through my things, takes the cartridges from my revolver. But when I lay my hands upon the leprechaun he tries to squiggle away by saying that he has read my book with admiration and would like to be friends. No, thank you. I'm having no traffic with leprechauns."

"The rebuke is merited," Westborough said humbly. "I am not offended but I am disappointed. Disappointed, Mr. O'Connor, because I realize I have no hope of ever inducing you to confide in me."

"None," the other returned, setting his strong jaw firmly. "Now get the hell out of here."

PART FOUR: SHADOWS IN CRYSTAL

THE JADE CHIME—a thin, carved fish of mutton-fat nephrite hanging from a wood frame—rang musically when struck by Madame Wu's wand. "Sweet is the voice of jade." (Her own voice, Westborough reflected, held much the same cool tinkle.) "But the lost was not here." The wand, a six-inch pencil of ebony, hovered laxly for an instant above the low oval table near the door, then pointed, seemingly of its own volition, across the room to the redwood curio cabinet.

"It was taken from here," Madame Wu announced with conviction. She wore a dark, short-sleeved dress modishly trimmed in red; her glossy black hair was waved and semi-bobbed.

Lydia Kroll glanced triumphantly toward her mother. "She's done half of it already."

The Chinese lady walked gracefully. Her lips were red and roguish, the small nose delicately upturned. Her flawless, pale gold skin was tinted with living rose. She was as lovely as Yang Tai-chen, that celebrated court beauty of the T'ang dynasty.

And as modern as Rockefeller Center.

Moving from shelf to shelf of the cabinet, the wand traveled slowly to a halt. "This is the spot on which the lost was standing."

"Ye-es," Mrs. Vayne reluctantly owned.

"She's won your test, Mama!" Lydia crowed. "None of us told her; she's never even been in this room before, but she walked straight to it. If that's not true clairvoyance what is it?"

"An example of lightning-quick facial reading," Westborough answered—but only mentally. The girl (she could scarcely be over twenty-three though it was difficult to gauge Oriental ages) was at least as keen-witted as she was beautiful.

That was undeniably saying a good deal.

56

"There's some trick to it," asserted Mrs. Vayne, unconvinced.

"I am not a trickster, madame." The jet-black eyes mirrored definite scorn. "It has taken me a long while to travel this far from the city, and my time is valuable to me. However, I will charge nothing for the trip unless you wish me to continue."

"Thasha fair offer." Eugene Vayne reeled tipsily into the living pavilion. "Give the little girl a chanshe."

Mrs. Vayne said coldly, "You're beginning early this morning, Eugene." On her granite-hewn face was no maternal tenderness, merely icy contempt.

"My money'sh on China! Give her a chanshe, I shay."

Madame Wu met the man's drunken stare with silent unconcern.

"Please tell Weng to make a pot of strong coffee, Jethro." Mrs. Vayne issued a queenly command.

"Don't wannany," her son snarled. "Wanna have a good look at shingshong girl."

"But *I* want coffee, dear. We'll go drink it together." Faith Vayne's soft voice was soothingly patient. The thin, plucked lines above Madame Wu's epicanthic eye folds arched slightly in disdain.

"Wanna shtay and lishen to shingshong girl."

"But she isn't a singsong girl, Gene. This is Madame Wu."

"Wu, Wu, Wu? Parrot shays to owl not you ..." Wife and secretary, one on each side, succeeded in escorting the inebriate to the dining pavilion.

Mrs. Eugene Vayne's duties, Westborough deliberated, were no more exacting than those of any trained nurse, and she was paid rather better than nursing wages. He reflected that he ought not to pity her. But he did.

Mrs. Vayne addressed the Chinese lady. "I do wish you to continue the search."

"I am now seeing inwardly." Madame Wu's voice deepened, took on the conventional trancelike quality. "The jade is of limpid gray streaked with green—water running over a mossy rock. I see the carved form of a woman. She is very severe: her brows frown; the nose is long and aristocratic, the chin sharp. She is the Taoist goddess of T'ai Shan, and she has many names. Among yourselves you call her the Green Shiver or the Jade Lady. I see above her head to her broken crown. I see below her feet: on her pedestal is the symbol of the Hare Who Dwells in the Moon."

"I didn't tell her what it was!" Lydia exulted. "It's genuine clairvoyance."

"Is it?" Westborough thought. "Dear me, I should like to know if this charming Chinese lady were not visited last night by a Chinese scholar of almost equal charm. Doctor Liao Po-ching did, as I recall, ask for her address."

"A hand is snatching at the statue," Madame Wu resumed. "I see it dimly. I cannot tell whether it is man's or woman's. But it belongs to someone who is either in this room now—or has been here very recently."

"It ought to be easier to recognize whether the hand was male or female," Westborough pondered. "But the occult, no doubt, works under strange laws."

"Someone in this room!" Lydia cried excitedly. "Jasper, did you hear that?"

"I did, my dear."

Mrs. Vayne inspected one by one her daughter, straw haired and shrill voiced, her gray, slight son-in-law, the tall, rugged O'Connor, and finally her glance wandered toward the dining pavilion, where her son, daughter-in-law and secretary had just gone.

"One of us? How do you know?"

"I know. Even though I could tell how in words you would not understand. A blind man may be led before the Night Watch but he will see nothing of Rembrandt. A deaf man hears nothing of Beethoven though a hundred men may be performing The Ninth Symphony. "

Westborough thought: "Night Watch? Rembrandt? The Ninth Symphony? Beethoven? The child has received an excellent education."

"I am neither blind nor deaf," Mrs. Vayne said grimly.

"Blindness and deafness are not merely of the body. I am sorry to speak so obscurely. Words are small bags which cannot hold big things. Only one who follows the Tao is able to grasp the nature of the highest truth."

"Is it true," Jasper Kroll inquired with scientific interest, "that a Taoist is able to project his soul in visible form through the top of his head?" His mother-in-law's stern frown hushed him immediately.

"Are you prepared, Madame Wu, to make a definite accusation?"

"As yet I cannot see. There are too many thought patterns vibrating in this room. Is there a smaller one I may use temporarily?"

"Why, yes, you may have the tea pavilion. What else?"

"In my car is a case containing articles I will need. Send one of your servants to fetch it."

"Is there anything else?"

Madame Wu's sensitive fingers were caressing the jade chime. "I should like to borrow this if I may. The experiments I am about to undertake are accompanied by an element of danger. To me more than to others. White jade is the essence of purity —the Yang principle. Forces of evil cannot enter the room it guards."

"You may have it. Is that all?"

"All the material things I will need, yes. But I want to talk to all here, each separately." Her wand pointed from Westborough to Kroll. "First to this man who believes only in his own senses; then to this one who is too credulous."

Mrs. Vayne made no attempt to conceal her amusement. "And the rest?"

"I do not care in what order they come to me. But I must see all—even yourself."

"My servants too?"

"Your gardener, no. I will not talk to a Japanese. The others you may send to me."

"I can promise for myself and the servants—and Mr. Coggin. Faith also, I believe. And Lydia and Jasper ought to be willing to cooperate."

They nodded eagerly.

"This sort of hocus-pocus is just the thing that would appeal to you," Mrs. Vayne gibed. "I can't answer for Gene, Madame Wu. Even if he does come he may not be in any condition to talk sensibly. And Mr. O'Connor and Mr. Westborough are guests. I cannot compel either of them to do anything."

"Count me in," O'Connor said.

"And I shall be happy also," the historian added.

"In five minutes I shall be ready for you, Mr. Westborough."

"I'll show you where the tea pavilion is," Mrs. Vayne offered.

Turning her glossy black head, the Chinese girl smiled enigmatically. "It is not necessary to show me. I can see it clearly from within."

She strolled through the doorway with the bearing of a Manchu princess.

II

When he reached the tea pavilion Westborough discovered that the shades had been unrolled, shutting out most of the magnificent views of ocean, primroses and bamboo grove which ordinarily made the little room so pleasant. The lacquered table had been conscripted to hold Mrs. Vayne's jade fish chime and a big quartz sphere Madame Wu had undoubtedly brought with her. Most striking of all, the sibyl had changed her costume. She was now robed in crimson silk embroidered with the broken octagons of the Book of Changes and the divided circles of Yin and Yang. It was a gown well becoming a daughter of Tao or fitting a sorceress of the more ancient Wu rites (from which perhaps the lady had borrowed her terse two-letter name).

"We will not speak for a few minutes." She was seated behind the table, a short distance to the left of the wholly transparent crystal. "But it is necessary to observe mental silence as well as physical. Try to make your mind an utter blank."

Westborough found that task extremely difficult. His eyes remarked the slenderness of the Chinese lady's wrists, her exquisite hands, the small, flat breasts almost concealed beneath the flowing robe. They were, he reflected, the breasts of a virgin. Despite the matronly title Madame Wu had probably never known marriage or a love affair. He wondered if she ever would. It was doubtful. She seemed so aloof, so untouchable. ... The oracle had commenced to frown.

"You are a difficult subject," she said severely.

"I am very sorry." He regarded the ball of quartz on its carved teak base while he waited for her to continue.

"A few things I can tell you," she said at length. "You are a scholar. You have devoted your life to learning and have learned much. That, however, is not the path of wisdom."

"I fear not," he concurred. "Since I am still so far from being wise."

"You are modest and yet proud in your scholar's pride. You do not follow the Way."

"No."

"You are in this household but not of it—just as you sleep apart. You did not take the missing statuette."

"Thank you."

Her sloe-black eyes scrutinized his face minutely. "But," she added quickly, "you are more than ordinarily interested in its recovery. Take care. It is dangerous. He who mounts the tiger dares not dismount."

"I have no intention of dismounting," he said.

She smiled faintly. "You are not a coward. Nor are you unintelligent."

"May I return the compliment? I have never in my life encountered a woman of such mental alertness. Is it a racial quality?"

"Perhaps. And perhaps it is the result of the discipline my father forced me to undergo. A long, arduous training. The Way is not easy to follow. You look upon me as a charlatan, do you not?"

"Yes," Westborough said. "But one whose intuition is almost as remarkable as the psychic powers she claims to profess."

She giggled softly—and changed at once from a mystic sibyl into a modern young woman in her early twenties.

"I like you for not lying. I also respect your intelligence. For me that is saying much, Mr. Westborough. I have found few intelligences which I am able to respect."

"Thank you, Miss Wu. I shall not call you madame any more because it so obviously does not fit you. Will you deliver a message for me?"

She nodded. "If I know the person."

"You do know him, I believe. A Chinese gentleman. We met informally on Monday morning and exchanged a few words. He might have caused me considerable embarrassment yesterday by alluding to that incident. I had no opportunity to caution him, but he did not mention our meeting. Will you be kind enough to extend my thanks for his innate understanding of a delicate situation?"

"What is the name of the Chinese?"

"Doctor Liao Po-ching of Peking."

"I am sorry." The girl's face quickly became expressionless. "I cannot deliver your message, Mr. Westborough. I am not acquainted with Doctor Liao Po-ching."

III

"She's even younger than I am," Faith Vayne thought. "Why, she looks as if she's still in her teens!"

"I am twenty-five," Madame Wu replied to the unspoken observation. "The same age as yourself. No, that is not psychic. Your sister-in-law has given me many enthusiastic reports of you. I have looked forward to this meeting. You speak Chinese, I believe?"

"I know a little Mandarin."

"I do not," Madame Wu returned, smiling. "My father was from Canton, but I do not speak even Cantonese fluently. I was born and educated in the United States."

"Well educated," Faith said.

Madame Wu lifted her slim shoulders expressively. "It matters little. Learning is not the highest road to wisdom. You know the purpose for which your sister-in-law invited me here, Mrs. Vayne?"

"Yes, of course."

"Before you this morning I have talked to Mr. Westborough, Mr. Kroll, Mrs. Kroll and Mr. O'Connor. As your sister-in-law has told you, I do not see with the eyes alone nor listen only with the ears."

"Yes," Faith said.

"Mr. Westborough, your sister-in-law and her husband are guiltless of the theft. This is not speculation on my part; it is definite knowledge. About Mr. O'Connor I cannot be so sure. The Irish are a strange, fey people. Have you studied their history and folklore?"

"Not very much."

"The extraordinary beings whom many in Ireland profess to have seen are not altogether imaginative. The Irish are sensitive. There is no race so naturally psychic—no, not even the Chinese." Madame Wu paused briefly. "Mr. O'Connor insists that a banshee—a supernatural visitor from another world—has actually appeared to him. Have you known him long?"

"Only a few days."

"No more than that?" The Chinese lady's delicate fingers toyed with the white jade fish. "It may be true. Perhaps he is sincere in claiming the power to see. I cannot read his thoughts."

"Can you read mine?"

"Partially. I know, for example, that you are not happy with your husband."

Faith thought, "How could Lydia be so disloyal to her brother?"

"You are thinking that I was given the information by your sister-in-law? Perhaps. But perhaps Mrs. Kroll did not know she was giving it." Madame Wu turned from the jade chime to the quartz sphere. "I should like you to look in there."

Faith drew back involuntarily.

"You are afraid? Why?"

"I'm not afraid. It's just—I don't believe in crystal gazing."

"If you do not believe nothing can harm you. So why not make the experiment? But you are afraid of what you may see."

"No. No, I'm not. But—"

Madame Wu smiled knowingly. "You are thinking of hypnotism, are you not? Don't be alarmed. Neither I nor anyone else can hypnotize you against your will. You will not go to sleep. You will remain wholly conscious. Are you still afraid?"

"I'll look," Faith promised. "Is there any special method?"

"Yes. Lean back in the most comfortable position you can find. Relax. Let your arms hang limply at your sides. Stretch out your legs and be comfortable. No, not that way." Madame Wu's voice was gently soothing. "You must not think of your arms and legs. You must not think of anything at all. You have been for a walk in the snow of winter—such snow as we do not have here. You are cold, chilled. Oh, you are so cold! Your fingers and toes ache; your cheeks are tingling. Now you come into the house—into a warm, cozy room with a log fire blazing in the fireplace. Such a warm room! You take off your snowy coat. You have enjoyed the walk, but it is good to be home again. You take off your high-heeled shoes and put on slippers—old, a little shabby, but so comfortable! You take off your dress and girdle. You do not need to bother about appearances. No one is coming tonight. You are glad that you will be alone to enjoy the warmth of your fireside. You are glad that you will not have to entertain visitors, to talk to anyone. You are tired from the long walk."

Faith found herself beginning to yawn. She half closed her eyes but continued to regard the crystal. It was as transparent as a substance made by man could ever be. There was nothing to be seen in it—not even a reflection from the room.

"Here is your favorite negligee," Madame Wu continued. "You slip it on your shoulders. The smooth silk clings but does not bind. Your body has never been more comfortable. But you are tired. You sink into the big armchair by the fire. Its cushions give under your weight, enveloping you in a nest of down. Here are cigarettes; you have only to stretch out your hand. You light one and allow the smoke to blow through your nostrils. It is good, that smoke, but you do not want another one. You do not want to do anything but sit there, cuddled like a purring kitten in the soft, soft chair. The heat from the flames bathes your whole body in its delicious warmth. You are drowsy—just a little drowsy, perhaps. You stretch out your arms and yawn. You clasp the tips of your fingers behind the back of your neck. It is good to stretch, good, good! Your head nods from side to side. But you do not fall asleep. You are not asleep, are you?"

"No," Faith whispered. "No, I am not asleep." She saw that a cloudy something was blurring the center of the crystal's pure transparency. A trick of tired eyes of course.

"You gaze into the fire," continued Madame Wu. "The flames have almost died into a heap of glowing coals. You remember that when you were a little girl you used to be able to see pictures in a fire. Wonderful visions of lakes and mountains and castles and dragons and knights in armor. You wonder if you can see them again. You feel that you can see them again. But you must not try too hard. You stare fixedly at the burning coals ... the minutes pass slowly. One minute, two, three. The fire grows larger the longer you look."

The crystal seemed to be growing larger. Black magic? Something in its interior moved and took form.

"The fire is as large as the wall." Madame Wu's voice seemed to be coming from entirely outside the room. "You are conscious of nothing in the world but that shimmering flame. And while you look it changes shape ..."

"It does," Faith whispered. "How can you make it do that?"

"Quiet, please. You must think only of the picture. You must not let it escape from you. Tell me what you see?"

"Grain rippling in the wind. It's too tall for wheat. It's as tall as the head of a man on horseback."

"How can you judge its height? Is there something for comparison?"

"There must be—yes, there are human figures."

"Can you see them clearly?"

"Hardly at all. It's like looking through a telescope that isn't in focus."

"But you do see the grain clearly?"

"Yes. It's kaoliang. But the center of the picture is clear. It's as if a path had been cut through. ... I see what it is now. We're walking on a railroad track."

"We?"

"One of the figures is I."

"Who is with you?"

"A man. I can't see him clearly. I never can."

"You have seen this place before?"

"Not actually. But it is like a dream I have. It *is* my dream."

"Look more closely at the man."

"I can't. When I try to do that the dream ends. But I can see a little more. He is carrying a suitcase. Not his, mine. Now I know lots of things. How did I learn them? We were tired of being cooped up on the train."

"What train?"

"I don't know where it came from ... where it's going. I feel I should know but I don't. The train had stopped for a long time. I think it had been switched onto a siding at a tiny Chinese village—a dream village without a name. We had been there for hours, it seemed. He asked me to walk through the town. It was stuffy in the compartment and so peaceful outside."

"Was it the man who asked you to take a walk?"

"Yes. I didn't want to go at first. I told him I couldn't leave my suitcase on the train unwatched. He said that he'd carry it. It was heavy, but he carried it quite easily. He was strong, I remember. But it isn't memory, is it? You can't remember things that never happened."

"Are you sure they didn't, Mrs. Vayne?"

"Oh yes! I *know* all of this is just a dream. I must be dreaming now ... but I can't be, can I? I'm wide awake."

"Don't think of that now, please. Look only at that man. Try to see his face."

"He—he has no face!"

"Fear hides it from you. Very well, let the picture form as it will. What else do you see?"

"A bridge—the bridge I always see. Soldiers are standing around little huts a short distance away. Japanese. One in front of the bridge yells at us ... a dark, bowlegged little man so mad over nothing ... his hand slaps my cheek. A Japanese soldier slaps me! I can feel the shock, the sting. Do you feel pain in a dream? The soldiers by the huts are laughing, jeering, pointing. I feel as if I were standing there naked before them. I want to die so I won't have to endure that—that awful shame. Then I see the man again. He is ghost-white, and his eyes are a cold, hard green. I've never in real life seen a man so angry.

"This is the part I dream over and over. It's something like a motion picture but running on a screen inside my head. I know that he is going to do something foolish, and I want to stop him. I try to stop him, but I don't have time. Before I can even call a warning he twists the rifle from the sentry's hand. He strikes the sentry with his fist and knocks him down.

"It all happens quickly, but I can see every detail. The other soldiers come running toward us from their huts. One—the nearest—raises his rifle to his shoulder. I know that the man who defended me is going to die. I know that, but I can do nothing except stand there, paralyzed with horror. But the soldier doesn't fire."

"Why doesn't he?" Madame Wu inquired.

"Something happens to him. Can you hear sounds in your dreams? I hear them in this one. The rattle of a machine gun—and the soldier clutches a red mark on his throat. The Japanese fall like little sacks stuffed with straw. But not all of them. Some run back to their huts. Then other soldiers spring out of the kaoliang. Chinese in ragged cotton uniforms. Perhaps they have crawled through the grain for miles—hidden for hours by the bridge waiting for the right minute to make the attack. I do not know in my dream. There is shooting all around us—bullets coming from both the grain and the huts. I'm running. I'm on the bridge, the river beneath me and nothing but empty space between the railroad ties. It always comes as a terrible shock to find myself there.

"It has to be a dream. I couldn't run over those long gaps between the ties even if my life depended on it. But in a dream you can do impossible things. I look down at the river, churning in yellow foam; it is like a monster reaching up for me with magnetic power. I start to fall ... oh, it's awful, that part! I'm actually in the air, screaming, but he always saves me. His arm keeps me from toppling over the edge."

"Do you recognize him yet?" asked Madame Wu.

"No."

"You saw his face. You said it was white with anger."

"It was only the anger I saw. Not the actual face."

"Look closely again."

"No, no, please. I can't."

"Why are you afraid of that man, Mrs. Vayne?"

"I'm not. Yes; yes, I am. Why? I don't know. Something I've done to him—no, I don't know what it is. It's just a deep black horror. Don't make me talk about it, please."

"Very well. Can you see any more pictures?"

"Yes. They go on even while I'm talking to you. Are they really in the crystal?"

"Don't think of that, Mrs. Vayne. What is it you see?"

"The bridge isn't at all distinct. A railway bridge without any footway— we have to jump over the ties. He helps me across. When we reach the end we run down an embankment and hide in a field by the tracks. More kaoliang. They are still fighting on the other side of the river, but the noise is growing fainter. He still has my suitcase. I thought that he'd dropped it to hit the sentry ... he must have picked it up afterward. There's a bullet hole through the leather. The dream always gets silly here."

"Why?"

"Because—because I want to open the suitcase. Insist on opening it. And there are—all the lovely things I bought on Jade Street. The bullet broke a little piece from the Jade Girl's crown. But it didn't really. She was damaged when I bought her."

"Are you sure?"

"She must have been damaged, or I couldn't have bought her so cheaply. This is only a dream, I know. He's laughing at me. He tells me we can thank our stars we got out of it with our lives. He says that if I'd started to run back to the town instead of across the bridge we'd have been in the line of fire from both sides. How do I know he's saying these things? I don't hear any words. There isn't much more to come—some sort of explosion. I always wake up at this point."

"Will you look at him now, Mrs. Vayne?"

"Yes. Yes, I'll try. I want to see him. I really do. I do see him! Just a glimpse and then his face faded away. But I was able to recognize him. Mr. O'Connor!"

Madame Wu nodded thoughtfully. "That man has power, Mrs. Vayne. He is able to impose himself on your mind."

"He *can* do that. How did you know? I—I'm afraid of him."

"You must forget him now. Look at the crystal."

"There's nothing there. Everything left when I saw Mr. O'Connor. I knew it would."

"Soon you will see again. Concentrate all your mind on the little statuette. That will help you to see."

"It does. Is this magic or what? A Chinese is holding the figurine in his hand. I know him. He is Yee Feh-lu. I bought the statuette from Yee."

"Are you in his shop?"

"I don't think so. I should be, but—why, he's in my hotel room! Yee never came there. My clothes are scattered over the bed. It doesn't look at all respectable. I'm packing, I think. No, I'm at the desk writing. I'm signing a paper. I write Faith Kingston in English. And I write my Chinese name too."

"What else is on the paper, Mrs. Vayne?"

"Columns of Chinese characters."

"What do they say?"

"I don't know."

"You know Chinese. Read them."

"I can't. I can't see clearly enough."

"Mrs. Vayne," Madame Wu said with strange intensity, "that paper is enormously important. To you and to Yee and to China—the China that is being crushed by Japanese gangsters and heroin. You must read those characters. You must—"

"What the devil's going on?" Eugene Vayne, halfway sober now, walked into the tea pavilion. "She's got you dopey as a sleepwalker, Faith. Snap out of it. Let her go, Miss Singsong. It's almost time for lunch."

Madame Wu smiled charmingly. "Perhaps you will take your wife's place for a few minutes, Mr. Vayne?"

Sinking into a chair, Eugene answered, "Sure, why not?"

PART FIVE: ALL ROADS LEAD TO MADAME WU

THE CHINESE GIRL'S interest in the recovery of the statuette appeared to have waned. She declined Mrs. Vayne's luncheon invitation and refused to see anyone else after Eugene Vayne, explaining that the powers of clear sight had temporarily deserted her. During the course of the midday meal Mrs. Vayne indulged heavily in sarcasm at the expense of her daughter. Finally Lydia, almost in tears, flung down her napkin and flounced from the table.

The Thursday afternoon whereabouts of those residing at the Vayne estate were afterward to become of some importance. Immediately after lunch Jasper Kroll departed in the Buick for Los Angeles. His wife took the station wagon and went to visit a friend called Charlotte. Eugene Vayne invited O'Connor to the Palmas Country Club for golf. Coggin had work to do in his little office, and Mrs. Vayne retired to her own pavilion for a nap. Westborough and Faith Vayne, left undisturbed by the influence of weightier suns, eventually gravitated into each other's orbits.

"Yes," Westborough agreed after they had talked for a time on the bench by the lotus pond, "the ambuscade at the Southwest Gate rendered Japanese retaliation almost inevitable. But how was it possible for you to escape on the following evening? Surely there were no passenger trains running?"

The late afternoon sun winked hazily through a fleece of cumulus clouds.

"There hadn't been for weeks," she owned. "But the Japanese army gave permission for a special train to leave Peiping for the evacuation of American citizens. Japan had promised to keep the railroad open for that—

something in the Boxer agreements."

An entomologically inclined warbler hunted insect life on the glossy greenery of the pittosporums. A flat-tailed mockingbird announced completion of a new apartment in full-throated song. As peaceful an afternoon as ever graced southern California's semitropical spring! But in Europe as in Asia civilization tottered to the roll of bombs and cannon. The myrmidons of death were marching in a mad world bent on self-destruction, and no one could foresee the outcome of it all.

"Reservations had to be made at the United States Embassy." She rested a palm against her cheek for a few seconds. "Baggage was strictly limited. I had to leave my trunk behind and I never did see it again. But I was able to pack all of Mrs. Vayne's jades into a suitcase. None of the pieces were very large, luckily."

"The Green Shiver statuette was among them, was it not?"

"Yes." She turned to him a staid young face with delicate nostrils and gently rounded chin. "It was only a three- or four-hour run from Peiping to Tientsin. I spent a night there at the American Consulate. Sandbags and barbed wire were all around the foreign concessions, and soldiers of every nationality were on guard. Japanese planes had bombed the Chinese quarter of the city that day and killed hundreds, maybe thousands. I didn't see them doing it, thank goodness! I was hurried out of Tientsin in a grand rush."

The world's warlords have seemingly decreed universal slaughter of the innocent, Westborough mused, thankful that his span of life was nearing its end. He had no wish to go on living in the New Dark Ages which appeared so alarmingly near. What was it she had just said? But it was impossible. Perhaps, he reconsidered, it was his own memory of recent Chinese history which was at fault.

"The Tientsin bombing was on the afternoon of July twenty-ninth, I believe."

Her deep blue eyes, candid as a truthful child's, widened in admiration. "You have a remarkable memory for dates, Mr. Westborough."

"It has been trained by many years of concentration upon such foolishness. Possibly, however, I am wrong."

A breeze stirred the murky water of the dragon lotus pond.

"I couldn't be sure of the day without looking it up. Early the next morning they herded a group of us women into a launch and raced us down the Pei Ho to Tangku. A Dutch steamer was anchored in the river mouth—near a sand bar, I remember. The Japanese had the situation under control by then, I think. We passed several of their armored cars patrolling the riverbanks and we heard only scattered bursts of shooting now and then. Not very much of it anywhere."

The latter part of her narrative seemed to accord with historical fact. But the other? He did not interrupt.

"We sailed in the afternoon for Shanghai, and that ended my war experience. By the time the fighting had reached the Whangpoo I was bound for home on an American liner."

This young woman, being far from stupid, would scarcely falsify on a point so readily verified, Westborough reflected. Doubtless her account was correct. He regretted, however, that he was then a distance of between twenty-five to thirty miles from the Los Angeles Public Library. He would have liked very much to see a file of, say, the New York *Times* for July 1937. Probably, though, there was nothing to be learned. After all, he told himself, *she* had been there. ... His mind refused to be satisfied.

She hastened to change the subject, asking his opinion of Madame Wu's psychic powers. He replied evasively. "She made pictures appear in her quartz globe," his companion confided, a trifle shyly.

"No?" he exclaimed.

"I actually saw them there."

"Indeed? Most interesting!" Westborough made other conventionalized noises expressive of surprise.

"I didn't think things like that were possible."

"Yes," he confirmed. "Crystal gazing is one of the so-called 'direct methods' of analysis and is employed by rather hardheaded specialists in abnormal psychology."

"I didn't know that," she said thoughtfully.

"Few people seem to be aware that crystal gazing, automatic writing and hypnotism are, to borrow from Disraeli, on the side of the scientific angels. Nevertheless, it is a fact."

"Hypnotism too?" she asked.

"Yes, decidedly."

"Is it possible for a person to hypnotize somebody with just a single look?"

Before he could answer the two golf players appeared unexpectedly on the path bordering the reptilian pond. O'Connor went on to the guest house after a casual greeting, but Eugene Vayne lingered to chat. "How was your game today, dear?" his wife made dutiful inquiry.

"Lousy." (Does there exist a golfer, Westborough meditated, who will acknowledge that he has played well?) "Had a devil of a slice and missed some nice easy putts, damn it! We called it a day after nine holes."

"Oh, that's why you're back so early?"

"I didn't quit because I was getting beaten." He laughed unpleasantly. "No matter what you may think, Faith. I've got to run into town tonight, and I haven't any too much time."

"Won't you please let Mike drive you, dear?"

"No, I won't let Mike drive me," he mocked. "Nor anyone else. This is business, and it's my business, and it's private business."

Westborough had been selfishly considering his own interests.

"May I trespass on your good nature by riding into the city with you, Mr. Vayne? I should like to visit the public library."

"We've got books here if you want to read."

"That is not quite it."

"Well, I've got to change my clothes first. And it's a good bit out of my way."

"I shall not impose upon you by asking to be taken the entire distance—merely to some point convenient to bus or tramway service."

"I might drop you at Wilshire and La Brea," Eugene acknowledged rather unwillingly. "You could catch a bus from there. I can't pick you up again though. I don't know when I'll be through."

"Doubtless I can arrange for the return trip with Mr. Kroll who, I believe, is dining in Hollywood tonight with Doctor Liao. I can telephone to the latter's hotel."

"Okay, it's a deal."

For a man in the hurry he claimed to be Eugene Vayne seemed loathe to depart from the lotus pond. He glanced several times, Westborough noted, toward the island of the bronze Lao Tzu. Finally he asked point-blank, "Don't you have to change your clothes?"

"Doubtless the library will admit me in these garments," the historian returned with a smile.

"Coming up to the pavilion with me, Faith?"

"Not just yet. I'll wait until after you've had your shower, dear."

As Eugene turned to go up the long flight of steps his sullen face held the expression of a man who has swallowed a hornet. Westborough's mind, however, was on other matters. He was upbraiding himself for his stupidity in mentioning the library before Faith Vayne. She seemed a sufficiently intelligent young woman to perform the arithmetical sum of two and two; it should not be difficult for her to guess that he doubted her veracity.

"What is the scientific explanation of crystal gazing, Mr. Westborough?"

He breathed freely again.

"I am not altogether sure of the technical terminology, but I shall endeavor to do my best. While you were looking at the crystal did not Madame Wu talk to you in a quiet, restful manner?"

"Yes, she did."

"This, no doubt, aided you to reach the mental state psychologists term abstraction, in which the mind—or at least a part of it—is withdrawn, shall we say, into itself. Naturally the hallucinations were of psychogenic origin."

"What does that mean?" she asked.

"Actually there was nothing whatsoever in the crystal. The visions you saw there had no objective reality. They proceeded entirely from your own consciousness."

"Like a dream," she said, sighing.

"Similar in character, yes. Except, of course, that sleep is not necessary."

"Oh no, I wasn't asleep. She asked questions and I was answering her all the time the visions lasted. And when she told me to look at certain things I could see them. Isn't that odd?"

"Yes, but by no means supernatural."

"You know a great deal about these things, don't you, Mr. Westborough?"

"I have barely scratched the surface of the existing literature."

"What does it mean," she asked, "if a person has the same dream night after night?"

"Dear me! You have hit upon one of psychology's most baffling problems."

"Does it mean anything serious?"

Studying her gravely anxious face, he decided not to tell her that the prevailing tendency was to regard the recurrent dream as indicating an abnormal mental condition.

"I shouldn't worry over it. How often does it visit you, Mrs. Vayne?"

"Sometimes two or three times a night, and then again not for a long, long while. Lately I've been having it more frequently than usual, I think."

"Are the details always the same?"

"Yes, always. And very, very clear. Most dreams are hazy. Did you ever read *Peter Ibbetson?*"

"With vast pleasure," he said.

"Do you remember his description of dreaming true? Ordinary dreams are gray, are they not? This one is in Technicolor with sound effects."

"Indeed? It is rather unusual, I believe, to dream sounds."

"I do. I can even smell odors. Oh, it's so vivid! As vivid as anything I've ever experienced. But I know it didn't happen—couldn't have happened. It always begins in a little village in North China when we—"

He was to ponder afterward that it was highly unfortunate Faith Vayne was not allowed to finish her dream. Possibly if she had related it to him then—it was idle speculation. They *were* interrupted. Kerry O'Connor *did* choose that particular instant to come bounding from the guest house. Faith Vayne, as she had done before, fled up the stairs at his approach. And Westborough was forced to drop the tenuous thread.

Boiling with anger, O'Connor issued his ultimatum: "I'll be giving you exactly two minutes to be returning that gun you stole from me."

II

Rising from the bench to confront the raging redhead, Westborough reflected how the Irish lilt seemed to come unconsciously to Kerry O'Connor's lips during moments of emotional stress. But only at such moments, it would appear. To the Celtic fury the elderly little scholar opposed his mild blue eyes.

"I was not aware that your weapon was missing."

"Two minutes." O'Connor emphasized the time limit by gazing sternly at the hands of his watch. "If I don't have it then 'tis in the pond you'll be going, clothes and all."

"'Tis in the pond you'll be going ..." Yes, the journalist was obviously in a state of high excitement. Ordinarily he spoke in a more prosaic fashion. The historian tranquilly regarded the shimmer of late afternoon sun on the water.

"Then I fear I shall receive a ducking."

"I wouldn't try to hold out if I were you."

"It is impossible for me to return what I did not take, nor, in so short a period as two minutes, can I hope to demonstrate my innocence to your satisfaction. Since I am sure that you are a man of your word the drenching is therefore inevitable." Removing his coat, Westborough folded it neatly on the bench. "I am ready now for the pond, Mr. O'Connor."

"The devil and all!" the Irishman fumed. "I could throw you in there with one hand."

"Most probably," Westborough agreed. "I am something on the scrawny side, and you are a powerful man. Yes, I am quite sure you could do it with one hand. Shall we make the experiment?"

"By Godfrey! If you were fifty years younger—"

"Unfortunately my age cannot be remedied."

"You're an old scalawag." O'Connor's greenish-gray eyes were, however, riant. "You play upon my feelings like one of the Shee. I know how deeply you're steeped in sin. I ought to keep that promise—oh hell! Tell me what you did with the gun, and we'll call it square."

"I have not seen your firearm since last evening, Mr. O'Connor. I give you my word of honor I did not enter your room today."

"Then who did?"

"No one to my knowledge. I have been seated on this spot for a large share of the afternoon. Possibly someone could approach the guest house without my seeing him or her, but—could your revolver have been taken in the forenoon?"

"Might have been, yes. I put it back in the drawer where you found it last night and I haven't seen it since early morning."

"May I be allowed to inspect your room?"

"Sure, come on over."

The guest house, a one-story creation of tiled walls, gilded beam ends, latticed windows and an upturned Chinese roof, snuggled cozily in a grove of Monterey cypress a short distance from the lotus pond. It stood apart from the other buildings of the estate, hidden to a large extent by the bushy cypress branches. They went inside.

It was, all things considered, a relatively simple job of burglary. Neither the veranda door nor the sliding door between the two rooms had been locked, and the weapon had been in an unlockable dresser drawer. One had only to enter and take it. The only prerequisite was knowledge of the firearm's presence in O'Connor's room. Assuming this, any of the three Chinese servants could have committed the theft. Or the Japanese gardener. Or Fry, the chauffeur. Or Jasper Kroll. Or Lydia. Or Eugene. Or Eugene's perplexing young wife. Or Jethro Coggin, provided that he wanted another revolver when he had one already in his desk.

And there remained another possibility: a green-eyed, flaming-haired, rugged-featured young man with the Christian name of a famous Irish county. One could think of reasons—sinister, to be sure—why the owner of a deadly weapon should wish others to believe that it was no longer in his possession.

Westborough put that theory by for the time being. "I am sorry," he apologized upon completing his brief examination. "I can tell nothing. With fingerprint equipment perhaps—" He saw O'Connor's quizzical stare as they walked toward the veranda door.

"Know all about fingerprints, do you? I had your number last night. A private dick."

"I have no professional standing whatsoever," Westborough denied. His eyes were on the steps leading to the hilltop pavilions. The gold-studded gate was opening slowly.

"I'll let you off the ducking, sleuth, if you tell me who sicked you onto me."

Eugene Vayne had just appeared at the head of the steps. He was descending in a manner which could be best described as stealthy. Moreover, he wore no coat.

"If I impart the information it will be for another purpose than to escape the pond. And I must stipulate that my confidences be treated strictly sub rosa. I shall deny my words unhesitantly if you attempt to use them as a basis for legal action."

"Don't worry." The younger man's jaw set at a fighting angle. "I can handle my affairs outside of court. So it was Mrs. Nicholas Vayne, eh? I suspected as much."

"It was clever of you to guess."

"You shouldn't have mentioned law suits. She's the only one here with money enough to make suing worthwhile. But why? I never saw the old girl in my life before I came here. Why does she want me watched?"

Eugene Vayne's right sleeve was rolled up to the elbow, and he carried under his arm a white cloth which looked like a towel.

"She suspects you of stealing her jade statuette," Westborough replied absently.

"Oh my Godfrey!" O'Connor shook with hearty laughter. "That's so funny I can't even get mad."

"It appeared equally ridiculous to me."

Vayne was now walking toward them on the stone-paved path. It *was* a towel he carried, Westborough saw through the half-open veranda door. Strange!

"Then why'd you take the job?" O'Connor queried belligerently.

"Because"—Vayne had turned right and was going toward the other side of the pond—"I was curious about some of your actions, Mr. O'Connor. Curiosity is the vice for which I shall most certainly be damned."

Eugene Vayne had halted near the island of the bronze Lao Tzu. He was bending over the water. Westborough bolted immediately through the doorway.

Though hardly a sprinter he had had sufficient start to beat Kerry O'Connor to the lotus beds. "Good evening, Mr. Vayne." He carefully averted his eyes from the other's bared forearm. "I am ready to leave whenever you are."

"For the love of God!" Eugene's bent back straightened like a bow when the string breaks. "Oh, it's you! Don't sneak up on me again, please. I'm too nervous."

The historian immediately apologized. "I shall not let it happen again."

Eugene said informatively, "Mother and Coggin are leaving for town right away. Wouldn't you rather ride in the Packard?"

"You put me in an embarrassing position, Mr. Vayne. If I say no I shall be guilty of discourtesy to your mother, if yes, of the same offense to yourself. Let us cut the Gordian knot by saying that the original arrangement still stands. Unless, of course, you do not care for my company." In the background Kerry O'Connor was suppressing laughter.

"Okay, suit yourself." Eugene crammed the towel into his hip pocket. "You'll have to be ready to leave in five minutes." Turning his back, he marched sulkily toward the stairs.

"Never met a fellow I cared for less than that one," O'Connor observed when the golden-hobbed gate above had banged shut. "Are you thinking the same thing I am?"

"I am thinking of Chinese mythology," Westborough replied, gazing meditatively at the feet of Lao Tzu.

"What's that got to do with it?"

"Nothing perhaps. I will tell you the story, and you may decide for yourself. In something like the year 1000 A.D. a Sung emperor, stooping at a pool to wash his hands, discovered the historic Han image of the Jade Lady which he enshrined in the temple on the sacred mountain of T'ai Shan."

O'Connor grinned knowingly. "History, they say, repeats itself. That's something you ought to know."

"Unfortunately the worst phases of human activity do seem to repeat themselves." Westborough rolled up his right sleeve, exposing an extremely skinny arm. "An Alexander, a Caesar, a Genghis Khan, a Tamerlane and now a Hitler have strewn the paths of conquest with corpses. 'What comes next?' as Browning once asked. Is it—"

Plunging his arm into the water, he probed below the lotus pads. Within a short time his fingers felt the cool smoothness of jade. He drew a dripping object from the pond.

"By Godfrey!" O'Connor shouted. "You've found it. Marvelous!"

Westborough carefully dried the little jade goddess with his handkerchief. "When Mrs. Vayne's property has been placed safely under lock and key I confess—"

Glancing across the pond, he saw that the big town car was parked before the gatehouse.

Jethro Coggin was just helping a lady, unmistakably Mrs. Vayne, inside. Westborough started at once to run. "Save your breath!" O'Connor advised. "Yell! We'll both yell."

The lusty waves of sound, however, failed to reach the Packard, just plunging through the vermilion gate. At length Westborough halted his vigorous yoo-hooing. "A pity!" he gasped. "Now you and I, Mr. O'Connor, are responsible for this article until Mrs. Vayne's return. And I must leave shortly."

"I'll watch it for you," the other volunteered. "I'll take it to my own room and—"

"Under no circumstances. That is exactly what you must not do. Take it to the living pavilion, Mr. O'Connor. Conceal it beneath your coat and let no one see what you are carrying. Hide it in the living pavilion, in any convenient spot which suggests itself. And if you do not mind staying there with it watch until—" Westborough broke off his instructions.

Eugene Vayne was again descending the steps. "What's all the noise about?" he demanded peevishly.

Then he spied the Jade Lady in Westborough's hands.

III

O'Connor knocked the ashes from his pipe as Faith Vayne entered the living pavilion. "Hello, New England," he called blithely. (She had changed into a demure navy blue dress with prim white ripples of organdy at neck and arms.) "Yes, it's the ogre."

Closing the door, she marched toward him determinedly.

"You're not running away?" he jeered. "Can it be possible?"

"I have been afraid of you, Mr. O'Connor." Her eyes blazed like sapphires in a carved ivory face. "I'm going to conquer my fear!"

She actually was frightened, he saw. Her body was shaking like a leaf in an autumn breeze. "I'm not a cannibal," he observed cuttingly. "I don't boil women for breakfast. Stop trembling, Sweet Alice with hair so brown. I smile; you weep with delight; remember?"

The nonsense didn't come off. Too many ghosts were with them, he sensed intuitively. Faith Kingston's ghost, for one.

"The Irish are a strange, fey race." Her soft voice was almost toneless. "Even Madame Wu was a little afraid of you, I think. You can hypnotize people."

Faithless little Faith! But now there was no such person. There was only this woman, Mrs. Eugene Vayne. What had he to do with her? And what was the woman saying? *Hypnotism?*

"Will you please be talking sense?" he ordered.

"You're an expert," she insisted. "You hypnotized me with a look the first time I saw you."

Her slim hands were tensely clasped—Faith's lovely hands, he had once thought of them. Some little watchman in his brain stirred to warn of formless horror haunting the room.

"Do you know what you're saying, mavourneen?"

"Wizard," she hissed. "That's what they would have called you a few hundred years ago. You made me follow you into the tea pavilion. I was only a puppet for you to pull the strings."

Faith Kingston, oh, Faith Kingston! He couldn't yet put a name to it, but the name was there, ready for utterance.

"You went of your own accord," he said. His lips had become dry, lifeless skin; he had to moisten them with his tongue in order to speak.

"Oh no! When I woke afterward I didn't have the least idea of what I'd done. You called me with this terrible power you have. Why did you use it on a stranger, Mr. O'Connor? Was it a kind of test?"

Silence lay heavily about the darkly rich mahogany and ebony of the big, dimly lit room.

"And Madame Wu said you were sensitive. You can see things hidden from other people, she said. Supernatural things. Is it true?"

He knew the name now. It hit like a physical fist in his face.

"It must be true," she continued. "You read my mind, I know. You didn't even need Madame Wu's crystal."

"Moonstruck," his thoughts ran. "The Hill People stole her real self, as the books claim they can do, and left a changeling. This is the shell of Faith Kingston. My Faith! *Mad as a March hare.*"

"You did read my mind," she maintained. "Otherwise you couldn't have known about my dream. Could you?"

"No wonder Gene is drinking himself to death. No wonder Coggin watches her like a hawk at the table. Jasper, Lydia, old Mrs. Vayne—they must be all half crazy with watching her. But why don't they put her in an asylum?"

He checked himself after taking an involuntary step backward. It was only the horror of madness that caused him to shrink, not Faith herself. Faith—poor, deranged Faith—couldn't harm anyone.

"The old lady," his thoughts answered, "holds the purse strings here. She wouldn't stand the disgrace of letting the world know her son is married to a daft woman. So they keep her shut up behind these walls, while Gene kills himself with drink, poor devil! Was the real reason they asked me here because of that statuette, as Westborough seems to think? Or was it because of the effect I had on Faith's mind?"

"But hypnotism isn't magic." Her smile was forced, strained. "It's scientific, Mr. Westborough said. Is it true you and he found the Jade Lady in the lotus pond?"

He forgot even her madness in his new astonishment.

Only three had seen it, and the other two had driven from the grounds an hour ago without communicating their knowledge to anyone within the walls. He could answer for their silence as for his own. And when he had carried the jade figure up the stairs it had been beneath his coat. No one had seen him bring it into this room. Faith couldn't possibly know of the discovery. But she did; she had even mentioned the lotus pond.

She knew still more.

"It was hidden under a lotus leaf near the Lao Tzu. Mr. Westborough had it first, but he gave it to you."

"*Ts'ao ni-ti ma!*" Hearing her laughter, he remembered sheepishly that she was able to understand the untranslatable vulgarity of his favorite Chinese oath.

"I forgot you knew the language," he apologized.

"Anyone would swear, I think, under the circumstances. Is it true?"

He pointed to the jade-mosaic screen. Peering behind it, she drew back, noticeably shaken. "It *is* true. I didn't believe her at first."

"Believe who?"

"Madame Wu. She called me on the telephone a few minutes ago."

"How did *she* know?"

"She said she'd had a psychic vision."

"Nuts!" He had forgotten in his indignation that you have to humor those whom God's finger has touched. "I don't believe it. I don't take any stock in this psychic buncombe."

"No?" Faith seemed surprised. "Don't you believe in banshees?"

"That's different!" he answered warmly. "Banshees *do* exist."

"Other people don't think so."

She didn't sound insane at all just then. Maybe, he reflected, it was some sort of periodical thing that came and went.

"Why are you so sure banshees exist?" she persisted.

"I've seen one. I can believe my eyes, I guess."

"Not always," she demurred. "Your eyes can play tricks on you; Madame Wu taught me that. How can I get there? I wonder. None of the cars are in the garage, Wing told me. And I promised to be at her apartment by eight o'clock."

He looked at her, wondering.

"Madame Wu," she explained, "asked me to bring the Jade Lady to her tonight."

Tardily he recalled that those suffering from mental disorders must be gently treated. "What does Madame Wu want it for, mavourneen?"

"To hold in her hands. Just to touch it."

Poor little Faith!

"She can learn things that way, she claims. Psychometry, isn't it?"

"Bunk!" he thought.

"Madame Wu said that if she had the Jade Lady she would be able to help me. Explain my—my—visions."

"What visions?" He knew when he asked the question he was treading on ground too delicate for his weight.

"Hallucinations," she replied promptly. "Pictures without objective reality. Psychogenic was his word, I think. I asked him what it meant."

"She knows," he thought. "It makes it worse, somehow, for her to know the state of her poor, sick mind."

"Don't you be worrying now, darling!" he crooned in compassion. "None of that can be hurting you. 'Tis Kerry who tells you so."

"Kerry," she repeated. "Kerry. It's a lovely name."

"A county in Ireland, sweetheart. My mother came from there."

"It's a song, too—the 'Kerry Dance.' That's what makes it seem so familiar to me, I suppose. Isn't it?"

He looked upon the glories of the Screen of Heaven.

"It is *so* familiar! Kerry. Kerry O'Connor. Madame Wu said you had the power of imposing yourself on my mind."

"It's a black liar Madame Wu is," he said hotly. "I can do no such thing. I never hypnotized a person in my life. I don't know the first thing about it."

"Is it," she asked pitifully, "something else?"

He raised his eyes from the Western Paradise to the silk-painted ceiling lockers. "Yes," he answered finally.

"My dream? But it's your dream, too, isn't it? You were always there before, the man whose face I couldn't see."

He regarded the ivory-sheathed swords on the south wall. And in them found no inspiration for speech.

"I shouldn't have been afraid of you, should I? You were good. You risked your life for me—in the dream."

His tongue—his facile Irish tongue—clung to the roof of his mouth, a useless thing. She smiled, holding out her hand to him.

"She trusts me now," he thought. "This trouble seems to have given her the trustfulness of a child. But does she know what she's saying? Does she have any idea?"

"Now I'm going to ask a favor of you," she said. "Do you mind?"

"Of course not, Faith."

"May I borrow your car tonight? I wouldn't ask, but there isn't another on the grounds, Wing said. I promised Madame Wu I'd go, and I like to keep my promises."

"But, but—" he stammered.

"I shan't be away more than three hours or so. And I'll be careful."

"Hell, it's impossible," he thought. "But I can't stand her pleading, wistful eyes. She wants to go so badly. Sweet little Faith! Like a child, of course. But I can't take her."

"You don't need to worry about your car. I can drive—I have a license."

"If she has a driver's license they must let her out of the grounds sometimes. Alone. If I could be certain—but there's a test. Wong. He'll know whether they do or not. Most Chinese are sticklers for obeying orders. Wong won't open the gate if she isn't allowed outside."

"Will you show me your license, Faith?"

"Of course. It's in my room now. I'll get it when I put on my hat and coat."

Remembering the supposed guile of the insane, suspicion smoldered within him. "But we won't take the Jade Lady, will we?"

"No," she agreed readily. "I wouldn't touch the statuette without asking

Gene's mother's permission. I forgot she wasn't here."

She kept him waiting only a minute or two outside the pavilion door. When she emerged she had on a silver fox jacket and a tiny half-a-hat, one of the usual silly things that women wear. The operator's license was in her hand. It had, he read, been issued to Faith Kingston Vayne in August 1938. "Are you married?" a line of type impertinently questioned. "Yes," she had printed in quavering lines. When he handed it back she slipped it into her handbag.

His car was parked in the motor court back of the garage. "Do you mind having company?" he asked as they were walking down the east steps. "It's bored I am at the thought of remaining here alone."

She turned her head; dusk prevented him from reading whatever expression it was had come to her face. "Thank you," she said softly. "I'll be glad to have you."

"Missy going out?" Wong inquired as they drove up to the vermilion portal.

"Yes, Wong. Will you open for us?" The gatetender immediately began to slide back the wooden bar which held the leaves.

"So I'm a buck passer, am I?" O'Connor thought. "That ought to settle that, but I can't help wondering ... It'll be all right, I suppose. There isn't anything can happen."

"Kerry," she asked as they turned into the highway, "what is this strange link between us?"

IV

Westborough ventured to remonstrate at Eugene Vayne's reckless driving on the winding peninsular road. "Not quite so fast if you please." A fishing boat was trawling in the quiet bay. A wisp of smoke marked the vanishing of a far-distant liner. Eugene's foot did not release its pressure on the throttle.

His face, obviously once handsome, had become puffy from indulgence. The fleshy lips had set in an apparently habitual sneer. Regarding the sullen profile, Westborough wondered if he had been altogether wise to surrender himself to such care. Yet was not the audacity of the move its greatest safeguard? The sinking sun dazzled the water.

They swept into a populous beach town. Palms flourished along a strip of sandy coast. Pepper trees shaded white-walled, red-roofed houses. They slowed into the business district. Gulls and a single pelican consorted sedately on the post of a long black pier. Stands cried the merits of fried shrimp and hamburger. Woolworth prospered in the conventional red-and-gilt front. Soon they were out of all this and on a four-lane highway among derricks, freight cars and giant tanks like gleaming metal mushrooms. The stink of petroleum stifled the air.

Oil! Westborough briefly traced the course of its eventful history. Oil begat the internal-combustion engine, which begat motorcar and airplane and minor progeny too numerous to mention, which altered the ways of the world. There flowered the mechanical civilization of the early twentieth century. And men worshiped Oil the Father and Internal Combustion the Son as gods who had set them free. They set up Temples of Salesmanship in all the lands, and the cities were strewn with shrines to the Sacred Emblem of the Gasoline Pump. To each shrine daily came hundreds of the devout, and the world resounded with hymns of praise to Oil the Father and Internal Combustion the Son. Men forsook all other gods but these. And for a time they prospered. But, lo, after several decades had passed there befell evil days.

From the seed of Oil were begotten tanks, bombers and troop-transport planes, the begetters of Blitzkrieg. And the latter is fecund in offspring: chaos, destruction and the iron grip of the dictator on the throats of free men. Yet Oil is still worshiped by the faithful, yea, though he shower his legions of death upon those who cherished him, to the valley of death will they follow. Great Pan's song is dead, the lyre of Apollo muted, the meek Jesus spurned, the sage Confucius a focus for obscenity, the gentle teachings of the Buddha all but forgotten. But Oil the Father sitteth still in his heaven and ruleth the earth, the sea and the sky. Mighty is Oil!

The ocean opened to receive a disk of glowing, dying orange. Clouds rioted in streaked pink, scarlet, lemon and amber. The morose Eugene, doing sixty-seven an hour, saw no colors, merely the dull gray of the highway. A true worshiper of Oil, hallowed be His glorious name.

"Is it not dangerous to drive at this speed when you are—" Checking himself from saying "under the influence of alcohol," Westborough hastily switched his question. "Why is it that you do not allow yourself to be driven by your mother's chauffeur?"

"Don't like him," Eugene returned curtly. His big, flabby hands tightened their grip on the wheel. He said nothing more.

The sun became an extinguished lamp. Above a belt of blended saffron and magenta the sky shaded from turquoise to indigo. Venus shone brilliantly; Sirius became visible. Westborough tried again.

"You have a charming wife, Mr. Vayne?"

"Yeah, Faith's all right."

"Have you been married long?"

"Nearly two years. What difference does it make?"

Westborough agreed that it made none. The subject was closed and silence reigned for a brief period. Mars and Jupiter entered the evening lists. Orion appeared—a shade closer to the western horizon than at the same time the day before. North the Great Bear faithfully pointed to Polaris. Westborough cleared his throat for his third and final conversational attempt.

"May I inquire the nature of your engagement tonight?"

"Personal business."

"The rebuke is justified," Westborough said, thoroughly squelched at last. They passed the airport, turned into the long diagonal of La Tijera and came to the corner where five roads meet. "Ay, but you must be sure to take only one of them," Westborough recalled from the directions of Tony Lumpkin to Hastings and Marlow. The one they took led past one of Oil's temples and a neon-etched drive-in; they forsook it shortly for a twisting road over the hills. Soon the city was stretching out its boulevards, long, broad tentacles to pull the unwary straight to its pullulating heart.

"Wilshire and La Brea," Eugene proclaimed, satisfaction evident in his voice. "Here's where you get off."

"Thank you very kindly," Westborough said as he descended. The door slammed shut; the Chrysler rocketed away. Consulting his watch, the little man found that the hour was six-thirty. He dined at the counter of a drive-in. Having a weakness for foreign dishes of the peppery variety, he consumed a large bowl of chile con carne con frijoles with sybaritic relish before taking the bus. Precisely at seven twenty-one he was turning into the south portal of the Los Angeles Public Library.

He filled out a slip in the magazine room, giving his name and stating that his object was historical research. The girl behind the desk, deciding he was not likely to cut pictures from the library's bound files, stamped her approval on the slip. Soon he was looking upon a huge green cloth-bound volume, bearing the dates July 15–31, 1937. Opening it, he began with the evening of July twenty-sixth.

About seven o'clock, he read, over a hundred Japanese warriors had been shut within the Kwang An Men, Peiping's southwest gate, while Chinese soldiers bestowed benedictions of hand grenades. On July twenty-seventh the Japanese army served notice that it had been grossly insulted and that "contemptible action on the part of Chinese troops" could never be forgiven. (How seldom, Westborough reflected, do strong nations ever forgive the weak.) At eleven o'clock that night the special train for the evacuation of American nationals departed from Peiping's Chien Gate. The passenger list, unfortunately, was not published.

On July twenty-eighth the Japanese reduced (a pleasantly euphemistic term) enemy barracks at Hsiyuan, Peiyuan and Nanyuan; soldiers in these various yuans found broadswords unsatisfactory in combating bombing planes. Generals named Sung Che-yuan, Chin Teh-chung and Feng Ch'ih-an thought it best to withdraw the thirty-seventh and thirty-eighth divisions, leaving the historic ex-capital a plum for the taking. Westborough jotted down a few words in his notebook.

The war came full blast to Tientsin at 2 A.M., July twenty-ninth, when the *Paoantui*—a corps of Chinese policemen—captured a number of strategic points in a surprise attack and besieged the Japanese garrison at the East Station. Alarmed foreigners, barricaded behind sandbags and barbed wire, thanked God for extraterritoriality. The United States Fifteenth Infantry, the grand old "Can Do" regiment, joined English forces in maintaining a cordon around the British concession. French and Italians unbelievably cooperated in guarding the approaches to the International Bridge. In the early afternoon the heaviest bombers of Dai, Dai Nippon's North

China air force went systematically about the production of a four-hour explosive and incendiary hell. (Yes, it is indeed difficult for the strong to forgive the weak. The camel would have a far easier time with the needle's eye, the rich in securing admission tickets to the Kingdom of Heaven.)

The world had gasped at the horrors of the Tientsin bombing, that fortunate world of 1937 which could not foresee that in comparison with subsequent actions by European nations the Japanese air assault might be termed a shower of mercy. Finding nothing more to interest him in the newspapers, Westborough walked upstairs to the history department.

He looked up the number of *Bombs and Bayonets* in the card index and took down the book from the open shelves. Refreshing his memory of Kerry O'Connor's breezy narration occupied him fully until he was ejected at the library's closing hour. Strolling rather aimlessly down Fifth Street, he began to think of the necessity of getting in touch with Jasper Kroll if he wished to return to the Palmas Peninsula that evening. He entered a drugstore telephone booth.

A rather bored voice informed him he was correct in his surmise that he had dialed the number of the Aubusson Hotel. He was correct also in his conjecture that a gentleman by the name of Dr. Liao Po-ching had selected the hostelry as his temporary headquarters. Was Dr. Liao in his room? The bored voice found that question rather more difficult to answer. Presently a different voice—one unmistakably Chinese—was saying, "Doctor Liao speaks. Who is it, please?"

Westborough stated his name and errand. Jasper Kroll was still there and was called immediately to the telephone. "But, my dear fellow, of course," he said enthusiastically. "Where can I pick you up?"

Westborough had a great dislike of causing anyone trouble. "Please stay where you are, Mr. Kroll, and continue your visit. I shall taxi to Hollywood."

Dr. Liao could not have more faithfully followed the Doctrine of the Mean in his choice of hotel, Westborough decided over half an hour later. The neighborhood was not precisely good, nor could it be called precisely bad. The Aubusson was neither large nor small. Its lobby, which held a deal of red plush and gilded picture frames, was not exactly atrocious but was certainly not elegant. The night clerk was neither short nor tall, not particularly alert, nor yet altogether inefficient. The elevator boy's uniform was not immaculate yet could hardly be termed slovenly. The hall carpeting was not new nor was it noticeably worn. Dr. Liao's own apartment—bedroom and sitting room—was neither squalor nor luxury.

Like a sensible gentleman of his extremely sensible race Dr. Liao had made himself comfortable for the evening in Chinese slippers and a long gray silk gown. He was smoking a pipe—one tamely filled with tobacco instead of opium. He greeted the visitor in a manner reserved but not unfriendly, bowing but not offering his hand. Nor did Westborough make the mistake of attempting to seize it.

Kroll, cheerfully garrulous, did the major part of the talking:

"But, my dear fellow, why didn't you let me know you were going to the library? I was there myself; I could have saved you the taxi ride. And I'm sure Doctor Liao would have been delighted to have had you join us at dinner. He ordered, I can assure you, a royal banquet—Peking duck so tender it fell to pieces when you touched a fork to it. I can't even begin to say what else we had: melon seeds, bamboo shoots, yellow rice wine, candied ginger, sugared walnuts—yes, even the famous black eggs. Not bad either; tasted something like a nice ripe Camembert."

"I enjoyed conversation of Mr. Kroll," the host added. "He is learned, 'read-book' gentleman as we say in my country."

" 'Read-book' isn't a bad way of putting it, do you think, Westborough? Speaking of books, why didn't I happen to see you there at the library? Were you in the art department? Newspapers and history, eh? Well, that explains it. I was in the seven-hundred numbers, digging into jade. I'm doing a series now on its esoteric significance in Chinese religion. Doctor Liao has been very helpful. I've learned a tremendous lot from him this evening."

"Shoe is fitted to other foot. It is ignorant self who has learned from Mr. Kroll."

"How delightful is Chinese modesty," Westborough reflected. It was at that moment their visit was interrupted by a knock on the door.

Opening it, Dr. Liao admitted a pair of obvious plainclothes men. "Are you Doctor Poaching?" one asked.

"I am Doctor Liao. Last name is first in Chinese."

"Okay, okay. Know a little gal named Wu on South Novella Street?"

"I am acquainted with that lady, yes."

"Well, you'd better trot along with us, Slant Eyes. That dame's just been shot. Her and a white guy."

PART SIX: ONE MINUTE FOR MURDER

HAVING by God's grace a free evening, Homicide Captain Michael P. Collins agreed to take wife, young son and younger daughter to a neighborhood movie. Unluckily Mrs. Collins was one of the annoyingly conscientious homemakers who insist that the dinner dishes come first. While the younger members of the family fretfully dried plates and spoons their father, deep within his favorite easy chair, skimmed rapidly through accounts of wholesale slaughter in Europe. He had just grunted his satisfaction on reaching the more satisfying news on the sports page when his literary pursuits were interrupted by an ominous jangling.

Collins decided to let the telephone ring on the dual grounds that Mrs. Collins was almost as close to it as he was and that the call was probably for her anyhow. The latter was wrong. Presently his wife appeared at the living-room door, her mouth twisted into an expression of apprehension by no means unfamiliar. Scowling, Collins threw down the paper and marched into the hall. He picked up the instrument and muttered darkly, "Might let a fellow alone for one night, or is that asking too much?"

"What? A double killing. Tsk, tsk! When will boys and girls learn to behave? All right, all right, Jim, gimme the dope. What's the name of the white man? Vayne? Not *Eugene* Vayne. The devil! Know who he was? Ever hear of the late Nicholas Vayne? Oi! Yeah, that's the guy. Known all over town as Old Nick. Gimme the whole setup. Sure, I place 685 Novella; it's a block south of Wilshire and just east of Vermont. What was the Wu dame's racket? Fortune-telling stuff around, huh? Just possible there's a blackmail angle. Look for her date book. If she don't keep a book ask her maid if—What? You don't know whether there *is* a maid or not? Are you on the premises or not? Oh, you are! Well, why don't you know? Do you know anything? Who found the bodies? All right, that's something. Hold those two till I get there. Sure I'm coming. How do you know it's a love killing? You can't jump to conclusions that way. Yeah, I know it might be; some fellows do have queer tastes in women. Check with the building manager to see if she had a servant; try the neighbors too. And you can call Vayne's family. Old Nick's dead, but Mrs. Nick isn't. Be polite if you get her on the telephone. She's no floozy from South Main Street, remember. Maybe you had better let me handle her. Sure, be there in fifteen minutes. So long, Jim."

Practice had made Mrs. Collins, who had lingered in the hall, an almost perfect interpreter of such rather cryptic monologues.

"This," she observed sourly when her spouse had hung up the telephone, "is the last night of *Pinocchio*. Ann and Freddy have been counting on seeing it."

"They can still see it. You can take them."

"And how, pray, when you have the car?"

"It's only three blocks." Collins peeked into the hall closet to see if he had left his suit coat there. "Don't women have feet any more?"

"That isn't funny," she sniffed. "I've been on my feet all day. Besides three blocks each way is six blocks, and six blocks is—"

"All right, then, call a taxi." He slipped his arms into the coat sleeves.

"A taxi to the movies! That's squandering money. You know our budget won't—"

"For Pete's sake!" Collins jammed a felt hat belligerently upon the back of his head. "Can I help this? Can I help it, Mildred, if a guy gets mixed up with a Chinese fortune-teller and they both get shot? Is it my fault?"

"You might be more considerate of your family," she wailed.

"All right, it's my fault! I did it, didn't I? Just so I could get out of taking you and the kids to *Pinocchio?*" With a burst of Pagliaccian laughter he slammed shut the front door.

A short time afterward he was standing in the vestibule of a rather old-fashioned three-story apartment house. Finding the name of Madame Wu on one of the mailboxes, he pressed the push button and picked up the intercommunicating telephone to announce himself. Presently a buzz informed him that the inner door had been electrically unlocked.

The first floor hall was long, narrow, dim and had a faint odor of fried onions. Collins turned right into a staircase and climbed to the third floor. A uniformed policeman was standing guard by one of three apartment entrances; Collins nodded his recognition of this underling and stepped inside.

The homicide captain's eyes, trained by many years of police work, registered the details eidetically. The front door led into a reception room just big enough for two chairs, a small round table for magazines and something under the sheet on the floor, which Collins did not bother to disturb at the moment. He noted the position of the intercommunicating telephone on the north wall before walking straight ahead to a moderately large living room.

It was furnished more lavishly and more richly than the onion fragrance in the lower hall would lead one to expect—a grand piano, Oriental rugs, a huge radio of polished rosewood, black and elaborately carved tables and cabinets, incense burners, vases, bearded and beardless china dolls and other porcelain gewgaws. All right if you liked that sort of thing, Collins supposed. There was a big Chinese gong and a couple of silk kimonos on the walls; it would have meant nothing to him if he had been told that they were Manchu mandarin coats. The second body—a man's—was at present being photographed under the supervision of Sergeant James Webber.

The squad leader asked a number of crisp questions. He also made a suggestion or two but found nothing to criticize. Under Jim's capable management the routine of the investigation was proceeding with machinelike precision.

The revolver was lying on the living-room floor approximately half a dozen feet away from the dead man. Collins didn't touch it. Apparently he had not even noticed it. A single sharp glance, however, had sufficed to fix in his mind the weapon's make, type, caliber and exact position with reference to its surroundings. He walked north into the little study which adjoined both living and reception rooms.

The study contained a number of weird-looking charts and diagrams on its walls, a crystal globe, several types of planchettes and a score or so of china dolls—idols, he supposed—scattered in various places. For the moment the position of the living-room door was a matter of greater importance. Collins decided that a person in the study could, if the spirit so moved him, toss the revolver through the door to the spot in the living room where it was at present lying. He strolled over to the deceased Chinese lady's desk and picked up the leather-bound, gold-lettered appointment book. After thumbing rapidly through its pages he yelled for Sergeant Webber.

"Jim, come take a look. Today's page is torn out."

"Sure, I know it." Webber made a clicking noise with tongue and teeth. "Now who do you think did that?"

"Moon Mullins," Collins conjectured. "Was this book here when you found it?"

"Naw! Under the dining-room table."

"Of all crazy places," Collins said. "Have you found any paper scraps around here with ink writing and blue ruling?"

"Not yet. Crumpled paper in the wastebaskets, sure, but no chunks of *that* page."

"What about burnt fragments in the ashtrays or in one of those damn incense burners?"

"Nothing but cigarette butts and incense ashes."

"Look in the garbage and in the drip pan of the range," Collins ordered.

"Already checked both of those." Webber looked slightly aggrieved. "And I've got Eskins and Rawley outside combing the ground under the windows."

The bureau commander nodded absently and continued to turn back the book's pages. "H'm. Last night she had a date with a Chinaman, Doctor Li-something Poaching. Funny."

"What's so funny about it?" Webber demanded. "She was a Chink herself."

"The sucker list wasn't," Collins retorted, brandishing the book in the air. "I've gone back for nearly two weeks now, and there's not another Chinese name here. When Eskins and Rawley get through with the paper chase send 'em to pick up Poaching."

"Pick him up where? There's no address here."

"Call headquarters and get someone on the Chinatown detail—no, wait. First ask the woman and the fellow who was with her."

"What makes you think either of those two knows the Chinaman?"

"If one of 'em does it won't hurt to find out, will it?"

"No, sure. Okay, I'll take care of it."

Webber went back through the south door, and Collins walked alone into the dining room. Finding nothing much to interest him there, he continued through the butler's pantry into the kitchen. Here he paused by a back window leading to a fire escape. The window was open about six inches from the bottom. Perhaps a hurried attempt had been made to close it from the outside, or, perhaps again, someone had merely schemed to make it appear that way. Collins removed his shoes and jumped onto the sill. Without altering the position of the lower sash he pushed the upper one down a sufficient distance to stick his head out and look below. The huge shining disk of a police floodlight rendered an acceptable approximation to daylight. The iron stairs stopped at the second floor, but a section would swing down under the weight of anyone descending into a small, paved yard. Collins, regarding the two men who were making meticulous inspection of the terrain, concluded that the yard's cobblestone pavement offered scant hope of identifiable footprints even if footprints were pertinent to the investigation, a fact by no means established.

Another kitchen door led into a hall, on the south side of which were two baths and two bedrooms. Collins peered first into the bedroom immediately across from the kitchen. It was small, plainly furnished and bore many signs of recent feminine tenancy. Probably belonged to the missing maid. The bathrooms—one large and elaborate, one small and containing only the minimum conveniences—were side by side between the bedrooms. Collins peeked briefly into each. The witnesses—suspects if you preferred that term—were being temporarily detained among the toilet facilities. Not such a bad idea at that. They were out of the way of busy men, and since the bathrooms didn't communicate they couldn't talk to each other.

The larger and more luxurious bath, he found, was at present occupied by a woman. She stood by the shower curtain with a scared expression on her face when Collins entered. Without a word, a nod or any other sign of acknowledging her existence he walked on into the adjoining bedroom, a sensuous silken boudoir that was quickly cloying to masculine taste. No Sherlockian brilliance was needed to deduce that it had been occupied by the dead mistress of the establishment. Collins shrewdly appraised the furniture, hangings and toilet accessories. To outfit this room in the way it was outfitted had taken dough. The living- and dining-room furniture wasn't exactly cheap stuff either. If Chinese fortune-telling didn't yield such sweet returns Madame Wu had without doubt engaged in profitable sidelines. Stooping, he picked up a glove.

A white glove for a woman's right hand. He examined it closely and when satisfied with what his eyes could tell resorted to his nose. Necessity had compelled the bluff, burly and indisputably masculine Captain Collins to acquire no little information on the various substances with which women scented themselves. After a number of long, deep sniffs at the glove he crossed to the dressing table and applied his olfactory organ to various crystal bottles. All held heavy, almost narcotically sweet blendings of jasmine, musk, sandalwood, patchouli and other perfumes beloved by the Orient. The glove, on the contrary, hinted delicately of the aromatic antisepsis of English lavender. The bedspread, Collins now saw, was indented slightly. He buried his nose into the shimmering pale-green taffeta and sniffed again. Clinging very, very faintly to the spread was the same hygienic fragrance of lavender.

The hall brought him back to the living room, thus completing the circuit of Madame Wu's apartment. The male corpse was now draped in white to show that the photographer had completed his grisly task. Another important change had taken place. The revolver had been removed, its former place on the rug being marked by a chalked white cross.

"Gun have any fingerprints?" Collins asked of his sergeant.

"Not a smidgen. She'd been wiped cleaner 'n a hound's tooth."

"What about the shells?"

"Five empties. And the autopsy surgeon hasn't left his card yet."

"Slow old buzzard!" Collins dropped to his knees and lifted the sheet. "Vayne looks the type to get into trouble over women all right," he remarked, viewing the body with more attention than he had previously bestowed upon it. "Too much money's a bad thing for a fellow sometimes." He raised the head roughly by its hair. "Shot twice. Both head and chest wounds. I'd say the hole in the face was made at damn close range."

Webber nodded confirmation. "You can see the powder tattooing with a magnifying glass," he added verbally. "My guess is the gun muzzle wasn't more 'n a foot from his head."

"Well, you don't plug a guy close up and then shoot him again from across the room," Collins theorized. "Not if you've got any sense. But you might take your second shot close up, just to make sure the job was finished." He released his hold, allowing the head to flop limply to the rug.

"Two bullets in the dame too. Both head wounds. The second shot was at close range too. Exactly the same technique."

"Killer's efficient," Collins observed impersonally. "Thought you said five shots were fired."

"Right. Two for him and two for her and one"—Webber jerked his thumb toward the reception room—"for the north wall in there."

"You might have a try at checking the angles. I'm going to have a look at Wu."

Walking back to the reception room, Collins flung aside the covering sheet. "Couple of slugs through the skull kinda spoil a woman's beauty," he generalized. "Swell-looking wren once though. Can't much blame Vayne if he did show interest."

Webber leered knowingly. "I'll take mine from white women, thanks."

"You and me both. Let's have your glass, Jim. Sure well-marked tattooing here all right. Killer did fire close-range second shots at both, it looks like."

He threw the sheet back over the dead psychic's face and walked through the door to the study. "This room's okay, Jim. Tell Olie to come in. I'll want the gun too. Then bring me Mrs. Eugene Vayne."

II

The newly made widow entered rather timidly. Collins let her stand a minute or so while he looked her over. Height about five feet six. Nice type. Well-proportioned features and delicate nostrils. Sensitive mouth. Small hands and wrists and slender ankles. Brown hair and a smooth white skin. Her eyes were still swollen and clouded with moisture. She didn't look like a husband killer, but looks meant exactly nothing. He had known a golden-haired angelic creature of nineteen who had fiendishly wiped out an entire family with a hatchet.

"Sit down, please," Collins ordered gruffly. He was a little sorry for her but he couldn't afford to show it. "First it's my duty to warn you that anything you say may be used against you."

"I have nothing to conceal," she said as she seated herself. Nice voice, shy but sweet.

"Let me look at your handkerchief, please," he commanded.

She had wadded it into a small, damp ball. Collins employed his sense of smell first and was rewarded immediately by the lavender odor he had earlier noted on the glove. Then he inspected the fabric minutely with the powerful magnifying glass he had borrowed from Webber. A handkerchief which has been employed to wipe the barrel and stock of a revolver may be expected to show slight traces of gun oil. He found none—merely negative evidence.

Collins pointed to Olie, the police stenographer, who was seated in a corner with his notebook. "Do you object, Mrs. Vayne, to having a record made of your statement?"

"No," she answered.

"All right. Begin by giving me your name, age and occupation."

"Mrs. Eugene Vayne."

"Christian and maiden names, please."

"Faith Kingston. I'm twenty-five. I don't have any occupation."

"State the date of your marriage to the deceased."

She winced slightly at the word "deceased."

"June 20, 1938."

"Your first marriage?"

"Yes."

"How many children?"

"None. Gene—" She broke the sentence quickly.

"Present place of abode?" Collins continued in matter-of-fact tones.

"At the home of my mother-in-law, Mrs. Nicholas Vayne, on the Palmas Peninsula."

"These preliminaries seem like a waste of time, don't they?" Collins had learned many little tricks for putting witnesses at their ease. "What made you come here tonight, Mrs. Vayne?"

"Madame Wu invited me over the telephone."

"Did you expect to find your husband with her?"

"That was the last thing I expected. I had no idea where Gene was going."

She sounded sincere—but Collins remembered the golden-haired hatchet wielder. "How long have you known Madame Wu?" he asked.

"I met her for the first time this morning. Gene's mother recently lost a valuable jade statuette. My sister-in-law invited Madame Wu to the house to find it by psychic means."

Collins kept his opinion of this from showing on his face.

"Had your sister-in-law visited Madame Wu at this address before?"

"Yes, several times. She and her husband are both interested in such subjects as clairvoyance and psychic research."

"Was your husband?"

"No, not at all. Quite the contrary. Gene was always scornful toward Lydia and Jasper when they mentioned the occult."

"How long had your husband known the Chinese woman?"

"Only since this morning. He met her at the same time I did."

"Are you sure of that?"

"Oh yes, very sure. May I have my handkerchief back, please? Thank you." She dabbed at the corners of her eyes.

"Had Gene ever stepped out on you before?" he flashed brutally.

"It isn't true." She looked as though he had just slapped her face. "Oh no, no! It couldn't be true."

"Why did your husband come here tonight?"

"I don't know," she answered in a bewildered tone. "I can't even guess."

He had to let it go at that. "What time tonight did Madame Wu telephone?"

"Shortly before seven o'clock, I think."

"After your husband had gone?"

"Yes. About an hour afterward."

"What was her reason for wanting to see you?"

"It pertained to—to a psychic vision she claimed to have had."

"Do you believe in that junk too?" he asked derisively.

"No," she replied. "Not ordinarily. But I was curious. And I was interested in Madame Wu."

"Why?"

"I—I just was."

"Because your husband was attracted to her sexually?"

She raised her eyes, blue and brimming with tears. "How can you say a thing like that, Captain Collins?"

Collins blew his nose, secretly a little ashamed. This girl, he recognized, had class, breeding and gentility. None of these qualities altered in any perceptible degree the chance that she might have killed husband and husband's Oriental ladylove, but he resumed the questioning in a gentler tone.

"Is Mr. O'Connor an old friend of yours?"

"A very recent one."

"How recent?"

"I saw him for the first time last Monday when he came to our jade exhibit."

"How long has he been staying with your husband's family?"

"He moved into the guest house yesterday morning."

Further investigation elicited the following:

After Madame Wu had telephoned, young Mrs. Vayne had asked a Chinese servant named Wing to call the chauffeur and direct that one of the cars be brought up to the gate. She learned from Wing that the chauffeur was absent and so were all four of the household's automobiles: the Krolls' Buick, her husband's Chrysler, her mother-in-law's Packard and the Ford station wagon. The only car remaining on the grounds belonged to the guest, Mr. O'Connor, whom she had found in the living pavilion and requested him to drive her to the city. (She had asked only to borrow his car at first, she said, but he had offered his services as chauffeur.) They had driven through the gate at ten minutes past seven. Yes, she had looked at her watch.

"I'm terribly old-fashioned about liking to be punctual," she explained. "I had promised to be there at eight o'clock, and I knew we didn't have a great deal of time."

Collins tried to discover what, if anything, had taken place during the journey to Madame Wu's. He was given little satisfaction. Apparently O'Connor had been in a taciturn mood or preoccupied with the task of driving. They had not talked a great deal, she said. They had not talked about anything really important. At two minutes of eight he had parked on Novella Street, making the long trip from the Palmas Peninsula in very good time. Yes, she had again looked at her watch while they were walking into the vestibule. She glanced at her wrist as she spoke.

Collins compared the hour her tiny jeweled timepiece then indicated with the hands of his own watch.

"Shall I go on now, Captain?"

"Let me say something first. I have to know all the details. I don't like to keep interrupting you, Mrs. Vayne, because I'd rather have your statement without any prompting. But I have to know every little thing that took place, no matter whether you think it's important or not. Even if you're sure it's unimportant. Do you understand?"

"I think so."

"I wonder if you do. Do you read magazine stories, Mrs. Vayne?"

"Yes, of course."

"I want you to tell me this exactly as if you were writing it up for a magazine. All the details you can remember. Everything. What you said to O'Connor and what he said to you; how the clock was ticking and how loud your heart was beating ... even your thoughts. Will you tell it like that, Mrs. Vayne?"

She nodded. "When Mr. O'Connor and I were going into the building I wasn't particularly alarmed or worried. I was curious. Not about my husband," she added hastily. "My reason for seeing Madame Wu had nothing to do with Gene. Nothing to do with anyone except myself. Madame Wu affected me strangely this morning. I don't quite know how to express it. She was a surprisingly gifted person. I don't mean she was genuinely psychic or clairvoyant or telepathic. I don't know whether there are such powers though Jasper insists their existence has been proved beyond doubt. I read *New Frontiers of the Mind* to please him and Lydia, but I couldn't get interested in the Rhine experiments. Running through pack after pack of stars and circles and crosses and wavy lines and squares seemed rather dull. This isn't important, I'll admit. But you wanted my thoughts.

"I'm more sure than ever now Madame Wu was not a genuine psychic. Perhaps her methods were like those of a psychologist. Someone told me they were—I wish I knew more about psychology. Whatever it was, though, she *could* reach into a person's mind. I agreed to see her tonight because of a dream. I had planned to ask her to use her crystal—this one on the desk—to make me see it again."

Collins frowned at a sly wink from the male stenographer, a little irritated by Olie's freshness. She might be screwy—probably was—but that wasn't Olie's business. His business was making pothooks in a notebook, and Collins frowned as a sign for Olie to attend to said business exclusively.

She had paused—either for breath or because a corner of an eye had intercepted Olie's wink. "You're doing okay," the homicide captain encouraged her. "Please go on."

"We stepped in the vestibule to read the names on the mailboxes. Madame Wu's box was numbered 3A. That meant the third floor, I remember thinking. As soon as I'd pressed the button above the box I picked up the little telephone. A woman's voice spoke to me. She only said a dozen or so words, but I think—I'm sure it was Madame Wu. She told me to come upstairs, and there was a buzzing noise almost immediately after she hung up. Mr. O'Connor opened the inner door. He insisted on going up there with me. I told him it wasn't necessary. He answered, I recall, 'You shouldn't go alone.' That was the last thing he said for quite a while. We couldn't talk with that horrible noise going on.

"The downstairs hall was badly lighted. Only two bulbs … no, three, one for each door. We had to go a little way to the stairs. Have I told you yet about hearing the radio? It started just after we'd stepped inside. When we reached the stairs, I remember, we looked at each other's faces. His forehead was puckered, and there were three little wrinkles above the root of his nose. The Irish are sensitive to mental conditions, Madame Wu told me this morning. I was worried too.

"I'm not just sure why. Lydia would say a premonition, but I don't like to be so definite. It wasn't that I actually expected anything unpleasant to happen. I didn't. Just a vague sensation of unease—probably because of that awful racket. The radio began as soon as we came into the first-floor hall—oh, I said that, didn't I? It was loud! I felt as though a lot of tiny dwarfs with hammers and drills were pounding at the side of my head. We couldn't talk at all. It was almost impossible to think. I had both hands over my ears all the time we were climbing the stairs. That's how loud it was.

"We turned left on the top floor and walked back toward the street. Madame Wu had told me to do that over the telephone—the apartment telephone, I mean. There was a light near her door, and I read the metal number, 3A. The noise kept growing louder all the time, and finally I realized the radio was in this apartment.

"We knocked—one of us did. I can't remember whether it was I or Mr. O'Connor. It wasn't any use; nobody could have heard us with that pandemonium going on inside. I can't tell you what program it was. I'm not even sure whether it was music or talking, both maybe. It was just noise to me, a blaring, bellowing noise. I wondered why people didn't come from one of the apartments across the hall to tell her to stop it. They didn't. Nobody came at all. The hall door was open about an inch.

"Mr. O'Connor opened it wider. He put his head in and then drew back, looking startled. Before I could ask him what it was he had gone in and slammed the door in my face. I didn't know what to make of that. I couldn't understand why he would do such a thing. It wasn't rudeness, I knew: Kerry—Mr. O'Connor—is a gentleman. I knew that he must have had a strong reason for shutting me outside. He wouldn't be deliberately discourteous. I wondered what he had seen. The radio quit almost at once. Mr. O'Connor had turned it off the very first thing. It was quiet then. Just as quiet as it had previously been noisy. I could hear my heart beating. When he didn't come back I became frightened."

"Why were you frightened, Mrs. Vayne?"

"I knew that Kerry had seen something—something he didn't want me to see."

"What did you think it was?"

"I didn't have any idea."

"Did you guess?"

"No, not at all. I thought of everything else but that. I even remembered the things that Jasper calls extra-dimensional beings."

"*What?*"

"I can't explain it to you. There are other universes than this one, he thinks, and people—not people, creatures—live in them. Jasper claims that if you genuinely believe in their existence they will be able to leave whatever world it is they inhabit and come into your world—materialize in the very room with you. That's the basis for all ghost stories and folklore, Jasper insists. He does believe in them and so does Lydia."

"Do you?"

"Oh no, how can I? But I couldn't help thinking of them then. Jasper said Madame Wu was able to see them sometimes—she even made others see them, he said. I wondered if Mr. O'Connor could have caught a glimpse—no, that's too silly. I didn't actually think such a thing. Or did I? I did remember what Madame Wu had said about the Irish: that there is no race in the world so naturally psychic. Mr. O'Connor told her he had seen a banshee. She came into his bedroom on the night before his father died."

"Madame Wu came into his room?"

"No, not Madame Wu. The banshee."

"A banshee's a ghost, isn't it?" Collins asked.

"Oh no, that's just what it isn't. She—a banshee is always feminine—isn't of human origin at all. An elemental being, one of the Tuatha da Danann. Mr. O'Connor told me all about it on your way down here."

Collins grew impatient. "When did you hear the shots, Mrs. Vayne?"

"I never did hear them."

"Five shots were fired. Do you mean to say you didn't hear one of them?"

"The radio drowned out everything else. That's why it had been turned on, don't you think? To mask the noise?"

"Humph!" Collins snorted. "How long was it between the time O'Connor left you and the time the radio stopped?"

"Only a few seconds. Hardly any time at all. The radio stopped almost instantly after he'd closed the door."

"Would you swear to that in court if you were asked to?"

"Of course. It's the truth."

"Do you think that O'Connor could have fired the revolver before shutting off the radio?"

"Oh no, no! That would have been utterly impossible."

"Could he have fired it afterward?"

"I would have heard the shots then. I couldn't have helped but hear them. It was so quiet. I could even hear my watch ticking, and it makes hardly any noise."

"How long was O'Connor inside the apartment alone?"

"About a minute."

"No longer than that?"

"It couldn't have been longer."

"How do you know? You're guessing the time, aren't you?"

"Not altogether. I looked at my watch again."

"When?"

"Just before he opened the door. It was a minute past eight."

"You're sure of that time?"

"Quite sure."

"And what time was it when you and he were entering the building?"

"I've already told you. Two minutes to eight."

"Altogether then you have three minutes between the first and second times you looked at your watch?"

"Yes."

"Break it down. How long do you think it took you to look at the mailboxes, find Madame Wu's button, talk to her over the house telephone and wait for the door to be unlocked?"

"At least a minute."

"At least," he agreed. "And another minute, you say, that O'Connor was gone from you?"

"Yes."

"How much time does that leave you to get to the third floor?"

"A minute," she answered promptly. "That's about right, I think."

"But you heard Madame Wu's voice over the telephone downstairs?"

"I think it was her voice I heard. Yes, I'm sure it was. She was killed while we were walking upstairs."

One minute for murder!

"Mrs. Vayne," Collins said solemnly, "a minute isn't long enough."

"A minute can be very long," she returned, sighing.

He grunted—whether approvingly or disapprovingly it was impossible to say. "Go on from the time O'Connor came back to the hall, Mrs. Vayne."

"He closed the door so quickly that I wasn't able to look inside. Almost closed it, that is. It was still a tiny crack open. 'I turned off the radio,' he said, and I saw that his face was dead-white—as if he'd just seen one of Jasper's extra-dimensional beings. I remember thinking that. He didn't speak again for quite a little while. I know now how difficult it was for him to tell me about—about the things he'd seen.

" 'Is anything wrong, Kerry?' I asked. He answered very slowly, 'Yes, Faith, there is. I wish I could think of a way to get you clear of this, but there isn't any. You could take the keys to the car and drive back home, but it wouldn't be any good. Wong knows that we left the grounds together, and they'd get that out of him somehow.'

" 'Who would get it out of him?' I asked.

" 'The police,' he said. 'Madame Wu's dead.' He tried to keep me from going in, but I ducked under his arm somehow and was inside the little reception room before he could stop me. Madame Wu was lying there on the floor. Poor little Chinese girl! She had been so beautiful and so—so alive.

"Most people go through life half dead, I think. Robots who do the work they have to do and answer mechanically when you speak to them. Or smoke or drink or play cards or golf or read newspapers if you press the proper buttons. I'm one of the robot kind myself, probably, but Madame Wu wasn't. She was really and not artificially alive. She had a quality of mental alertness that's hard to describe. You felt that all of her senses were keener than most people's and more perfectly adjusted to the brain. I began crying, I think, and Mr. O'Connor said, 'Faith, you've got to get out of here.' "

"Does he call you Faith?"

"He calls everybody by first name or some nickname." The question had put her definitely on the defensive.

"Go on, please."

"I happened then to look through the door into the living room, and I saw Gene. Lying on the floor, not moving at all. I ran to him. I saw then there was a damp splotch on the front of his coat and the side of his face was bloody, and I tried to scream, but my tongue wouldn't move and I couldn't make a sound. You'll have to ask Mr. O'Connor what happened after that. The next thing I know I was on the bed and he was just coming out of the bathroom with a glass of water in his hand."

III

The redheaded Irishman inspected the revolver—a .38 "Bankers' Special" with a checked walnut stock and a grotesquely stumpy barrel. "Mine," he acknowledged tersely. "I'll save you the trouble of tracing the number."

"Well, that's just fine!" Collins declared sarcastically. "Now all you have to explain, O'Connor, is how your gun got here."

"I wouldn't be knowing that. Someone stole it from my room today."

"Yeah?" the officer queried dubiously. "Who?"

"Practically everyone at the Vayne place had the chance."

"Including Mrs. Eugene Vayne?"

O'Connor jumped angrily to his feet. "She couldn't have brought it here without my knowing."

"Why not?"

"How many places has a woman to hide such a thing? Their clothes don't have pockets."

"They carry handbags," Collins retorted meaningly. "Mrs. Vayne has one with her tonight."

"There wasn't any gun in it."

"Now don't tell me you peeked inside her pocketbook?"

"No-o," O'Connor admitted hesitantly. "But it wasn't necessary to look. This spalpeen of mine weighs nineteen ounces. I would have felt the weight when I picked her bag up from the floor."

"It fell on the floor, did it?"

"It did that."

"When and where?"

"In the vestibule downstairs. While we were waiting for the buzzer to sound."

"Mrs. Vayne didn't tell me that she dropped her bag."

"She didn't? Well, don't be calling me a liar on that account. A little detail like that can slip a woman's memory."

"This particular woman," Collins asserted, "has a good memory for detail. A very good memory, O'Connor."

"You don't scare me, Copper."

"Captain Collins," the officer snapped.

"All right, Captain. Truth is truth, you'll admit. It's gospel truth that from the time we left the Palmas Peninsula until we found those two dead I didn't leave Faith—Mrs. Vayne—alone for a single second."

"You might as well go on calling her Faith," Collins suggested. "You know her that well, I guess."

O'Connor's gray-green eyes glinted dangerously. "It doesn't mean a thing. I called her husband Gene, too, and I've known one almost as long as the other."

"How long?"

"I met Mrs. Vayne for the first time at Monday's jade exhibit. How many times," he demanded testily, "do I have to say a thing before you will take my word?"

"All right, I'll take it now. It's not important anyway. You've had two full days at the house to get acquainted. A lot can happen in two days."

O'Connor slammed his fist against the dead Chinese girl's desk. "Good Godfrey! Foul minds must run naturally in your profession."

"We see the seamy side of life," Collins asserted. "Some of it's plenty seamy. A woman might fall for you, O'Connor."

"This woman didn't."

"You tried, huh?"

"I did not. Ask anyone in the Vayne household if I've had more than a dozen words with her. I scarcely knew her."

"You call her Faith though."

"Hell, I call everybody by first name. Just a habit of mine."

"What did she really say when she asked you to drive her here?"

"I've already told you about the jade statuette."

"She didn't mention her husband?"

"She did not."

"She didn't hint that she expected to find him?"

"Of course not."

"Did she tell you that she was unhappy with her husband?"

"She did not."

"Do you think she was unhappy with him?"

"How should I be knowing? Gene drank a bit—lots of men do. She seemed happy enough to me."

"Did you have any idea that he was playing around with this Chinese girl?"

"How the devil would I learn such a thing? If it were true—but I don't think it was. Little Madame Wu struck me as being rather fastidious."

"Then why did he come to her apartment?"

"Probably for advice from one of her tame spirits."

Collins smirked triumphantly. "Wrong! He didn't take any stock in that bunk, Mrs. Vayne said."

"Then you've got me, Captain. Why did he come here?"

Collins didn't answer.

"What happened after you went inside the apartment and left Mrs. Vayne in the hall?"

"The first thing I did was to have a better look at poor little Madame Wu. I couldn't tell for sure that she was dead. I remembered the mirror trick, but I don't carry one with me. I started to go into the bedroom to get one, and that's when I saw Vayne. The living-room door was open."

"When did you turn off the radio?"

"Immediately after that. On my way to the bedroom."

"How did you know where the bedroom was?"

"I didn't. I saw a hall and walked down there and turned into the first door I came to. It was the bedroom, and I found a hand mirror."

"Was the door between this room and the reception room open?"

"Closed. So was the door between this and the living room. Only the door between reception and living rooms was open. After I'd experimented with the mirror I went back to the outside hall to break the news to Mrs. Vayne. I tried to keep her out, but she was too quick for me. Then I tried to keep her from seeing her husband and failed there too. She started to keel over, and I caught her just in time. I carried her into the bedroom and went to get some water to throw on her face. She came to before I could throw it. Then I thought about searching the place."

Collins waxed sardonic. "All this time you were playing around with mirrors and turning off radios and carrying women into bedrooms and hunting for water did it ever occur to you there might be a killer loose in the apartment?"

"All right, I pulled a boner," O'Connor acknowledged, shrugging. "You can't think of everything at once. Even you can't, Cop—Captain. I had plenty on my mind. That doesn't excuse me, though, for letting the murderer escape."

"You're pretty sure, aren't you, you did let him escape?"

"Well, I didn't find him. There wasn't anyone in the apartment but ourselves."

"Did you see anything else wrong besides two corpses?"

"Madame Wu's appointment book was in a queer place. Under the dining-room table."

"Anything else?"

"The kitchen window—the window that opens on the fire escape—had been raised about six inches."

"A man can't crawl through a slit that narrow, O'Connor."

"A man in a hurry might try to slam down the window from outside and rush away without finishing the job if it jammed."

"And run down the stairs into the yard?"

"To wherever the fire escape goes."

"And from there where?"

"How should I be knowing that? I didn't leave the apartment."

"Not even to look in the yard for this murderer of yours?"

"I didn't want to touch the kitchen window. I know better than to be monkeying with a window a murderer used."

"You monkeyed with the radio, O'Connor."

"Sure, and I'd do it the next time. The noise was bothering Mrs. Vayne."

Collins smiled in satisfaction. "Chivalrous guy, huh? Knight in tin pants. That's just what I wanted to find out about you. Now I know."

"Know what?"

"Plenty. Suppose the murderer didn't go down the fire escape, O'Connor?"

"He had to. He couldn't get out of the apartment otherwise."

"Yeah? Well, what if the killer didn't leave the apartment?"

"I see what you mean, Captain. A suicide pact. One shot one and then killed himself or herself, whichever it was. Sure, that could have happened."

"Could it?"

"Why not?"

"If Wu was the last alive she'd have to take a shot at herself from a distance, then a second shot close up and finally throw the gun at least fifteen feet in a curve to clear the living-room door. That's out, I'd say. If Vayne killed Wu he'd have to shoot himself first in the chest and then in the face and toss the gun almost six feet away afterward. It's usually found close to the body in a suicide or still held in the hand. Also it takes guts for a man to shoot himself twice—real guts. Think Vayne had them?"

"I wouldn't think so," the other answered. "Not that I mean to say anything against Gene, rest his soul. Well, if suicide's out then there was a third party here—had to be."

"An outside murderer?" Collins asked sarcastically. "Do you know what's wrong with that theory, O'Connor?"

"Nothing that I can see."

"No? Just to argue about it we'll say Mrs. Vayne's story—and your story—is true."

"It is," the redhead maintained. "In every particular."

"All right it is. Now what do you have to begin with?"

"That would be depending on where you want to begin."

"This is no time for wisecracking," Collins said severely. "Begin with the time you were in the vestibule. Mrs. Vayne heard Madame Wu on the house telephone—swears it was Wu's voice she heard."

"Faith was right, I'm thinking. Who else would be pushing the buzzer to let us in?"

"All right, she was right and Wu was alive then. How long did it take you to walk upstairs?"

"I'd say a minute would cover it."

"Mrs. Vayne says a minute too. When you peeked in the door Wu was dead."

"She was that."

"Your murderer has just one minute to operate. Sixty seconds. And he has to fire five shots."

"Now wait a bit there, Captain," O'Connor pleaded. "Don't be jumping at conclusions. I've visited a police pistol range when the boys were practicing timed firing. Some fellows could make five bull's-eyes at twenty-five yards in under ten seconds. I'm thinking maybe you could be doing the same yourself."

"You're talking about expert shots. My time's twelve."

"I'm not in your class, Captain, but I could myself fire the five-shot string in twenty seconds. Even rank beginners, they told me, needed no more than thirty to thirty-five. And we have sixty." He grinned disarmingly. "Would you mind telling me where all the time's been wasted?"

"Wasted!" Collins exploded. "*Wasted!* Do you know all the things this phony murderer of yours has to do in that sixty seconds? He has to walk over to Wu to make the closeup shot. He has to walk back to Vayne to do the same thing. He has to wipe the gun—and it was wiped pretty clean. He has to come into this room, find this appointment book and tear out the page with his name. That last alone would take a good many seconds. To say nothing of going into the kitchen, opening a window and making his getaway down the fire escape. I tell you, O'Connor, a minute isn't long enough. Do you know what I think?"

"I'd be dumb if I didn't, Captain. You've been hinting at it for a goodish while. Your idea, I take it, is—"

Sergeant Webber stuck his head into the study from the living-room door. "They're here, Skipper. The Chinaman and—"

"Poaching?" Collins interrupted.

"That's the right guy, Skipper, but he calls himself Liao. Doctor Liao Bo-Jing."

"He can call himself Mickey Mouse if he wants to. Is Mrs. Nicholas Vayne here?"

"Not yet. She's on the way, though—with her secretary. Say, there was a couple of white guys visiting the Chinaman."

"No crime, is it?" Collins asked brusquely.

"One is Vayne's brother-in-law and the other is a little old guy who's a guest of theirs. Eskins and Rawley brought 'em both over."

"I'll talk to them *later*." The homicide captain significantly emphasized the last word, causing the sergeant immediately to withdraw his head. "All right, O'Connor, where were we?"

"You were telling me your theory, Captain, or I was telling you. You believe I did this thing myself and Mrs. Vayne, out of the goodness of her heart, told lies to save me."

"The other way round, I think," Collins retorted. "*You* lied. You didn't pick up her bag in the vestibule. Think I can't tell when a fellow is lying to me? You didn't have any way of knowing that she had the gun in there. She did have it."

"She did not."

"She fired the five shots before you could stop her."

"'Tis a wonderful imagination you have, Captain."

"And you were a sucker for a sob story afterward. Young wife abused by dipsomaniacal husband who kept Oriental love nest. She fed you that angle, and you swallowed it like cream."

"Not one word has Faith Vayne ever said against her husband," O'Connor declared indignantly.

"You promised to see her through. You wiped the gun clean of prints; a woman like Mrs. Vayne wouldn't be likely to think of it. And you planted the fake clues—the kitchen window and the appointment book."

"I did not."

"You crazy Irishman! Do you have any idea of the mess you've got yourself into?"

IV

The Chinaman was taller than most of them Collins had known, a good deal taller than the usual run of Japanese. He might have been anywhere from fifty to sixty. The closely cropped, grizzled hair suggested the upper age limit; on the other hand the high-cheekboned olive face was practically wrinkleless. Collins waved him toward a chair.

Bowing politely, the Oriental inquired, "What is your esteemed age?" Collins snapped, "Forty-five." He had been a little sensitive on the topic since passing the forty mark. "Not yet great age, but it will grow with years," the Chinaman commented—as if *that* was something to be happy about! Collins, somewhat disconcerted, took shelter behind a wall of routine questions.

He learned that the man's last name was his first and vice versa; that Dr. "Lee-ah-oh" had been born in Peking (later Peiping; now Peking again); that he was not a citizen of the United States; finally that his insignificant age was sixty (sixty after all). Collins, not in the least fooled by the courteous patience with which all these particulars were explained, asked bluntly.

"Ever been at this address before?"

Dr. Liao lowered his head affirmatively. "Last night I called on unfortunate occupier of unlucky premises."

"Why?"

The Chinese silently regarded a row of six-inch porcelain dolls—they were called the "Eight Immortals," Collins afterward learned—standing on a narrow shelf immediately above the reception-room door.

"You heard me," Collins said warningly. "You savvy English all right."

"I do. Though not yet with complete mastery of difficult idioms."

"Well, you know enough idioms to answer my questions. What was the reason you called on this girl last night?"

"Ignorant self apologizes for offending one of exalted station," Dr. Liao replied—no answer at all. Realizing that only a hose squad could force this sphinx to speak against its will, Collins subtly reworded the question.

"What did you two talk about?"

"Does the tiger concern himself with the twittering of wood birds?"

"Sure, if one of the wood birds has been murdered." Collins was pleased with his adroit response. "Personally, Liao, I don't think you had anything to do with this job, but just the same I've got to file a report on you. Be a good sport, will you, and give me the dope?"

"Does the tiger seek aid of the rat?" Dr. Liao's black eyes remained firmly fixed on the row of porcelain immortals.

"I'm no tiger, and you're no rat. Let's get down to cases."

"How can humble Chinese assist high-ranking magistrate?"

Collins had never been called a high-ranking magistrate before. The funny thing about the Chinese, he mused, was that you usually couldn't help liking them.

"Just answer a few questions, please. What was your business with Madame Wu?"

"A matter too small to be worthy of important official's notice."

Being a humane man, Collins didn't want to arrange for the hose squad.

"How many times have you been here before?" he asked.

"Yesterday was only time."

"You mean you hadn't known her before last night?"

"Situation is correctly stated." Dr. Liao peacefully contemplated the image of an ugly looking black-faced doll balancing itself on one foot above the dining-room door.

"Who told you about Madame Wu?"

"Mrs. Kroll. I met her yesterday at home of venerable mother, Mrs. Nicholas Vayne, who had kindly invited me to tea."

A gold mine! Delving into the newly opened drift, however, Collins soon found the vein petering out. Dr. Liao's acquaintance with the family was apparently both brief and casual. He had not known any of the Vaynes or the Krolls prior to yesterday. He had not, since the deceased Eugene had absented himself from the tea party, met the slaughtered son at all. However, Collins wasn't yet prepared to write the gentleman from Peking off entirely. The Chinese sphinx had had *some* reason for consulting with the supposed psychic—a reason all the more important because he chose to keep it carefully guarded behind his impassive countenance.

On other topics Dr. Liao spoke freely. He was willing to discuss in detail his movements for that afternoon and evening. An afternoon lecture before a Pasadena women's club had been followed by a late tea at the home of the club's president. Escaping at last, he had driven from Pasadena to Hollywood in the small car which he had purchased upon starting his lecture career. No, he had made no note of the time when he retired to the privacy of his own quarters. But it had been before eight o'clock. He had had an engagement to dine with Mr. Kroll at that hour, and Mr. Kroll had arrived with American punctuality. No, there was no one else to testify that the two actually were in Dr. Liao's sitting room at eight o'clock. The other gentleman had not been there during dinner; he had not called until just before the arrival of the police. Dr. Liao and Mr. Kroll had dined *à deux* as the French say. Collins, concealing his surprise on finding that a Chinaman could speak French, requested the name and address of the restaurant which had supplied the dinner.

There being no more information to be extracted from Dr. Liao—except his secret which couldn't be extracted—Collins allowed him to depart (from the study, not the apartment) and sent down to the squad car for the Los Angeles map which was always carried there. Spreading the large-scale map over the surface of the little desk, he circled with a soft pencil the block in which Madame Wu's apartment was located and the block on Hollywood Boulevard wherein was situated the Aubusson Hotel. The distance intervening between the two circles represented close to three and a half miles, nearly three miles of which was through Vermont Avenue traffic. If Dr. Liao had actually been in his sitting room within twenty-five minutes after eight o'clock he was innocent of this grim affair. Collins sent for Jasper Kroll.

Besides being able to confirm or disprove Dr. Liao's alibi, Kroll was important to the investigation for two other reasons: He was Vayne's brother-in-law and he had also been well acquainted with the murdered woman, according to Mrs. Vayne. Collins asked Olie to turn back to her statement. Olie grinned and found the places in short order.

> *I even remembered the things that Jasper calls extra-dimensional beings. Jasper claims that if you genuinely believe in their existence they will be able to leave whatever world it is they inhabit and come into your world—materialize in the very room with you. That's the basis for all ghost stories and folklore, Jasper insists. Jasper said Madame Wu was able to see them sometimes—she even made others see them.*

"That's about all of it," Olie said as he concluded his reading.

"Extra-dimensional beings! Extra-dimensional nuts!" Collins snorted, preparing for the worst.

Jasper Kroll turned out to be a shrimp with a big head and a fluttery manner. He looked like a nut all right. "Good evening, Captain, a terrible tragedy." The shrimp talked rapidly in a rather high tenor, illustrating his words with frequent gestures. "One completely inexplicable to me. Poor

Gene was—to say the least—a scoffer. I cannot understand why he was calling upon our dear friend Madame Wu."

Guessing that Kroll (who was only the murdered man's brother-in-law) would not deem himself personally insulted, Collins ventured a question concerning the deceased Eugene. It was a bad guess. The shrimp was immediately transformed into a crackling electric eel.

"Oh, my dear captain, absurd! Much too absurd, preposterous, impossible! You have wronged both of them deeply by those vulgar suspicions. And you wrong poor Faith as well! Out of the question, I assure you. I refuse to listen to such vile slander."

Collins decided it would be well to direct the interrogation into a less controversial channel. Unfortunately the channel he picked was Madame Wu's profession. Kroll spluttered wrathfully again. No, Madame Wu was not a racketeer. She was a genuine, unusually gifted psychic. The powers of clairvoyance, cryptoscopy and telepathy, Collins was informed, have the same objective reality as the senses of sight, smell and hearing. Kroll did not ask anyone to take his unsupported word upon the point. He was content to refer all doubters to Professor Rhine's experiments. Certainly no one could question the validity of the scientific method nor doubt the good faith of Duke University. This sort of thing went on for quite a while.

"All right," Collins cut in finally. "Maybe there is such a thing as ESP, I don't know. But at least ninety-nine per cent of all mediums are fakes. You won't argue that, will you?"

Kroll would. He objected in the first place to the word "medium"—an obsolete and inaccurate term—and he questioned Collins' estimate of ninety-nine per cent. Ninety per cent, perhaps, he was willing to allow, but Madame Wu had been numbered among the angelic ten per cent. Moreover, Kroll insisted, she had been under the protection of powerful occult forces. Collins asked for a detailed explanation.

Jasper Kroll, only too happy to oblige, began by citing the monsters of mythology. It didn't matter which mythology you took, he declared; you found much the same sort of creatures in all. Dragons, demons, devils, giants, trolls, vampires, etc., if folklore were to be believed, had once ranged across the Eurasian continent from Hibernia to Cathay. And what were these horrors actually? Distorted images of reality. Reflections glimpsed from a concave-and-convex mirror, the imperfect mirror of early man's unformed mind.

"The reality which created these crude images exists today as it did then. We are less likely to be touched by it, largely because we have lost primitive man's simple faith."

Collins decided to have as little more to do with this screwball as possible.

"Where were you this afternoon and evening?"

"Immediately after lunch I drove into town and went to the public library. I remained in the art department, consulting several reference works on jade, until almost seven-thirty when I remembered I had a dinner engagement with Doctor Liao in Hollywood."

"Were you late?" Collins put the question casually.

"I was a minute or two early."

"Let's see your watch." It checked within a few seconds of Collins' timepiece, which only a little while ago had been compared with Faith Vayne's jeweled wristwatch.

"Was Doctor Liao at the hotel when you got there?"

"Yes, but we had to wait a few minutes before the waiter from the restaurant brought our dinner. A most delightful Chinese repast."

Having finished with Jasper Kroll, Collins wanted to hustle him outside, see the few other people he had to talk to and go on home for some sleep, but Kroll insisted upon continuing his long-winded harangue, the gist of which was that Madame Wu had been in telepathic communication with extra-dimensional beings who had taken her under their psychic wing. A screwball, a screwball!

"The equilibrium of psychic tensions has been disturbed—a bad condition."

"Bad for who?" Collins demanded.

"Principally the creator of that disturbed condition. In other words, the killer of Madame Wu."

"You mean that one of your funny things is going to reach right out of thin air and choke him in his sleep?"

"Not exactly. If you'll pardon me, the analogy is rather crude. To a certain extent, though, it does convey my meaning. Most certainly the murderer will soon be made to answer for the consequences."

V

"Tell Kroll and the Chinaman to go on home," Collins said to Webber. "Fewer people cluttering up the place the better. How many more have I got to see?"

"The old guy and—"

"What old guy?"

"The one that was at the Chinaman's with Kroll."

"Oh, sure. What's his name?"

"West-something. He's staying at the Vayne's guest house, and he says he rode into town with Eugene Vayne tonight. Claims Vayne dropped him at Wilshire and La Brea at six-thirty."

"If that's so he's one of the last fellows to see Vayne alive. Bring him in."

Webber halted on his way to the living-room door. "I don't like to butt in on your business, Skipper, but maybe you'd better see the old girl first. The other Mrs. Vayne."

"Is she here now?"

"Blew in a little while ago with her secretary. She's getting pretty mad about waiting."

"What do you expect?" Collins demanded. "You can't keep ten or so million dollars standing around like a sack of flour. Bring her in right away."

He prepared himself for a deluge of tears and hysterics, but he received neither. The bereaved mother was as calm as an iceberg. With her snowy hair, cold blue eyes and stern features she looked something on the iceberg order too. Collins pulled out a chair for her with the courtesy of a Chesterfield.

"Mrs. Vayne, I am very sorry."

"Don't be a hypocrite," she snapped. "Anybody can bear up under a stranger's troubles."

Collins didn't quite know what to say to that tart truism.

"Gene never amounted to much," the astonishing mother went on. "All he was good for was to drink and spend money. No, I can't be sentimental over him. Not after this last thing."

Collins assumed an air of innocence. "I don't know what you mean, Mrs. Vayne."

"Don't play the fool, Captain. It's obvious, isn't it, Gene was having an affair with this Chinese girl?"

"I know just how you feel," Collins said soothingly.

"You don't," she contradicted him. "You're not a woman, and you're not my age and you haven't had a worthless son to plague you for years. I'm not a weepy, sentimental mother," she continued, glowering. "But I've paid Gene's debts and supported him in idleness; I've got him out of I don't know how many scrapes; yes, I even found a wife for him. I was foolish enough to hope that marriage to a sweet, intelligent girl might make something out of him. Worst mistake I ever made. Mud stays mud no matter what you do with it."

"Weren't they happy together?" Collins asked.

"How could they be? Faith tried. No one could have been more patient. I wanted to slap her sometimes for being so meek. But she—why do you want to know, Captain? Do you think that has anything to do with this?"

"Not necessarily," he parried.

"Come into the open," she ordered waspishly. "I like plain speaking. It's not very ladylike, but I never pretended to be a lady. I'm a rancher's daughter and I married a cowhand who had the brains and the push to make money out of oil. I don't suppose that Nick and I together had more than eight years of school. There's truth for you. Pay me back in the same coin."

"Mrs. Vayne, you're upset now."

"Of course I am." She choked down something suspiciously like a sob. "I'm not made of iron and steel. But if you think you can sidetrack me you're mistaken. I heard a woman crying. Faith's here now, isn't she?"

"Yes." Collins was forced into the admission.

"Thought so!" Mrs. Vayne exclaimed. "When your man stopped me from going into the bathroom I was almost sure it was because Faith was there. How long has she been in this apartment?"

"Awhile."

"Answer a question, can't you? Was she here before your men?"

"Yes."

"Alone?"

"Not exactly alone."

"Who was with her?"

"A man."

"Doesn't he have a name?"

"Yes, an Irish one."

"O'Connor? She came with *him?*"

"That's not all." Collins had stopped feeling sorry for the old hellion. "The shooting was done with O'Connor's gun. He's admitted ownership. How well do you know this fellow, Mrs. Vayne?"

"Not well enough to vouch for his honesty." She clasped her big, strong hands together as though squeezing a walnut between them.

"His story checks in practically every detail with your daughter-in-law's."

"I want the truth, Captain." Her pale, shrewd eyes fixed upon him penetratingly. "How strong a case do you have against Faith?"

"She was here," Collins replied evasively.

"Anything else?"

"She had access to O'Connor's revolver."

"How could she?"

"He claims it was stolen from him at your house."

"I see," Jocasta Vayne declared coldly. "Is that all?"

"Not quite. There's her motive. It's very powerful."

"Did Faith confess?"

"No," he admitted. "She says the shooting was done before she got here."

"Then it was. Faith never lies. And didn't I hear you say O'Connor bears her out?"

"Yes, he does."

"A witness!" she cried triumphantly. "What more do you want?"

"There's some circumstantial evidence on the other side," Collins mumbled uncomfortably.

"Circumstantial fiddlesticks!" she jeered. "Do you know anything about Faith's character? She's one of the turn-the-other-cheek-when-slapped kind. I slap back. So do you. Faith doesn't. It isn't weakness; weaklings whine or go to pieces when trouble comes. Faith is brave, uncomplaining. But there simply isn't a grain of rancor in her entire makeup."

"I have to deal in facts," Collins asserted, not very happy.

"Does that mean you're planning to put her in jail?" the oil queen's harsh voice demanded.

"We'll have to hold both of them till this thing's cleared up."

"I'll fight." Her lips set in a stern line of threat. "If you do this to her, Captain, I'll fight you personally with every weapon I can buy."

Collins regarded the woman's hawklike nose. Ten million dollars, he cogitated, ought to buy a few choice weapons among politicians. Enough, probably, to take away his stripes. To put him back in uniform or even out of the force altogether. Such things had happened to fellows for being too honest. Hell, that wasn't the right way to look at it! The right way was—he'd tell this ex-cow hand's widow what it was.

"With me it's only the facts of a case that count, Mrs. Vayne. Not wealth or social position."

"You're frank," she acknowledged. "I can respect even a pigheaded fool who has courage."

"Thanks for the compliment," he said ironically. "Now tell me, Mrs. Vayne, where *you* were between six and nine this evening."

The hysterics came then when he didn't in the least expect them.

VI

"Her nerves have been keyed up to tremendous tension," explained the secretary, who talked in a funny kind of whisper. "An emotional breakdown was almost inevitable. She has quieted since you gave permission for Mrs. Eugene Vayne to remain in the room with her, but she should be in bed. May I send her home with the chauffeur?"

The secretary, a tall, skinny bird, had a thin long nose pinched at the root from wearing glasses. Nothing remarkable about that. His eyes, too, had the glasses look, also nothing remarkable, but the flesh surrounding the right optic was darkly discolored.

"I can talk to you in her stead," he continued.

"All right," Collins assented. "Let me have five minutes alone with the chauffeur first."

"Is it necessary to delay her at all? I can give you the information you need."

"Including the black eye," thought Collins, studying the discoloration. He said aloud, "I'll have to see the chauffeur, Coggin. I'll talk to you afterward."

The chauffeur wore a tight-fitting green uniform with a peaked cap and black leather leggings. He was older than Collins had expected him to be. His name, he said, was Mike Fry.

Having the Christian name of Michael himself, Collins wasn't particularly prejudiced against it. "How old are you, Mike?" he asked genially.

"Forty-seven."

"Getting along in years for your kind of work."

"Maybe. Mrs. Vayne ain't kicking though."

"Good boss, is she?"

"I ain't kicking any. Neither are the rest, I reckon."

"Who are the rest?"

"All Orientals. Three Chinamen and a Jap."

"Well I'll be damned!" Collins exclaimed. "Wonder you don't have a young war."

"Naw, they don't bother one another. The Chinks they don't have nothing to do with the grounds and Eiichi—the Japanese gardener—ain't allowed to go inside none of the buildings except the garage. Him and me sleep over the cars, and the Chinks sleep in the gatehouse. There ain't no danger of any rumpus. Besides Ichi—I call him that for short—is a good little guy. You should see how he keeps his room. A whole lot cleaner 'n I can keep mine. My daughter stayed there a few days last summer, and she didn't find nothing to complain about."

"How did your daughter happen to be sleeping in the Jap's room?" Collins wanted to know.

"Well, sir, that's quite a story. It seems that one of Ichi's folks—they live in the Jap colony out on Terminal Island—was sick and like to die, and Ichi, he wants to know if he can have a few days off, and the missus, she says sure, take the week, and me, well, I pluck up my nerve, and I say to her, 'Mrs. Vayne, my daughter Coral, you know, the one that works for the candy store in Hollywood, she's on vacation right now, and she ain't got no money to go no place and if she could stay in Ichi's room—Ichi won't mind 'cause I just asked him—well, it would be just swell.' So she says, 'All right, Mike, you can take the Packard and pick her up tonight if you want to.' So that's what I did. And maybe you think Coral didn't have one swell time! They couldn't-a treated her nicer if she was one of the family, honest."

"All right," Collins said, shutting off the faucet. "What time did you start out with Mrs. Vayne tonight, Mike?"

"Maybe five-thirty. We drove to a joint on Wilshire."

"What kind of a joint?"

"A store. Damn 'f I know what kind to call it. The kind where you buy jade and stuff. There's a Chinaman runs it. Lee's his name, F. C. Lee."

"Ever been to the place before, Mike?"

"Like to have a nickel for every time. She is pals with Lee, the guy that owns it. He's Chink, even if the name ain't, little dried-up old muggins with big horn-rimmed specs. Seen him lots of times. Mrs. Vayne's bought a pile of junk from him."

"Do you know the time you got there and how long she stayed?"

"Maybe I can figure it out. She never wants me to let the Packard out much so it takes a good hour to run into town. Yes sir, an hour; an hour at least. That would make the time we parked six-thirty. Say six thirty-five, which sounds more like it to me. Six thirty-five. Then I waited with the car. Let's see, how long did I wait? Once I looked at my watch and it was seven o'clock, and she hadn't come out then. I was beginning to get kinda hungry, wondering if we was going to eat on the way home or what. She buys me a dinner when we eat out, but Ichi and me, we take our chow over the garage when I'm home. She had a kitchenette fixed up for us after the China war broke out so we could do our own cooking. Idea is to keep Ichi away from the house. If he had to go in the kitchen to eat the cook might get sore. Maybe even use a knife, I don't know. They don't like each other a-tall, them Chinks and Japs. I don't like the Japs none either, as a general thing, but Ichi's all right. He's a good little guy."

Collins steered the conversation back to Mrs. Vayne.

"Let me see." The chauffeur resumed deliberation. "Maybe I was wait-ing for her an hour. Say an hour. That would make it seven-thirty, no seven thirty-five. Maybe it was a mite after that. Maybe it was seven-forty—no, I don't think it was that late. Say seven thirty-five. Are you checking up on her alibi, Captain?"

"Just answer the questions, Mike. Were Mrs. Vayne and Coggin in the store all that time?"

"She was so far as I know. Couldn't see the back door though. Lee might have a secret passage too. Don't a Chinaman's house always have a secret passage into an opium den or somewhere? But unless he took her out through one of those she was in the store. Not Mr. Coggin though. He didn't go in—not even after he got back."

"Back from where?"

"Damn 'f I know. He told her he was going to walk over to a drugstore and get a bromo. She didn't like him leaving her a-tall. She told him to come in as soon as he got back, but he didn't. He got in the car instead. Wouldn't talk none; just sat there. Funny!"

Collins leaned forward attentively. "When did he pick up the shiner, Mike?"

"He didn't have it when he started out. But he did afterward, yes sir. She asked him the very same question, Captain, when she come out, and he pulled the old one about bumping into the car door. But that was just a stall. I coulda told her that, but it wasn't none of my business so I kept my mouth shut. I don't like to monkey with what ain't none of my business."

"How long was Coggin gone from the car, Mike?"

"Twenty minutes, maybe, or twenty-five. Say twenty-two."

"All right," Collins agreed. "Say twenty-two." He unfolded the large-scale city map. "Will you do me a favor, Mike?"

"Sure, what is it?"

"Take this pencil and mark a cross on the block where Lee's store is located."

The distance between the chauffeur's X and the circle which Collins had earlier drawn to designate Madame Wu's apartment measured a shade under three eights inches. On the map scale that was less than a quarter of a mile. Collins sent immediately for Jethro Coggin.

VII

"She drove all the way into town just to look at a jade-handled whip?" Collins demanded incredulously.

"But Mr. Lee assured her over the telephone this afternoon," explained the secretary, "that the whip had once been the personal property of Ch'ien Lung."

"Who's that fellow?"

"The fourth Manchu emperor."

"Yeh, sure. One of the big guns in the jade game?"

"The biggest gun of the lot perhaps. The Ch'ien Lung period, 1736–96, is generally considered to be the peak of the art."

"You seem pretty well posted," Collins observed thoughtfully.

"Naturally. One could hardly catalogue the Vayne collection without becoming informed on the fundamentals."

"Interested in the stuff yourself?"

"Yes." Apparently Jethro Coggin had failed to see the trap. "No one can help but be when he gets into it. The study of jade is the study of Chinese culture."

Collins lured the victim to set a few more stakes on which to impale himself. "Was all the best work done in Ch'ien Lung's time?"

"Not all but unquestionably a large share. Ch'ien Lung was a magnificent patron of all the arts. The Maecenas of China, you might say."

The homicide captain grunted. "Go on and tell me about him," he ordered. "I like to know these things."

"The emperor—one of the greatest, most able rulers, by the way—loved to work on a piece of jade with his own hands and was, in fact, an expert craftsman in his own right. He encouraged jade carving in every possible way—awarded prizes to the artists and staged exhibitions of their products in the imperial palace, behind the violet walls of the Forbidden City itself."

Collins allowed the trap to spring. "If all this is so, Coggin, you should have been interested in having a look at that whip. Why didn't you go into the store?"

The secretary apprehended the pit—too late to save himself. "Why—er—uh—" He writhed helplessly upon the stakes. "Ch'ien Lung things are no particular treat to me. I've seen so many of them."

"Not a whip old Ch'ien himself had owned, I'll bet."

"But it wasn't genuine." Coggin clung desperately to that straw. "Mrs. Vayne didn't purchase it. Lee couldn't guarantee its authenticity, and he apologized for having misled her over the telephone."

"That's not the point. Mrs. Vayne was so anxious for a squint at this particular whip that she bounced out of the house right away and drove twenty-five miles or so into town on the strength of what she'd been told about it. Until she'd seen her man Lee she thought it was the real McCoy, and you didn't have any reason to think different about it either. You're interested in jade and you admit Ch'ien Lung is the kingpin of the game. According to all the rules, you should've broken your neck trying to get through Lee's front door. But you didn't give a damn about seeing the emperor's whip. Why the hell didn't you?"

"I had a little stomach upset," Coggin parried weakly. "I thought a bromoseltzer might help, and I walked over to a drugstore."

"If that's true it still doesn't fit all the facts. You didn't go into Lee's at all, not even after you got back, Fry said. Why not then?"

"My eye," Coggin said, placing his index finger upon the discolored ocular socket. "I bruised it getting out of the car."

"Oh, that was it, huh?"

"Yes, that's right. I ran carelessly against a corner of the rear door." He seemed more confident now. "When I reached the drugstore I saw my face in a mirror. The flesh had commenced to turn livid. Naturally I didn't wish to embarrass Mrs. Vayne by appearing in public with her."

Collins snorted in contempt. "That's what you told her. Don't try to pass that story off on me too. I've got my facts from the right source, Coggin. Cute stunt you tried, rushing the chauffeur away before I could talk to him, but it didn't work. When you began to show signs of being anxious about it I was sure you had a good reason for wanting to keep Mike away from me, and I was dead right. You picked up the shiner during that trip to the drugstore, didn't you?"

"Yes," Coggin whispered, a whisper softer than usual.

"Who hit you?"

"I'd prefer not to say."

"Why didn't you tell Mrs. Vayne someone hit you?"

"I—uh—she might have misunderstood."

"Misunderstood what?"

"She might have thought that I had been fighting."

"Well, hadn't you?"

"No. I was struck but delivered nothing in return."

"Why not?"

"The blow was totally unexpected." The secretary gingerly touched the area of the ecchymosis. "When I picked myself up he had gone."

"Who had gone?"

"I would rather not mention the name, Captain."

"You didn't want Mrs. Vayne to worm it out of you either. Did you?"

"No, I did not."

"Why do you want to hide it?" Collins demanded.

The secretary didn't answer. The homicide officer shifted the attack swiftly to a new direction.

"How far would you say it is from this apartment to Lee's place?"

"Why, I don't know."

"You can guess. A long ways or not?"

"I don't think it's very far."

"It isn't. Not more than a quarter of a mile. Want to do a problem in arithmetic? A man can walk four miles an hour; how long will it take him to walk a quarter of a mile?"

"Three and three quarters minutes," Cobbin calculated promptly.

"Double it for going and coming—seven and a half minutes. Fry said you were gone twenty-two. Did you know that Madame Wu lived at this address? Quick! Yes or no?"

"Yes," the secretary replied after a brief deliberation. "I've typed letters to her for Mrs. Kroll."

"Were you coming here to see her or not?"

"I—er—no."

"Coggin, you're a lousy liar. You were. You've been in this apartment before."

"No. No, I haven't. I've never been here."

"You weren't even on this street, I suppose?" Collins asked sarcastically.

"Yes, I was on Novella Street today. Why should I conceal it?"

"You passed right by this building."

"I—I probably did."

"There's no drugstore within several blocks of here," Collins informed him ominously.

"I didn't know. I turned into the street at random. Purely a coincidence."

"Random, hell! Coincidence, hell! It stands out like a boil on the nose that you were coming here to see Madame Wu. You did see her."

"No. I didn't. I've never seen her in private. I saw her only a few minutes this morning with the others. Not before or afterward. I wasn't acquainted with her at all."

"Don't interrupt me, Coggin. I know what I'm talking about. You found Vayne here with her. It had to be Vayne; that's the reason you lied to his mother about your eye. It was Vayne who hit you. Wasn't it?"

"Yes." The secretary's lips were curiously white. "But not in here—outside in front of the building. I was just walking by when he jumped out of his car and saw me."

VIII

"Professor Westborough!" Collins jumped up and held out his hand. "Man alive! How did you get here?"

"I sadly fear that I was arrested. It is worth the temporary inconvenience, however, to discover you have not yet forgotten me."

"Forgotten the Launay case! Not in a hurry. Why didn't somebody tell me you were here?"

"Those of your men whom I saw were strangers to me."

"Yes, that's right. Big shake-up in the department about a year ago—hit us like an earthquake. I was lucky enough to be able to hang on though; even got a promotion out of it."

"I congratulate you, Captain."

"Thanks."

"The city was also lucky to be able to retain your valuable services." While uttering the compliment Westborough stared with undisguised curiosity about the little room.

It was a weird combination of modern office and Oriental temple. The desk and chairs were twentieth-century American. Other things were not: the altar, incense burner, wooden tube of bamboo splints, kidney-shaped fortune-telling blocks, planchette for sand writing under spiritual control,

porcelain images of Taoist deities, drawings of the twenty-eight constella-
tions and the thirty-six heavens. The little Chinese lady seemed very close
to Westborough at that instant.

Without doubt it was in here that she had entertained her clients. She
had assisted them to shake the tube of numbered sticks. She had instructed
them in the proper method of tossing the halves of the divining bamboo
root. She had inscribed Chinese characters in the sand dish under the V-
shaped planchette. She had burned incense and prayers to the porcelain
gods. Pretty little fortune-teller! What could she have done to have merited
her swift decease? Or had she merited it?

"Still interested in murder cases?" Collins asked.

"I am very much interested in this one." Westborough's mind was on
Miss Wu's soft, mischievous giggle. So much intelligence, beauty, charm
gone from a world which needed these qualities so sorely!

"Maybe I can use you on it."

"If you can I shall be very happy," the historian declared with fervor.

"You tell me what you know, and I'll tell you what I know. How's that?"

It was mutually satisfactory.

"So you think," Collins pondered after a time, "that Eugene Vayne was
the crook who stole his mother's statue?"

"I am reasonably certain that, whether or not he actually consigned the
Green Shiver to her watery grave, his actions indicated that he at least
knew her whereabouts."

"What made him hide it in the lotus pond?"

"I am at a total loss to explain."

"Screwy business!" Collins grumbled. "Doesn't fit with the rest of the
case at all."

"May I offer a slight contradiction? It does, to a limited extent, confirm
Mrs. Eugene Vayne's story of Madame Wu's telephone call. The alleged
'psychic vision' may be explained without the necessity of invoking clairvoyance or telepathy. I should prefer not to invoke either. I should much
prefer to believe that Miss Wu derived her knowledge of the statue's recovery in more ordinary fashion from Mr. Vayne's lips."

"But did she really know?" Collins countered. "I've only young Mrs.
Vayne's word that the Chinese woman telephoned her."

"Would not it be possible to ascertain from the telephone company
whether or not a call from this number was made to the Palmas Peninsula
today?"

"Yes, that can be done. The peninsula is served by a different company
from the city so a record would have to be kept for billing. But if it checks—
well, we get into difficulties."

"We do, indeed," Westborough concurred. "Shall I state a few of them?
The crime must be premeditated at the time Mr. O'Connor's revolver was
stolen. But a Mrs. Eugene Vayne telling the truth about her reason for visiting Madame Wu could not foresee, when the revolver was taken, that she
would discover her husband with the Chinese lady, for she could not know

then that she would be going to Madame Wu's apartment herself. On the other hand, how else could a falsifying Mrs. Vayne learn that the statuette had been recovered? That fact was known only to myself, Mr. Vayne and Mr. O'Connor."

"It's a problem all right," Collins admitted. "But there must be an answer somewhere."

"The theory of the escaped murderer perhaps?"

"No, I can't check on that. The wife's the only logical suspect. She had motive, method and opportunity. She must have found out somehow that her husband was going to be here. Maybe he told her so himself before he left. If I could only prove it!"

"Is it your intention to arrest Mrs. Vayne?"

Collins said doggedly, "If I didn't hold her I'd be as crazy as she is. And she *is* crazy. I wish you could have heard her statement. The facts were mixed up with the damnedest gibberish about ghosts and premonitions and extra-dimensional beings and dreams and crystal gazing and God knows what all. Even Olie thought she was nuts. Isn't that right, Olie?"

"She didn't sound any too sane," the stenographer confirmed.

"The woman's loony. There's just no other answer. She shoots her husband and his Chinese girlfriend, and O'Connor gets a sudden attack of chivalry and decides to go the limit for her. Damnfool impulsive Irishman!"

"Did your investigation uncover no other possible motive?"

"One. Vayne took a poke at the secretary and gave him a black eye. Right out in front of this building, too, Coggin admitted, but the time's wrong. It happened at six forty-five. Ten minutes later Coggin was back in the car with the chauffeur and stayed there until eight-thirty when they were all in Redondo Beach, having sizzling steaks at the Rolling Wheel Restaurant. The shooting, according to Mrs. Vayne's watch, was at eight o'clock."

"Could it be possible," Westborough inquired, "that the crimes actually were perpetrated earlier?"

PART SEVEN: GOBLIN TURNS GLADIATOR

JASPER KROLL, after retrieving the Buick sedan he had left near the Aubusson Hotel, returned to the Novella Street apartment for Westborough and Jethro Coggin. It was 2 A.M. before the three finally reached the Vayne estate, and the vermilion gate was naturally barred. Taking a flashlight from a car pocket, Kroll directed the beam upon one of the black-lacquer Chinese characters.

"A photoelectric cell is hidden in a recess," Coggin explained. "When the light strikes it a bell rings in Wong's room."

"Excellent!" Westborough commented. "May I ask who thought of this ingenious idea?"

"I did," Coggin said.

"Yes, Jethro is an electrical engineer," Kroll added while they waited.

"Twenty-five years ago I thought I might be one," Coggin amended. "Instead I—"

The circular *Shou* character unexpectedly swung inward. There peered through the aperture the head of a yawning Chinese.

"All right, you come in," Wong said after a brief inspection. "You come late; Missy in bed." The little wicket was slammed shut before the heavy leaves of the gate were opened.

After bidding his companions a good night at the garage Westborough followed the winding path by the lotus pond to the guest house. In his room he saw a sealed envelope pinned to his pillow.

Immediately he recalled the previous note hinting of dire things if he persisted in his prying. "I thought," he recollected, "that there would be no second warning. Yet here it is. Dear me!"

He slit the envelope open. There was neither salutation nor signature to the short page of sprawling handwriting. He read:

I must see you alone. If you return tonight wait an hour to make sure the others are asleep. Where is Oregon? If you know open my door without knocking. Absence of light must not mislead you; I shall not be sleeping tonight. Destroy this, please.

The name "Oregon" had been underlined twice; the word "alone" three times. Touching a match to the missive Westborough burned it in the jade ashtray on the night table. "Most inhabitants of the United States," he mused, watching the flame, "would unquestionably declare Oregon to be northwest. Ergo, I am sure that this is the answer meant. Understandable. What I do not understand, however, is why this of all times is chosen for cryptograms. Nevertheless, I shall certainly keep the—it would be scarcely accurate to say assignation."

Exactly an hour and five minutes from the time the paper had been reduced to crumbling curls of carbon his groping fingers encountered branches which could belong only to the aged dwarf cypress in the center of the ocean court. Praised be the tree spirit who must surely have guided a mere mortal's fumbling touch through this opacity! Fog blotted out the stars' tiny lanterns and beclouded a moon which should have been shining brilliantly. Moreover, the night's turbidity was unmarred by the faintest glimmer from any of the seven pavilions. Westborough, trusting largely to his nose, moved in the direction in which he fancied the scent of brine was the strongest. He pushed open a door into a darkened room. As he crossed the threshold a beam of light dazzled his eyes.

"Close the door behind you," ordered a deep-toned but feminine voice. The light flickered away to rest momentarily upon a chair near the head of the bed. "Sit down there." When he had complied the flashlight was extinguished. "We'll talk in the dark," Jocasta Vayne continued. "Less risk. I don't know who to trust any more."

"I know where Oregon is," Westborough said.

"If you didn't you wouldn't be here. That was to test you. I had to know whether you really had sense or not."

She was certainly an unusual woman. Westborough decided that he would not offer condolences or say any of the supposedly comforting things usually said to a mother who has just lost a son. "I burned your note," he informed her instead. "And your statuette has been recovered."

"What's that?"

"More through good luck than through any unusual perspicuity on my part," he confessed apologetically. "It is now somewhere in the living pavilion. I am not sure exactly where. I have not had the chance to confer with Mr. O'Connor since we said good-by at the foot of the steps. Do you wish me to look for it now?"

"No, don't bother with it tonight. It isn't important now."

"Very well, I shall allow it to remain wherever it may be," Westborough murmured. "I am sure that Mr. O'Connor put it in a safe place. Moreover, unless he talked indiscreetly before quitting the grounds this evening, I do not see how anyone here can know that the Green Shiver was found."

"Stop harping on that fool piece of jade," she ordered.

"I am sorry if I offend. I was merely trying to convey the impression that Mr. O'Connor had nothing to do with the theft. I would rather not tell you at present whom I believe to be the guilty party."

"I would rather not know," she retorted in a fierce whisper. "Westborough"—she omitted the customary title, addressing him in the blunt manner of men—"will you work on this case? I want you to show that Collins up for the fool he is."

("But," the historian objected to himself, "I recently pledged myself to enlistment under the Collins' banner. Alas, what tangled webs we weave!")

"I'll pay any fee to see Faith cleared of this charge."

Amazing woman! To her a murdered son apparently meant far less than the plight of a living daughter-in-law.

"Before I make a rash promise allow me to inquire your reasons for so strongly believing in that young woman's innocence."

"You've met Faith," she rejoined acidly. "That's all that's necessary."

"True, she is sweet, gentle and considerate. These qualities, however—"
She interrupted at once.

"If my own eyes had seen Faith standing over Gene's body, the weapon still smoking in her hand, I would refuse to believe her guilty."

"Dear me!" Westborough was considerably jolted by this remarkable demonstration of loyalty from Naomi to Ruth. It was queer to be conversing with a woman one could not see—their voices bodiless in the darkness. "You have been extremely kind to her," he observed.

"Kind!" she repeated. "You call it kind to wreck a person's life? That's what I did to Faith."

"I—I cannot understand," he faltered.

He found her explanation fully as remarkable as other developments in this bewildering case.

"When Faith returned from Peking she was in a state of emotional shock. She had seen too much, I think, and it had affected her in ways so subtle that it took quite a while before I could even see them. She wasn't her old self, but there was little you could put your finger upon: a listlessness she hadn't had before, an occasional spell of absentmindedness and then the terror that sometimes showed on her face. I saw it the first time when I was questioning her about the bombing of Tientsin; her eyes cringed as if someone was about to strike her. That's what China had done to Faith."

"The responsibility is scarcely yours."

"Perhaps not. But I should have let her alone afterward. I should have given her time to recover in her own way. I didn't because my son had been attracted to her. I made her marry Eugene."

"How is it possible to force an adult woman into marriage against her will?"

"It's difficult to explain to a man. Faith was wavering; a little pressure one way or the other would turn the trick. I wanted her to marry him. She has all the qualities I most admire: courage, affection, intelligence, loyalty. I knew that Gene loved her. I thought that he might do for her what he had never been able to do for himself or for anyone else. He didn't. It didn't work out at all."

"No?" Westborough questioned.

"Gene lost interest within a few months. He treated the child abominably though she never complained. I never understood what made him turn against her so completely. Gene had loved her genuinely in the beginning, I believe."

"Perhaps a displacement of hatred," the historian meditated to himself. "A man may take revenge upon a wife for a mother's sins, psychoanalysts claim." Aloud he inquired, "Did she also love your son?"

"Why else did she marry him?" the unseen voice countered raspingly. "Money? Some would say so, but I know better. Money means nothing to Faith. She was miserable here with Gene."

Westborough could think of nothing whatsoever to say.

"It hasn't been easy to tell you this," she continued slowly. "I'm as proud as the next person about washing family linen in public. But I want you to know why I feel obligated to Faith. I want you to promise that you will do all in your power to help her."

"It will be very little," he temporized.

"I'm not so sure. At first, I'll admit, I didn't have much confidence in you, Westborough, but you grow upon a person somehow."

"Thank you. That is a very nice compliment. I will look where I can in the interests of truth, but I can promise to accomplish nothing. While I have the opportunity may I ask you a few more or less personal questions?"

"Yes, go ahead." It seemed to him that her breathing deepened.

"What was the errand which took you away this evening?" He thought it best to pretend complete ignorance.

"A Chinese dealer in Oriental art objects invited me to his gallery to look at a Ch'ien Lung whip. He had another purchaser, he insisted, so it was urgent that I come immediately. But the whip wasn't genuine."

"Not of the Ch'ien Lung period?"

"Of the period, perhaps, but it had not been owned by the emperor as Lee had represented it to me. We had quite an argument over it."

"You have dealt with this dealer before?"

"I have bought thousands of dollars' worth of jade from him."

"Therefore you are sure of his reliability?"

"I have never known him to do anything remotely dishonest. Even in this last matter he didn't actually deceive me. He might have sold me the whip at a fancy price; I would have taken his word for its authenticity. But he refused to confirm the things he told me over the telephone; denied, in fact, having made such claims."

"Is it possible that you misunderstood him?"

"Possible but not probable. 'I personally can guarantee that the whip was one of Ch'ien Lung's own riding crops,' is exactly what he said over the telephone. That's pretty definite."

"Extremely definite. Did he deny those words afterward?"

"He certainly did. He said that he had only told me the whip was of the Ch'ien Lung period, a vastly different thing."

"Vastly different," Westborough agreed. "I do not wish to sound alarming, Mrs. Vayne, but does it occur to you that you might have been the victim of a hoax?"

"A hoax? But it was Lee's voice I heard on the telephone and he admitted that he had called. Why should Lee try to hoax me?"

"Perhaps he wished to sell you some other article which he knew you would not make a special trip to see."

"He did show me a ring I wouldn't buy. Very beautiful emerald-green jadeite but not worth seven thousand. Lee acted a little put out when I refused. He insisted that the stone was the most perfect piece of imperial jade in the world except the 108 matched beads in the Ch'ien Lung necklace."

"But that is almost legendary!" Westborough exclaimed.

"No, it isn't a legend. The necklace really was given to Ch'ien Lung and descended from sovereign to sovereign until it was finally taken over with the other imperial treasures when Henry Pu-yi was driven from the Forbidden City by the troops of the Christian General."

"That was in 1924, I believe," Westborough annotated.

"It stayed in Peking until after the establishment of Manchoukuo. Then all the imperial treasures, I understand, were packed and shipped to a foreign warehouse in the French concession of Shanghai. That's where it is now, I suppose, though Lee claims to have heard a grapevine rumor that some Peking jade dealers bought it from the central government just before the outbreak of the present war. Scarcely believable, but Lee seemed sure. In fact, he acted almost as if he had it on hand to sell to me. He even mentioned a price."

"Indeed?" Westborough murmured. "What price was mentioned?"

"A good stiff one—one hundred thousand dollars."

"Dear me! Would you buy it for that exceedingly large sum?"

"How do I know? The very idea is so much moonshine. That's what I told Lee."

"Were you with him long?"

"Something like an hour—he insisted that I stay for tea. Lee loves to make tea."

"A true Chinese. Did you and he discuss other topics?"

"Nothing important except one thing. He wanted to know if I had found the Jade Lady. That rather startled me."

"I should think it would be surprising," Westborough concurred. "The theft, I believe, was not mentioned in any newspaper."

"Jethro succeeded in keeping the story out. Not much of a trick. Nick's oil company spends quite a big sum every years to advertise, and I'm still holding onto the bulk of Nick's stock. No, I can't guess where Lee could have heard about the loss."

"Did he not reveal his source of information?"

"No. He was very mysterious about it. 'We Chinese have ways of learning things' was the best I could get out of him. Madame Wu knew (thanks to Lydia's foolishness) but it's not likely he was acquainted with her. Educated Chinese such as Lee and Doctor Liao don't go to fortune-tellers."

"Not often," Westborough agreed. "May I now ask why we are talking under such extreme conditions of secrecy?"

"I thought I made that clear in my note."

"I am sorry, Mrs. Vayne, but you did not. You hinted a great deal but actually told nothing. May I inquire if you definitely suspect a person in this household as being involved in the evening's tragedy?"

Before she could answer an excited little dog shattered the night's silence with a series of shrill yelps.

II

Mindful of the reputation of his hostess, Westborough slipped at once from her sleeping quarters to the glassed porch spanning the gap between Mrs. Vayne's pavilion and the smaller one occupied by her secretary. Jethro Coggin continued to slumber, but a light was shining in one of the little houses. The dog had ceased barking. As Westborough walked toward the lighted pavilion words floated to him through an open window.

"Jasper!" wailed the voice of Lydia Kroll. "Goblin isn't in his little basket. Oh, my sweet darling is so brave! He heard something with his little ears, and he ran out all by himself. Do you think anyone could be so mean as to hurt a little doggie?"

"I'll see, pet," her husband promised in a sleep-muffled voice. "Just let me find my trousers."

"Jasper, you mustn't look for him alone!" she cried, noticeably frightened. "Wake Jethro, please. He has a revolver."

"Very well, pet."

It occurred to the historian that his own position was not enviable. He had no way of accounting for his presence in the compound at such an hour without compromising a lady. Though he and she were of an age where such compromise would be, perhaps, somewhat impracticable, the little scholar did not dwell upon that unpleasant aspect of the circumstances. A strategic retreat was assuredly in order. The only question was how.

The most direct route, down the stairs to the lotus pond, involved two major difficulties. He must unbar the gate, which could not be done quietly, and, furthermore, he could not even reach the gate without passing perilously close to the Kroll pavilion. While he was hesitating Kroll himself emerged from the door. Westborough hurriedly fled into the shadows.

He skirted the living pavilion unseen, but his lead was slight. Strictly speaking, it was no lead at all. Coggin's office connected by telephone with both garage and gatehouse. The logical action under the circumstances would be to notify the servants at both buildings. In that event, Westborough quickly realized, he would be trapped between two forces. Haste was imperative. He raced through the doorless gate on the south.

Luckily he knew the turns of the zigzag path fairly well by this time. He did not stumble, fortunately, but he could go at only a gentle dogtrot. The telephone was much faster. By the time he reached the wishing well he saw lights glowing in the windows of the gatehouse. Nor was that all. He also heard Wing, Wong and Weng conversing in high-pitched, excited voices. The three Chinese might rush out at any instant, and he could scarcely fail to run directly into them if he kept on the path. He ducked under the railing and entered the bushes.

Flopping to hands and knees, he endeavored to crawl around the slope of the hill to the eastern stairs. His snakelike progress was extremely slow, but he was thankful that the leaves he disturbed did not rustle loudly. The servants passed within a few feet of him on their way to the compound. There were only two; Wong, doubtless, had remained to guard the gate.

Noise would have been fatal. Westborough held his breath as they walked by, a quartet of softly swishing legs. When they were out of earshot he resumed his wriggling through the orange-fragrant pittosporums. He was not sure at all of direction; the shrubbery was a veritable maze, and there were no paths. His fingers, groping ahead in the soft dirt, came suddenly into contact with warm hairiness.

By a supreme effort of will he stifled the natural impulse to cry out. It could be nothing more alarming than a dead Peke. He brushed his hand lightly over the silky fur, paying a silent tribute to Black Goblin's spunky ancestry. No breed of canine is so packed per cubic inch with ferocious courage as the Pekingese, hateful lap dogs as they may appear to the general run of American masculinity. One of these bowlegged, snub-nosed midgets will challenge unhesitantly a dog three times his size and frequently is allowed to get away with it.

So Goblin, a silken-haired gladiator knowing not the meaning of fear, had rashly rushed to battle and paid the full penalty which lack of judgment exacts. It might be important to know how he had been slain, but Touch refused to yield the information. Sight was at present useless. Hearing, the only major sense available, informed him of an anxious consultation taking place in the courtyard immediately above his head. He could not linger in the shrubbery with the tiny warrior's body near by to accuse him if he were caught. He must reach the guest house before they looked there and discovered his empty room. The hillside steps could not be far away.

Neither could the dog-killer, a human animal savagely taut with fear, crawling as soundlessly as himself. Westborough tried not to think of encountering the prowler. He told himself that peril is doubled, never lessened, when the mind is forced to meet it in advance of the body. Presently his fingers grazed the gratifying hardness of concrete.

He edged, inch by inch, toward the foot of the stairs. Emerging from the pittosporums, he paused to brush the dirt from his clothing. The guest house remained a shadowy hulk, but a light shone mistily in the upper story of the garage. Chauffeur and gardener had also been aroused. The hum of acrimonious dispute above traveled faintly to his ears. Instinct—the instinct of the hunted—whispered that the hue and cry would not be on in force until the contending voices were united under one leader. Kroll? Coggin? Jocasta Vayne? The question of who led the pack was unimportant to the fox scuttling to reach his burrow.

The fog, luckily, continued to opaque the moon. But shoes, Westborough realized, might betray his presence on the stone-paved pathway. He removed them, tucking one under each arm. Shoeless feet could move silently. Not fast, however; he must carefully feel each separate step or risk a disastrous tumble on the dank, slick flags. A glow, springing suddenly into visibility, caused him to turn his head. The decorative gate at the head of the stairs had just been thrown open, and flashlighted searchers were descending the steps.

Beams stabbed the fog behind him. Fortunately, the electrically minded Mr. Coggin had not thought of the installation of a garden floodlighting system or else the suggestion had been vetoed. The guest house loomed abruptly before him, and he darted through the veranda door.

He made some noise upon entering, but it did not much matter. He had the little building to himself that night. No hotheaded young O'Connor could come storming from the adjacent room to collar him. Strangely he regretted the Irishman's absence. But he had no time to think of anything except disrobing. He must be in bed, apparently sleeping, by the time they came. Contrary to his usual neatness, coat, trousers, tie, shirt, socks, underwear were flung helter-skelter. He won his race, but only by the narrowest of margins.

"Yoo-hoo, Mr. Westborough!"

He allowed them to repeat the call, then answered yawningly, "Yes, who is it?"

"Let us in."

He turned on the small lamp by his bedside. "One minute, please." He was able to restore some semblance of order to his scattered clothing before he admitted them. "Has something serious happened?"

The intruders were Jasper Kroll and the Japanese gardener. Kroll had incongruously armed himself with that rubber implement on a stick known as the plumber's friend, and the squat Japanese carried a spade. Both had electric lanterns, and neither was fully clad.

"Put on something and come with us," Kroll ordered tensely. "We need every available hand. There's a prowler on the grounds." The gardener, a dark, dour little man, significantly brandished his spade.

Westborough was extremely thankful that he had earlier taken the precaution of brushing the soil from his trousers. He prayed fervently that the dirt upon his Oxfords might pass unperceived. Under pretense of tying the laces he contrived a surreptitious cleaning while Kroll was explaining the *modus operandi*.

"Wing and Weng are beating toward the gate; Mike and Jethro are taking the territory by the garage; and the rest of us will handle this end. Wong is at the gate with his shotgun."

"Are the women left unguarded?"

"Lydia is with her mother, who has the only revolver on the premises. You'd better find a stick or something."

Westborough searched throughout the room for an article that might serve the purpose of a club. "May I ask how the prowling gentleman made his presence known?"

"Goblin heard him; his barking woke up Lydia and me. He must have pushed open the door with his nose and run outside because he wasn't in the room when we turned on the light. We haven't found any trace of him yet, and I'm afraid we won't find him alive. Evil is at large tonight." Kroll's elfin face was the color of a blanched almond.

Westborough discovered a pocket flashlight among his belongings but no weapon of any description. He was secretly pleased. "I shall walk over to the garage to arm myself," he said.

Kroll volunteered to accompany him. "It isn't safe for a man of your age to wander around alone, my dear fellow." Westborough was slightly nettled by the reference to his age. He was not, after all, precisely doddering. He insisted upon going alone and after some little argument succeeded in winning his case.

"Be careful, please." Kroll's voice was oddly concerned. "I can almost smell the danger."

"I can smell nothing except the salt of the sea," Westborough replied as he took the path to the garage.

He had gone only as far as the pond before he was challenged. The challenger was the chauffeur, Fry, who carried an iron jack handle. Thankful that it had not split his skull, Westborough asked if he could find a similar weapon. Fry went back with him to the garage, stepped inside and came out with a foot-long wrench.

"That ought to do you, sir," he said.

Westborough quoted gravely, " 'Tis not so deep as a well or so wide as a church door, but 'tis enough; 'twill serve.' " The chauffeur tipped his cap and returned to patrol duty.

Though he had promised to rejoin the party on the northern side of the grounds Westborough continued in the opposite direction, following the drive along the south wall. Shortly a light was flashed on him. "Who goes there?" he hailed.

"Coggin," was the answer. "Who are you? Oh, Mr. Westborough! If you want to be helpful you might take the motor court behind the garage."

Westborough, dropping his wrench silently into the grass, told a falsehood.

"It is first necessary for me to go up to the compound to procure a weapon of some nature. I am now defenseless. I shall hurry back."

"All right," Coggin agreed, "but be careful not to startle Wong when you pass the gate unless you want a charge of buckshot."

Westborough did not. Neither did he want his throat slit by the butcher knife Weng carried, nor any of the many things which might have been done to him by Wing's hatchet. In all three of these encounters, however, his name was the only password needed, and he reached the summit of the hill without serious mishap. Four of the pavilions were lighted, three dark. The living pavilion was among the dark, but it was the one Westborough elected to visit.

His torch flickered over the ebony and mahogany furniture. Somewhere in here Kerry O'Connor had promised to leave it. In that pearl-inlaid teak cabinet perhaps? It contained nothing but a ceremonial scepter and a few other knickknacks. Then behind the Screen of Heaven ... his eyes glimpsed at once the little jade goddess standing proudly on the floor.

Was she the object the prowler sought? At any rate she had not been discovered. Westborough stepped out from behind the screen. He wished that he knew a more secure abode for Mistress Green Shiver, but the ceiling lockers, where she properly belonged, were inaccessible to him. Under a sofa cushion might be a trifle less obvious. Or perhaps under the sofa itself. As the tiny beam of his light was traversing the shimmering blue field of the Tientsin rug he halted in sudden surprise.

A slight indentation in the thick Mongolian wool indicated that the circular base of a heavy bronze floor lamp had been shifted an inch or so. The lamp had been moved recently, Westborough believed; otherwise the resilient fibers would probably have effaced the traces. He eyed the dome of the base meditatively. Why had the lamp been moved? He stooped for a closer examination.

Curiosity had blunted his sense of danger. He did not recognize the peril stealing silently into the room. His fingers closed around the shaft of the lamp. He was just about to look under the convex base when a heavy missile hurtled through the air. It struck the side of his head, and he fell unconscious.

PART EIGHT: PUZZLES FROM PEKING

IN A HOTEL sitting room two Chinese conversed in the singsong tones of the Pekingese dialect. They said, in effect:

"Crab swallowed bait. Yesterday evening honored lady was lured to my valueless shop."

"Venerated merchant, did you speak to her of what it is not necessary to mention between us?"

"Illustrious scholar, this person so conducted himself."

"What did you learn in your glorious emporium?"

"The superior man values truth. In my wretched hovel I failed most miserably. Honored lady whose face is like crab may have that for which you seek. I do not know. She admitted nothing."

"Did not her face mirror her soul's knowledge?"

"I am a worthless reader of the soul, or she is deeply versed in the art of concealment."

"How truly it has been said: 'The fish that swims deeply in the water may be taken with the hook. The bird that flies high in the air is not beyond the arrow's reach. The heavens may be measured, the earth surveyed; the human heart alone is not to be known.' "

"True, illustrious one. I have failed to know the heart of this woman."

"Esteemed merchant, I have failed also. But it is bootless, said the great Kung, to protest against things past remedy. An army may be deprived of its commander, but men like ourselves cannot be robbed of will. For the cause we must redouble our efforts."

126

"What I can do will be done, revered scholar. For the cause."

"It is unwise for you to visit me here. Last night I barely escaped arrest. Even now the police may be spying upon us."

"My heart laments for your misfortune. How shall I get in touch with you if I have news?"

"This paper contains my schedule for this week and the next. If you have a message to deliver let your noble son visit one of my lectures."

"My worthless son shall do as you suggest. Are you, honored one, in personal danger?"

"It matters not. When the horse has run to the edge of the precipice it is too late to pull the rein."

"It is said that on the brink of peril we must rely upon our friends. You may rely upon me, illustrious one!"

"For the cause I thank you, noble merchant. Now go quickly, lest the police be watching."

II

A shimmering waterfall cascaded in the marble fountain by the Babylonian tower of the city hall. An elderly little man, walking from the corner of First and Spring streets, halted a second to watch the sparrows drinking. Beneath the brim of his soft felt hat the white gauze of a bandage was visible. Climbing the two flights of weather-stained stairs, he read the Cicero quotation graven above the entrance:

"He that violates his oath profanes the divinity of faith here."

"Faith," he meditated, treating the abstract quality as a proper noun, "has already profaned her divinity by violation of the truth, I sadly fear." He entered the long vaulted corridor traversing the ground floor.

Two plainclothes detectives emerged from a double door lettered "Record and Identification Division." The elderly man, passing them on his way, guessed their profession from the aggressiveness with which broad shoulders were squared and the look of power on heavyset faces. Taking the corridor they had quitted, he followed it a short distance to another door. Before going further, he perused its inscription twice:

Room 42
Homicide Bureau

The man with the bandaged head turned the knob and walked inside. A clerk with blue jowls and a pencil behind his right ear stepped from behind a frosted-glass partition to inform the visitor that Captain Collins could not at present be disturbed. Politely removing his hat, the little man apologized for the intrusion. He gave his name and added that he would gladly await the convenience of the homicide captain. The period of waiting was employed in a study of the relics in the big glass case.

Remarkable relics they were, exhibits worthy of any chamber of horrors. A grinning skull neighbored a big can of cyanide. A small bottle of bichloride of mercury had figured in a poisoning case. There were razors and revolvers, the pocket knife a Japanese had employed in the sacred obligation of hara-kiri, a butcher knife which had also cut into human intestines. A length of flexible tubing had aided another suicide, less traditionally minded than the Japanese, to perish with comparative painlessness from carbon-monoxide fumes.

"Captain Collins will see you now," the blue-jowled clerk said as he opened the gate to the inner sanctum.

An entire wall of the not overly large private office was taken up with four-drawer, sectional steel filing cabinets. A neutral-toned carpet, a desk, several plain wooden chairs and a swivel chair with armrests completed the furnishings. "Westborough!" Collins ejaculated, arising from the padded seat of the swivel chair. "What happened to your head?"

The little man turned his hat shyly in his hands. "I had a slight accident."

"Who slugged you?"

"That I do not know." Westborough inquired if he might deposit his headgear upon the unused top of one of the filing cabinets.

"Sure, anywhere. When and where'd it happen?"

"About 4 A.M. this morning in Mrs. Vayne's living pavilion." He related the circumstances.

"How long were you out?" Collins asked after a time.

"Only a few minutes. Fortunately there was no fracture. The doctor whom I visited this afternoon complimented me upon the hardness of my skull. It is true that I do feel a little groggy."

"You ought to be in bed," Collins declared severely. "A man of your age, Professor, has no business running around after a shock like that. What sort of thing was it that hit you?"

"A green jade buffalo. Being normally employed as a doorstop, it was readily available from the front entrance."

"Might've been killed," Collins snorted.

"Luckily the missile merely grazed the right side of my head. A laceration of the skin was the only damage the doctor was able to find. I am rather fatalistic on the question of death, I confess. When the time comes it comes. Shall I continue?"

"Go ahead."

"When I recovered consciousness I discovered that Wing, Mrs. Vayne's number-one boy, was bathing my head. I endeavored to question him. He had hurried up to the court, he said, hearing the noise of someone running. The door of the living pavilion was wide open, and this prompted him to look within. He saw my inert body, noticed that my head was bleeding and rushed immediately to the kitchen for a pan of water."

"And let the slugger get away completely!" Collins looked his disgust at the delinquency of the Chinese Samaritan. "How about the prowler all of you were hunting?"

"We failed to find him."

"How was the dog killed?"

"Throttled."

Collins frowned, rocking in his swivel chair. "Rawley was out there this morning to look over the grounds."

"Yes, I talked with him for a few minutes before leaving for the doctor's office. I am sorry that I am unable to bring you fresh news."

"You fill in details; Rawley's report was rather sketchy. However, he did give the place a going over. He swears that no one could get in or out unless by the main gate. Ten-foot walls, cliffs on two sides ... Rawley claims it's almost an impossibility to get in any other way."

"Walls built by man may be surmounted by man's ingenuity," Westborough contended.

"Any theories?"

"None. I am baffled by the ramifications of this perplexing case."

"Ramifications!" Collins echoed. "I'll say there are—some that I don't think even you know about. The bureau has had a busy day."

"I am anxious to hear. But first of all may I ask a favor? I should like greatly to speak to Mr. O'Connor."

"Try over there." Collins jerked his thumb in the direction of the county jail.

"I did. I was not permitted to see him. Furthermore, if it be possible, I should like to converse with him alone."

Collins picked up his telephone. "They'll bring O'Connor over in half an hour," he was able to promise a few minutes later. "You can talk to him in here." He locked the office door leading into the outside corridor and put the key in his pocket. "I'll clear out when he comes."

"You do not know how honored I am by your confidence."

"You're working with me," Collins said brusquely. "I wouldn't invite you in on this case if I couldn't trust you. Think you were slugged by the same fellow who choked the dog?"

"I cannot say. The assumption is a reasonable one, however."

"If it's an outside job, Rawley says, the gatekeeper had to be in on it. What do you know about this Wong?"

"He has held his responsible position for, I believe, five years," Westborough answered. "Certainly that is long enough to demonstrate his loyalty."

"For a white man, yes. But he's Chinese."

"Dear me, Captain, the Chinese are on the whole more honest than we—not less so." Westborough spoke a little heatedly. "Personally, it is my opinion that Wong is a wholly reliable servant."

"Well, if he is we're up against an inside job."

"Yes, I see."

"An inside job. Someone inside the grounds. Or maybe two persons. To save time we'll call the dog-killer P and the slugger Q."

"Or P-Q if a single person," Westborough suggested.

"Yeh, good idea. Give me the names of everyone there last night."

"Mrs. Vayne, Mr. and Mrs. Kroll, Mr. Coggin, Wing, Weng and Wong, Mr. Fry, the gardener and myself. That completes the list."

"Can you make any eliminations from it?"

"As to P: Mrs. Vayne, who was talking to me when the dog barked; Mr. and Mrs. Kroll, whom I know from personal observation were in their pavilion at the time. As to Q: Mrs. Vayne and Mrs. Kroll, who remained together in Mrs. Vayne's pavilion while the men searched the grounds. Possibly, though not certainly, Wong."

"No others off for Q?"

"I can think of none. The men scattered; in the darkness any of them might have run up the hillside stairs to surprise me in the living pavilion."

Collins scribbled on a scratch-pad. "Now we come to the question of motive. Was it to steal the jade statuette again?"

"Apparently not. I looked immediately behind the screen and discovered it had not been touched."

"Did you find anything under the lamp?"

"Nothing."

"H'm. This problem is a stinger! Well, one thing's certain. It couldn't have been the other Mrs. Vayne or O'Connor last night." He chuckled at the grim jest.

"Have you considered the possibility that P-Q may also be the murderer?" Westborough inquired.

"Sure I have—considered everything—but it's no go. It's the wife all right. Got to be."

"But Mr. O'Connor, I believe you told me, confirms her story most positively."

"Covering up," Collins said succinctly.

"If so is he not rendering himself liable for criminal punishment?"

"Damn right. The charge is accessory to a felony, and it's a penitentiary offense. I pointed out to him this morning that he could get up to five years for it. To say nothing of getting another one to fourteen years on top of that for perjury. I offered to help square things with the D.A.'s office if he came clean. Well, what do you think he said?"

"A sentence containing the word 'hell,' " Westborough conjectured.

"That's where he told me to go all right," Collins admitted. "Damn stubborn Irish mule! I know he's lying, and he knows I know it, but he won't budge an inch. Faith Vayne is guilty as hell. We had a good case against her last night, and it's stronger today. Much stronger in fact. We've been able to eliminate every other possible suspect."

"Upon what basis?"

"First the ballistics report," Collins answered, picking up a sheaf of papers. "It's now a hundred per cent certain that O'Connor's gun killed both victims. So the murderer has to be a person with access to the gun. That lets out everybody who wasn't at the Vayne estate yesterday. Young Mrs. Vayne swears she heard the noise of the radio at eight o'clock. That's one thing she's not lying about—the couple who live in the single across from Wu's apartment heard it at the same time. The radio was turned on to mask the noise of the shots. Check?"

"A reasonable hypothesis."

"Mrs. Vayne insists that the three Chinese and the Jap were all present and accounted for when she and O'Connor drove away yesterday evening. That lets out four of the five servants. None of them could have possibly got to Wu's apartment before Mrs. Vayne and O'Connor. After his car had gone there wasn't any other means of transportation left on the grounds. Check?"

"Yes."

"Now we come to the alibis—I've had practically every man on the bureau working on those today. I'll begin with the best ones and work down. Mrs. Kroll told Rawley that she had driven over in the station wagon to spend the afternoon with one of her friends, Charlotte somebody-or-other, some married woman with lots of dough who lives on the peninsula about three miles from the Vaynes. Rawley had a talk with her. Mrs. Kroll was there, she told him, and not only in the afternoon. She stayed to dinner with them, and they all sat down to the table at seven-thirty. So she's out. Right?"

"Unquestionably right."

"Kroll was in the Aubusson Hotel with Doctor Liao Po-ching during the murders. Doctor Liao confirms it; he had ordered dinner for eight o'clock, he said, and Kroll came a few minutes before the dinner. Dinner might be late, you think. Well, it would have to be at least twenty or twenty-five minutes late. I had Eskins make a test run from Madame Wu's apartment, and it took twenty-five to cover the distance. Eskins checked with the restaurant also, a Chink joint, but they could all speak English. The dinner went out of there at one minute to eight, swears John Chinaman, the proprietor. Eskins talked to the waiter and the cook, and he got the same story. One minute to eight, they both said without any hesitation about it. And the restaurant clock is electric and running okay. So that lets Kroll out. One Chinaman might be lying out of pure cussedness maybe, but not three. You said yourself a little while ago that the Chinese were more honest than we are."

"Yes," Westborough confirmed.

"Who else is left? Only Mrs. Vayne, Coggin and the chauffeur. They claim to be at the Rolling Wheel in Redondo eating sizzling steaks at eight-thirty. If it's true those three are out; Rawley says the best time he could make on the trip from Wu's apartment to Redondo Beach was forty minutes. Rawley checked up at the Rolling Wheel. Manager recognized the description of the party all right; he said the chauffeur sat at the counter and the old lady and her secretary had a booth. Rawley asked the time they came in; manager says eight-thirty. Rawley says, 'How do you know?' Manager says—here, let me read it to you: 'Because there was an argument about it, Buddy. We stop serving the table d'hôte at eight, but the dinner was what the lady wanted. Waitress says no, she'll have to order à la carte, so the lady says, "Send for the manager." I told her it was eight-thirty and we'd stopped serving dinner half an hour ago, but we could fix them up with some nice steaks. She says, cold like: "Do you know who I am? I am Mrs. Nicholas Vayne." I said, "Lady you can be Mrs. John D. Rockefeller, but we're not serving dinner." So they took steaks.' "

Collins laid down the report. "That lets everyone out but young Mrs. Vayne and O'Connor. Check?"

"Not yet. Do you remember that we discussed the possibility of the murders occurring at an earlier hour than eight?"

"You bet I remember. You had an idea that some electrical dinkus might have been fixed up on the intercommunicating telephone system so that when someone downstairs pressed the button it would buzz and release the door lock. Also that there might have been a hookup with the radio so it turned on at the same time."

"I did speculate upon such a possibility."

"Smart idea, but it didn't happen. I had an electrician up there this morning to tear the walls apart. No wires that shouldn't have been there."

"I am extremely sorry that I put you to such fruitless expense."

"You didn't put me to any expense. Nor the department either. It was a city electrician, and he has to do something to earn his salary. So that brings us right back to eight o'clock for the time of the murders."

Westborough said hesitantly, "Your police work has certainly been thoroughly efficient. In your reasoning, however, I perceive a slight flaw. Do you mind if I take the liberty of pointing it out?"

"Go right ahead."

"Your assumption that the murderer must be a person with the opportunity to steal the revolver from Mr. O'Connor's room is not wholly valid. The murderer might also be one who had access to the weapon *only at Madame Wu's*."

Collins looked puzzled. "You'll have to explain it, Professor."

"The deceased Mr. Vayne was among those who might have stolen the revolver, was he not? Ergo, there remains the possibility—doubtless slight—but nevertheless existent—that it was he who brought it to the deceased lady's apartment."

"Sure, sure. Why in hell didn't I think of that myself?"

"It is a matter easily overlooked. If true, however, the field of suspects is materially widened."

"You're right about that." Collins bit viciously at the end of a cigar. "As a matter of fact, Professor, I've already got three more suspects. Well, maybe they're not all suspects. One has an alibi and another doesn't even have a name yet."

III

"Before we proceed further," Westborough said, "I should like to show you something." He unfolded an oblong slip of pale orange paper.

"Five hundred bucks!" Collins exclaimed, reading the figures. "What did you do to rate it?"

"Mrs. Vayne insisted upon paying me the reward promised for the recovery of her statuette."

"You're a lucky old coot, Professor. That paper's good anywhere with *her* signature."

"Unfortunately it is not. A check—even with the Vayne signature—is useless to an unknown stranger until it has been exchanged for United States notes. The banks, moreover, have been closed for nearly two hours. May I ask a truly great favor? Could you, perhaps—"

Collins chuckled mordantly. "If it was five hundred cents I might handle it myself. Five hundred nickels, and the bureau jointly might be able to swing it. But five hundred bucks! Well, anyway, thanks for the compliment."

"I am extremely reluctant to press the matter," Westborough said shyly. "Is there not, however, among your business acquaintances one who might possibly have so large a sum on hand?"

"Sure. A jewelry loan company on Fifth Street keeps lots of jack in its safe all the time. Want me to have a try at cashing your check?"

"It is an imposition, I know." Westborough wrote his signature on the back of the orange slip. "I should not dream of troubling you were I not in urgent need of funds. What can I ever do to repay your kindness?"

"Forget it," Collins said gruffly. "Walk'll do me good. Been cooped up in here most of the day. How'll you take your dough?"

"Hundred-dollar bills will do. Or bills of any denomination that is convenient. I beg your pardon for the interruption. Who are the three suspects you mentioned?"

"The first is Madame Wu's maid."

"Oh, you have found her?"

"She came back to the apartment last night after you'd left. Chinese, naturally; goes by the name of Pearl Blossom. Pearl told a straight story. Thursday is her day off—it is most maids', I guess—so she spent the afternoon and evening with a boyfriend. Same nationality. And the boyfriend took her to call on his folks. Golly, the Chinamen that have been questioned today!"

"Miss Blossom's alibi was checked, I presume?"

"I put Anderson on it this afternoon. He used to be on the Chinatown detail and can gabble a little Cantonese. Only man in the homicide bureau who can. He found the boyfriend's folks in a dark alley off North Broadway: Ma, Pa, two sisters and Grandma. Grandma seemed to rule the roost. The sisters talked good English and Pa talked it after a fashion. Ma and Grandma didn't speak it at all. The three who understood English swore to it that Blossom had been there with them last night. Anderson put the question to the non-English speakers and got the same answer. Grandma, he says, was so tickled that he could talk their lingo she invited him to have chow with them—he settled for a cup of tea. Hospitable people, the Chinese!"

"Indeed yes."

"I would have believed Blossom without any alibi, though," Collins continued. "It was plain that she worshiped the ground Wu walked on. When I told her what had happened to the madame you should have heard her take on. Don't let anyone ever tell you that race isn't emotional!"

"Yes, the so-called Chinese stolidity is only a surface quality," Westborough confirmed. "This case is beginning to assume a markedly Oriental flavor, is it not?"

"More so than you think. The next suspect is still another one."

"Not Doctor Liao, I hope."

"No, but he ties into it. This morning I planted Anderson in the lobby of the Aubusson Hotel, hidden behind a newspaper, to tail Liao when he stuck his nose out. He was too cute to leave his room but another Chinaman dropped in—little old fellow with a gray, straggly beard of about twenty hairs. The beard asked for Liao and went on up to his room. Anderson followed and listened outside the door. Their confab lasted for quite a while, he said, but he couldn't make out a word of their jargon. I was plenty sore when he reported. Here I'd put him on Liao because of all his bragging about knowing Cantonese, and the first thing he did was to let me down. But he claims they spoke an altogether different language."

"Doubtless Doctor Liao, who hails from Peking, would speak Mandarin."

"What's that?"

"The official language of North China. The lingual differences between Cantonese and northern Mandarin, I have been told, are rather greater than those between English and Norwegian."

"If that's so I guess I gave Anderson a bawling out for nothing. I couldn't understand what a Norse was saying. Could you?"

"I fear not."

"The kick in Anderson's report is yet to come. Pretty soon, he said, the number-two Chinaman came out and walked downstairs. Anderson had a tough time shadowing him because the number-two seemed to have the idea he was being tailed. Every now and then he'd turn his head, but Anderson knows his business. I'm going to recommend him for a sergeant's stripes one of these days. He followed the number-two outside and saw him climb into about as smart a looking job of automobile as you can hope to find—even at Palm Springs during the winter. Anderson got the license number. The owner is—ever hear the name of F. C. Lee before?"

"Yes," Westborough replied.

"So have I, and you know where. What the devil tie-in does *he* have with Liao?"

"An interesting question."

"Not much use asking it though. You can't get anywhere with Chinese when they don't want to talk. Lee, come to think of it, could have done last night's job as far as opportunity goes. Mrs. Vayne left him at seven thirty-five, and it's only a ten-minute walk from his place to Wu's apartment. He'll bear looking into—thanks to your idea that Vayne did the gun toting himself."

"Not *did* but *might*," the historian stressed. "Auxiliary verbs may make a tremendous difference. Who is the third suspect you mentioned? The nameless one?"

"I'll have to tell you the whole story," Collins answered, putting his feet on the desk. "The boys gave Vayne's Chrysler a going over early this morning at the city garage, and they found a coupon crumpled up into a ball behind the front-seat cushion. It was from one of those photographic outfits that snap you on the street. You know the racket? If you want the picture you send a quarter with the coupon the see-the-birdie man hands you. Well, I rushed Jim Webber up to the address, and he made 'em dig out the negative and make half a dozen prints right away." Collins opened his top desk drawer. "You might take a gander at the evidence."

The background of the photograph was obviously one of the large race tracks—Westborough was not well enough acquainted with Hollywood Park or Santa Anita to be able to distinguish which. In the foreground were two human figures. The male was readily recognizable as Eugene Vayne. The woman, clinging intimately to her companion's arm, was neither Madame Wu nor Faith Vayne. She was young, blonde, slender, rather flashily dressed, by no means ill-looking.

"Dear me, this is an extremely interesting find. Was the picture taken last Monday?"

Collins regarded the parchment-pale face of the elderly little scholar with noticeable awe. "How in the devil did you know that?"

"Mr. Vayne, in order to escape attendance at his mother's jade exhibition, went to the races that afternoon."

"He didn't go alone."

"It would appear that he did not. Moreover, if I recall rightly, he dined that night at the apartment of a friend whose name and address he refused to divulge to Captain Cranston. Is it unreasonable to assume that the friend is here?"

"Sounds damn reasonable to me."

"You informed me, I believe, that half a dozen prints had been made? Might I borrow this one for a few days?"

Collins' eyes narrowed. "Any more big ideas, Professor?"

"I have a nebular hypothesis. Dear me, that sounds so astronomical! I should not like to commit myself until I have tested it empirically."

"All right, take it along."

Westborough put the photograph into his breast pocket. "Thank you very much for the favor."

"If that's a favor you can pay me back."

"Gladly."

"There's one ragged end on this case that I'd like to see cleaned up. Do you know why Coggin was going to Madame Wu's last night?"

"No, I do not."

"Will you find out?"

"I will try. It will be a matter of some difficulty. Mr. Coggin is not pre-cisely—"

The blue-jowled clerk with the pencil inserted his head in the door. "They're bringing in the prisoner, Captain."

IV

"Godfrey, the leprechaun!" O'Connor's face, haggard and unshaven, yet reflected the unquenchable mirth of Eire. "So you're running the cops now?"

"No," Westborough replied. "Will you please sit down?"

The prisoner accepted the chair on the opposite side of Collins' desk. "A razor might help," he ruminated, fingering the reddish stubble. "Pressed pants would be a help, too, I'm thinking; I slept in these garments of mine last night. Otherwise I'm doing well, thank you. To what am I indebted for this honor?"

"First would you like a cigarette?"

"If you have one. I have not."

Westborough (who seldom smoked cigarettes) produced two unopened packs from his coat pocket. "I brought these especially for you. I do hope that I picked the right brand."

"Yes, thanks." O'Connor split the cellophane with his thumbnail. "Didn't I ask you a question?" he demanded.

"Yes, you did."

"I am waiting for my answer."

"In due time," Westborough said. "Here are the matches."

"Thanks." Lighting his cigarette, O'Connor asked humorously, "Aren't you afraid to be alone with such a desperate character?"

"Not in the least. You cannot bolt through that door at which you are looking, Mr. O'Connor; it is locked. The key is in Captain Collins' pocket. And I strenuously advise against escape through the outer office. Dear me, if you attempted it you might very easily be shot."

"And do you think I would not be knowing it?" The prisoner tossed his half-smoked cigarette into the cuspidor where it sizzled out. "Hold the lep-rechaun tightly, they say, and he has to tell you where he has hidden his gold."

"So they say," Westborough agreed, faintly uneasy.

"It's time for the showdown." O'Connor's jaw shot forward in sharp, hot anger. "I know your game—stooling for the cops."

"I am not familiar with that particular use of the verb 'stool.' "

"Derived from the noun 'stool pigeon.' You'll be knowing your name, I hope?"

"That is almost an insult," Westborough protested.

"It is and it was meant to be. There seems to be doubt in your mind, however, so I'll word it in blunter language. You can go to hell."

"Dear me, sir!" The historian's face flushed.

"And so can the cop you're working for and the dictograph he has planted here."

"To my knowledge there is no dictograph in this office."

"Isn't there now? And would you be expecting me to believe it?"

"I give you my word that I do not know of any dictograph here, Kerry."

"Kerry is it?" O'Connor belligerently flipped the two packs of cigarettes across the desk to their donor. "Only friends are permitted to call me that."

"I should like to be one of them."

"While you plot with Collins to trap me?"

"Captain Collins did not arrange this meeting."

"No? Was it Santa Claus?"

"It was the leprechaun." Westborough's mild blue eyes twinkled through his bifocals. "Captain Collins made it possible, true, but only at my urgent request."

"I don't believe it."

The historian finally lost his patience. "A little while ago Captain Collins referred to you as a 'damn stubborn Irish mule.' That is no exaggeration, Mr. O'Connor."

"So it's a damn mule that I am, is it?" The tall redhead broke into a grin, wrath disappearing from his face almost as quickly as it had come there. "I have been called worse things."

"I don't have the least doubt of it," Westborough observed. "*Timeo Danaos et dona ferentes.* 'I fear the Greeks even when bringing gifts.' Do you understand, Mr. O'Connor?"

"I do not."

"Mrs. Nicholas Vayne today conferred with the finest legal talent available in an effort to secure your early release."

"She sent a lawyer to see me," the prisoner acknowledged morosely. "What's it to you?"

"It is not the charm of your personality. You might as well take the cigarettes; I will only have to leave them here. Do not delude yourself, please, that Mrs. Vayne has contrived a secret passion for you."

"Hasn't she now?" O'Connor asked jauntily.

"Her interest is strictly a business one. You are a most important witness for the defense; one might almost say that without your testimony there *is* no defense. Except, of course, a plea of insanity."

The mercurial Celt veered again in the direction of anger. "We will not be discussing that. She—" His lips closed as tightly as the jaws of a beaver trap. "Would you mind taking a message to Mrs. Vayne for me?" he asked after a few seconds had passed.

"Gladly. What do you wish me to say?"

"The same thing I've already told her lawyer. I'm sticking to my story till hell raises icicles."

"But—" Westborough suddenly realized the hopelessness of attempting to counsel the headstrong Irishman. "I will convey those words to Mrs. Vayne. Your chivalry will make her happy."

"Chivalry, hell! Don't you know truth when it slaps your face?"

"What is truth, Mr. O'Connor?"

"Truth is that Faith Vayne is being railroaded by cops too stupid to look beyond their noses. And 'tis you who are helping—helping to convict an innocent woman who has harmed neither you nor anyone in her sweet young life. You should be ashamed of yourself!"

"May I ask a few questions on another subject?"

"I won't be guaranteeing to furnish answers."

"Yesterday evening I reread *Bombs and Bayonets*—at least a portion of it—at the public library. Parts of your narrative seemed rather vague."

"I write as I please," O'Connor muttered irately. "If anything is vague it's because I meant it to be."

"I am not criticizing, merely seeking information. Were you on the train that evacuated American citizens from Peiping? Wait, I will be more specific. Were you on the special train which left the East Station at the Chien Gate at eleven o'clock in the evening of July 27, 1937?"

"I was."

"Was Mrs. Vayne also?"

"She was not."

"I beg your pardon for ambiguity. I meant to ask, 'Was Miss Faith Kingston on that train?' "

"How the hell should I be knowing? I saw only the passengers in my compartment."

"Was Miss Kingston in your compartment?"

"She was not."

"Did you at any time see her upon the journey to Tientsin?"

"I did not. Now are you satisfied?"

"I fear," Westborough returned sadly, "that I shall have to be."

V

Riding in the luxurious town car which Mrs. Vayne had placed at his disposal, Westborough asked through the speaking tube, "Is the shop of F. C. Lee greatly out of your way?" When they drew near to the address he handed the chauffeur a bill. "Please park a block or so away if you do not mind and wait for me there."

The store did not resemble a commercial edifice at all but appeared to be a large old-fashioned house upon which Oriental grace notes had been incongruously superimposed. Turning into the walk, Westborough sauntered under a bright red crossbeam and climbed a short flight of steps. The porch was guarded by a pair of bulging-eyed, open-mouthed stone lions which looked rather like enlarged, permanently petrified versions of Lydia Kroll's dead Goblin. A sign on the door proclaimed in bold letters: "This is an all-Chinese store; we handle no Japanese goods."

Westborough entered a cavern of teak and blackwood, bronze and porcelain, cinnabar and lapis lazuli, glowing amber and waxy jade. Its treasures were heaped higgledy-piggledy on tables, hung from the walls or locked in glass counter cases. Temple incense and sandalwood scented the air. There were two Chinese clerks, both busy with belated female customers. Westborough's eyes roved from specimen to specimen of the many arts of Cathay.

Lustrous, mellow silks. Rice-cloth mandarin coats. Ivory snuff bottles. Ancestor portraits. Bronze incense burners. A globular peach-bloom vase. A bowl of duskily veined agate. Scrolls which had been written with long, ink-dipped fingernails.

A young Chinese, completing the sale of a lettuce-jade cigarette box, stepped forward to ask in a flat voice, "May I assist you, sir?"

"Do I have the honor of addressing Mr. F. C. Lee?"

"I am Charles Lee. Can I take care of you, or is it necessary for you to see my father?"

"Do you mind asking your father if he will be so kind as to receive me?"

"One minute, please." The youth disappeared behind a silk-painted spirit screen.

There was much to occupy the time of waiting. Pendants, rings, earrings, bracelets of jade, amethyst, amber, topaz, carnelian. A ruby-red K'ang Hsi vase. An apple-green jade pagoda. A bulbous blue-and-white ginger jar with prunus blossoms over ice flakes. Tiny silver junks and rickshaws. Brass candlesticks. "Temple of Heaven" incense cones. Hollow painted eggs nesting endlessly one within another. Mushroom-hatted mandarins carved from cherry wood. A gilded Buddha with supernaturally long ears.

A small, elderly Chinese emerged from behind the spirit screen. "Do you wish to see me, sir?"

"Do I have the honor of addressing Mr. F. C. Lee?"

The dealer bowed. He had a face like a wrinkled lichee nut, horn-rimmed spectacles and a sparse gray beard. His western garb scarcely fitted the surroundings. He belonged in a long silken gown, arms interlocked within its capacious sleeves while he calmly awaited the pleasure of his customers. Westborough began the conversation.

"Today I came into a sum of money for which I have no immediate need. My life expectancy is not long and, unlike yourself, I have no descendants."

The Chinese stood silently as a temple image against a background composed of white and turquoise Kuan Yins, cinnabar lacquer boxes, silk-robed porcelain puppets and the fragrance of burning aloewood.

"I wish to give the whole of this sum to Chinese relief," Westborough continued. "Will you be so kind as to see my donation reaches the proper hands?"

"With pleasure, sir."

After he had counted out the five one-hundred dollar bills Westborough waived the merchant's tender of a receipt. "One needs no receipt from an honest man," he asserted.

Representatives of the yellow and white races smiled in friendly under-standing. "In the name of my race I thank you," said F. C. Lee, whose name long ago had been Li Feng-chou. "I shall be greatly honored, sir, if you will join me in a cup of tea."

"It is I who am honored by the invitation," Westborough replied, fol-lowing his mentor through a door behind the spirit screen.

The inner room might have been the office of an American businessman except for two characteristically Chinese touches: a silk painting of a crane in a bamboo grove and a hyacinth blooming in a white jade bowl. A wall panel opened to reveal a miniature kitchenette. The senior Lee personally prepared the tea, a delicately flavored, pale golden-yellow beverage. West-borough reflected that at five hundred dollars it was probably the most expensive pot ever brewed.

But though the price had been high he had attained his desire. "This is worthy of the dragon spring, Lung Tsing!" he exclaimed as he sipped.

"You are too kind." The host beamed in pleasure at the compliment. "The water of the dragon spring is beyond compare. You are learned as well as generous, I perceive. May I ask your name?"

"West," the historian replied, employing an alias which had served him before. He added, not quite truthfully, "I am an antiquarian by profession."

From there it was an easy task to reach the history of jade. The merchant was well informed, having a Chinese memory, and he expressed his thoughts fluently. Westborough, listening attentively, now and then tossed in a few words to direct the conversation in the direction he wished.

"It is a rare pleasure, Mr. Lee, to meet so great an authority as yourself. Am I correct in my belief that the bulk of Chinese jade in the world today is the nephrite of Turkestan?"

"You are altogether correct, Mr. West. For some two thousand years practically our entire supply of raw material was obtained from the river beds and gorges of Chinese Turkestan. Much of it still comes from there. For centuries camel trains transported the uncut boulders two thousand miles across the Central Asian desert. Jade caravans from Khotan still travel the same route, passing through the historic 'Jade Gate' on their way to Peking. We Chinese are nothing if not conservative. Until two hundred years ago we would not hear that any other jade was the equal of the 'water stones' of Sinkiang."

"The Burmese product was, then, unknown?"

"It was scorned. We Chinese are worshipers of tradition. The hard, glassy jadeite was generally held to be of poor quality in comparison with our duller, softer nephrite. We are also instinctive isolationists. For a long pe-riod of time the importation of Burmese jade was forbidden."

"It was during the reign of Ch'ien Lung, was it not, that the condition was altered?"

"Yes." Lee nibbled a piece of preserved ginger.

Westborough deemed that the time was ripe if it ever would be. "Many years ago," he ventured, "I ran across a most romantic explanation of this, concerning the fourth Ch'ing emperor and a contemporary king of Burma. The latter's name, if I recall rightly, was Bodawpaya, and he suffered somewhat from delusions of grandeur. Doubtless the fable is familiar to you?"

"Yes, I know the story you refer to, but you are mistaken in calling it a fable." The aged Chinese daintily touched his lips with a napkin.

Westborough mentally balanced Daring against Caution. If he pressed too hard he would probably learn nothing. On the other hand, if he did not press he was virtually certain to learn nothing. On the whole, Daring seemed to be the more profitable course.

"It is authentic? Dear me, that is most interesting!" He hesitated, remembering that of all the world's races his host's was the most wary. "May I, please, hear your version, Mr. Lee? I am anxious to learn if it differs from mine."

"King Bodawpaya ruled Burma from 1782 to 1819. I believe those dates are correct."

Westborough was sure of it, knowing that the wonderful Chinese memory makes nothing of absorbing verbatim the contents of entire books. He made an effort to conceal his elation over this early and perhaps only temporary success.

"He was, as you have stated, in the earlier years of his reign a contemporary of Ch'ien Lung," Lee continued. "As you have also mentioned, Bodawpaya experienced delusions of grandeur. He talked lightly of adding both India and China to his kingdom, which was much the same as if Poland, in the years when there was a Poland, had decided to annex Russia and Germany. It was madness even to dream of such an idea. But Bodawpaya was a provincial sovereign who knew little of the civilizations outside his barbaric court. As a mere prologue to his program of world empire he set about the conquest of Siam. His army was defeated, and the invasion ignominiously collapsed. Bodawpaya, realizing then the magnitude of his task, became frightened." The old merchant paused reflectively. "Hitler might have felt the same fear if he had been given a similar setback by the Czechs."

"I do not have the least doubt of it," Westborough said.

"Under the able Ch'ien Lung the Middle Kingdom was then at the zenith of its military power. Burma was looked upon merely as a vassal state. Spies brought to Peking the tale of Bodawpaya's senseless folly. The emperor was angered. And word of his imperial displeasure traveled to distant Mandalay.

"Now Bodawpaya knew a greater fear than before. If he could not defeat his neighbors of Siam what chance had he against the disciplined legions of China? He saw no hope of preserving his kingdom unless the mighty Ch'ien Lung could be appeased. It was a custom of the Burmese court to bestow trinkets and golden vessels on public officers when they were raised to higher rank. Bodawpaya, a barbarian, thought in these terms. But what gift was worthy of the great Manchu emperor? What could insignificant Burma present to him that he did not already have ten and a hundredfold?

"Of all the sovereigns who have sat upon the dragon throne Ch'ien Lung was the most devoted to jade. Even the jungle capital on the Irrawaddy had heard of the emperor's love for the substance that he carved into objects of beauty with his own imperial hands. Burma had jade. Bodawpaya the ignorant knew nothing of the scorn with which the local stone was regarded at Peking. He hired twenty Chinese craftsmen—the Burmese, far below their neighbors in culture, could make few things themselves—and ordered them to fashion for him the most marvelous creation of jade the world had yet seen. He stipulated that it must be finished before Ch'ien Lung issued the order for his troops to march.

"It was an impossible assignment. The finest articles of jade, as these men well knew, require years of patient labor, and they had at the best but a few months. Moreover, the Chinese artists had none of their beloved, softly glowing Turkestan nephrite to work with, only this glassy, valueless Burmese stuff. It must have seemed almost hopeless until one—his name has not been preserved for posterity—recognized the possibilities of that rare, rich green we now call *fei ts'ui* because to us it is the same shade as the kingfisher's plumage.

"They fashioned a necklace of 108 beads—the number in a Buddhist rosary and also the official number for a mandarin chain under the Manchu Empire. Each stone was the gleaming grass green of the most perfect emerald. They were perfectly matched in shade, it is said; this in itself is a miracle to one who knows the many variations in color which both jadeite and nephrite can assume. The gift was completed; from the golden court at Mandalay the king's embassy set out on the long overland journey to Peking.

"The mission accomplished its purpose, for Bodawpaya was left undisturbed on his throne, but it accomplished also something which had not been planned. It is said that as the aged Ch'ien Lung took into his hands the Burmese king's present and allowed the glorious green jewels to trickle slowly through his imperial fingers a revolution was wrought within his imperial soul. And he called for a scented scroll and brushed in his own beautifully formed characters a decree that the jade of Burma should henceforth be considered the equal of the jade of Turkestan. And the edict was signed with the emperor's vermilion pencil and ended with his, 'Tremble and obey.' All of this is historically true, Mr. West. Does my account agree with the story you know?"

"Yes," Westborough said, "except that mine was not related nearly so well." He took a deep breath before plunging into the dangerous waters. "May I ask what later became of that famous necklace?"

VI

Shortly after dinner on Friday night Westborough contrived to happen casually upon Jethro Coggin, who had retired to the north terrace for a postprandial cigar. With a word of apology for the intrusion the historian preempted the next chair. It was a cloudless night. Venus was low in the west— a planet of brilliance and beauty. Westborough turned from the evening star to the glowing tip of his neighbor's cigar.

"Mrs. Vayne is bearing up admirably, is she not?"

"She isn't the iron woman she pretends to be," the secretary dissented. "She is carrying on under tremendous inner tension. Gene's death has affected her deeply, and she is very much worried over Faith."

"The newspapers have not been consoling," Westborough observed, bringing out his pipe and tobacco pouch.

"The hints about Gene's relations with the Chinese girl are gall and wormwood," Coggin declared.

"*De mortuis nil nisi bonum* is a somewhat difficult rule to observe," Westborough ventured, "when the dead possess the unpleasant traits of the late Mr. Vayne." His cast flickered the fly lightly over the surface of the trout pool.

The trout spurned it. "It will save time if you ask directly about my eye. Though the homicide bureau has probably already informed you. You forget that I have known your avocation since you came here."

"Dear me!" Westborough exclaimed in dismay. "I am exceedingly clumsy. Does anyone else besides you and Mrs. Vayne know that I am sailing under false colors?"

"I didn't tell anyone."

Puffing upon his pipe, Westborough decided that he had nothing to lose by continuing the interrogation.

"It was fortunate that you were not wearing your glasses when Eugene Vayne struck you."

"Yes, wasn't it?" Coggin casually flicked the ashes from his cigar.

"May I know the circumstances?"

"Don't you know them?"

"Only that Mr. Vayne made a brutal assault upon you outside Madame Wu's apartment building. May I ask what prompted it?"

"Gene never liked me. I had acted as his mother's agent in certain rather unpleasant personal matters. When he jumped out of his car last night he accused me of having followed him. Which I had not. When I denied the allegation he struck me. Then he ran heroically into the shelter of the vestibule. I didn't go after him."

"Naturally not."

"Why naturally?" Coggin asked. "Your friend, Captain Collins, seemed to think that I acted in a rather cowardly fashion."

"I cannot agree with that opinion. A public brawl might have led to most unpleasant publicity for Mrs. Vayne. Having the foresight to perceive this, you also had the strength of character to control yourself. Am I not right?"

"Something like it," the secretary admitted.

"May I ask why you were calling upon Madame Wu?"

"I wasn't calling on her."

"You didn't call upon her," Westborough corrected. "Such, however, had been your intent. Come, Mr. Coggin, denial is stupid, and you are a man of intelligence."

The surf beat rhythmically against the rocks at the base of the cliff.

"Is it any crime to consult a fortune-teller?" Coggin demanded.

"None. May I inquire, however, if it were your own fortune which you wished to be predicted?"

"What? Of course it was."

"Of course it was not," Westborough contradicted. "Is it not true that on yesterday morning the deceased Chinese lady had had rather a remarkable effect upon Faith Vayne?"

Coggin jumped angrily to his feet. "Is that any concern of yours?"

"None," Westborough replied. "You have been in love with her for some time, have you not?"

"You devil, you've guessed the truth. I pitied her at first, and then—she doesn't know, of course. Even if she had been free I should never have told her."

Poor angular Mr. Grewgious! Westborough felt singularly guilty at having trespassed upon the man's most intimate secret.

"Some time I shall kill myself," Coggin continued in his queer, toneless whisper. "It would be easy! A single jump would do it." He gestured toward the cliffs.

"Don't!" Westborough shuddered. "Don't dwell on suicide, please."

"Why not?"

"It's not normal."

"Why do you assume that I *am* normal?" Coggin's laugh was almost soundless. "This funny voice of mine! Do you have any idea what a handicap it is to a man not to be able to talk like other people?"

"My dear sir, we must stop this," Westborough said insistently. "A man cannot be permitted to drown himself in an ocean of self-pity. You are not a weakling. If you did not possess moral courage you would have done the natural thing and returned Eugene Vayne's unprovoked blow. You said a while ago that you pitied Faith Vayne. Because her husband was a dipsomaniac?"

"Largely that."

"Did you not also have grounds for believing that Mr. Vayne was keeping a mistress?"

"Some grounds, yes. Gene had a liberal allowance, practically no expenses and was always in debt. A woman is one of the answers. However, I don't think it was Madame Wu."

"Do you know who she was?"

"No."

"Do you suspect who she was?"

"No, I do not."

"Come over to the light," Westborough requested. "I have something to show you." He exhibited the print which he had that afternoon borrowed from Captain Collins. "Do you recognize this young lady?"

"I certainly do," Coggin answered grimly. "She's Coral Fry, the chauffeur's daughter."

Westborough nodded in satisfaction.

PART NINE: MERCHANT, THIEF

AT NINE O'CLOCK Saturday morning the inquest room in the Hall of Justice was packed to capacity with quietly tense spectators. As the hearing opened the district attorney stepped forward and requested the presiding deputy coroner to issue certain instructions to the witnesses.

"This is a dual proceeding," the latter were consequently informed. "The county grand jury is simultaneously investigating the same case. As soon as each of you has given his or her testimony here please go directly to the grand jury room on the fifth floor of this building."

The medical evidence presented at the inquest confirmed on the whole, though in more technical language, the homicide bureau's previous opinions concerning the double shooting. A ballistic expert swore with positive assurance that the weapon exhibited to the jury was the weapon which had fired the shots which had penetrated the skull and chest of the deceased Eugene Vayne and twice penetrated the skull of the likewise deceased lady known as Wu. The testimony of Faith Vayne, Kerry O'Connor and other witnesses did not differ in any material particulars from their earlier statements to Captain Collins. When Westborough had been dismissed by both the deputy coroner and the grand jury he hastened away from the building. The historian was extremely anxious to reach his destination before noon.

A considerable crowd of the curious, who had arrived too late to secure places in the inquest room, waited on the sidewalk outside the Hall of Justice in the hope of picking up tidbits of information. Public interest in the dramatic murder case had been well whetted by the newspapers; even reports of fresh and appalling carnage in Europe had failed to move the "love-triangle killings" from the morning's front page. Listening to arguments he could not help but overhear as he made his way through the throng, Westborough found it clear that this section of vox populi firmly believed:

(a) That the dead Mr. Vayne had cherished, caressed, fondled, petted, feasted his eyes upon and otherwise conducted himself with a woman of the Chinese race.

(b) That the said Faith Vayne, tracking her errant spouse to his rendezvous, had shot him and his Oriental mistress with promptitude and efficiency.

(c) That no one could blame her for thus emulating Frankie in the song. (There was interjected some rather salacious speculation concerning the sexual union.)

Westborough was a little ashamed for the moment of belonging to the self-styled "superior" race. "Do these good people," he pondered, "realize that to the Chinese such an *affaire d'amour* is even more repugnant than they seem to find it?" Hailing a canary-hued taxi, he gave the driver an address on Hollywood Boulevard.

It was a candy store. There were long glass counters of products deliciously compounded of chocolate, sugar, cream, honey, corn syrup, egg whites, cream of tartar, molasses, coconut oil, citrus pectin, almonds, peanuts, pecans, walnuts, tartaric acid, invertase, gelatin, gum arabic and a variety of natural and artificial flavors. The human inhabitants of the establishment were female, youthful, sexually attractive and definitely hygienic in starched white uniforms. With no little trepidation Westborough ventured to approach one of them.

"Do I have the pleasure of addressing Miss Coral Fry?"

He recognized her immediately from the picture, however. She was patently a xanthochroid, fair-haired and fair-skinned, a product of her age and century, kept slim by dieting and witless by confessional magazines.

"Who told ja?" she retorted. Upon a structure which nature had not designed too badly artifice had imposed seemingly needless trimmings. Her cheeks were red, her mouth more so and her gleaming nails the reddest of all. Her yellow locks were shorn, waved, frizzed at the back of the head ... Westborough did not know the technical term for the hairdress.

"Ja come here to buy *can*-dy?"

The elderly scholar, discomfited, felt himself to be the source of innocent merriment and the cynosure of not-so-innocent eyes.

"In the hope of inducing you to lunch with me." The bold response elicited a second, much louder titter from Miss Fry's fellow workers.

"Well, at chour age!" the recipient of the invitation exclaimed. "And ya never did say how ya knew my name."

"Through the late Mr. Eugene Vayne," Westborough replied in a low voice. The color upon her cheeks was not the type to vary with emotional stresses. Her face remained on the whole much as it was. She lowered her eyes to the counter, however, thus telling him she had heard.

"From Mr. Applebury," he said in a louder tone for the benefit of the listeners. "You remember Mr. Applebury, I am sure. He insisted that I see you when I next visited this city." In a whisper he added, "It is urgent that we talk in private."

"Sure, Tom Applebury! Okay, you can buy me a lunch if you want to, Mr..—"

"Brown," the little man supplied promptly. "John Brown, but my body does not yet lie moldering in the—" He halted immediately upon seeing her stricken look. Could it be possible that this young woman had felt a genuine affection for the late Mr. Vayne? In a gentler tone he inquired, "When is your lunch hour, Miss Fry?"

"Two."

"Dear me, that is most disastrous!" Westborough recalled the note he had that morning slipped, covertly he hoped, into the hands of one of his fellow witnesses. "I have an important engagement at two. Is there no way in which you can manage to leave now?"

"I might. Marge's off now. Marge, will ya trade lunch hours with me? Mr. Brown's gotta date for my time."

"Sure, Coral, go ahead."

While he waited for his luncheon companion to doff uniform and replenish complexion at the rear of the shop Westborough endeavored to compensate the young woman addressed as Marge by purchasing five pounds of assorted chocolates. These he ordered to be mailed to Mrs. John Launay, the hostess whom he had so shamefully deserted upon hearing the siren call of a fresh mystery. The postage had just been calculated when Coral Fry reappeared in a saucy red hat something on the order of an organ grinder's monkey's cap. Her short skirt concealed very little of shapely, silk-clad legs.

"Youth, youth," Westborough reflected. He took her to a restaurant that was more famous for the cinema luminaries who occasionally lunched there than its cuisine. A tip to the headwaiter netted the private booth the elderly gallant found needful. She ordered a daiquiri, lobster salad and Washington cream pie. Unhesitantly the historian duplicated the gastronomic horror.

"Who told ja about us?" she demanded after the waiter had brought their cocktails.

"Your own picture."

"Gene never had one of me."

"The picture was taken by a peripatetic photographer," Westborough elucidated, "when you attended the races with Mr. Vayne last Monday afternoon."

"Oh, that thing! I shoulda thrown the slip away like Gene wanted me to do."

"Why didn't you?"

"I crumpled it up like I was going to, and then I thought it'd be kinda nice to have a picture of him and me together. I was going ta put the coupon in my purse, but it got away from me somewhere."

"The police found it in Mr. Vayne's car."

"P'lice?" she wailed. "Are you a plainclothes man, mister?"

"No." He hesitated, finding himself in something of a quandary. "But I have a friend in the homicide bureau."

"Oh yeah?" she queried suspiciously. "That friend's yourself, I bet."

The considerable time that might be required to disabuse her of the illusion could be more fruitfully invested. He solaced his conscience with the reflection that he had not deliberately tried to impersonate an officer.

"It does not matter what my profession is, Miss Fry. I promise you that I shall not harm you. Merely answer my questions truthfully."

"I'll answer what I can," she said.

"You met Mr. Vayne last summer, did you not? The occasion, I believe, was during a visit to your father made possible by the temporary absence of the gardener?"

"Pop's the chauffeur there, and I slept in the Jap's room above the garage. You needn't rub it in. I know I wasn't in Gene's class."

She was not, Westborough cogitated. She was in a class manifestly superior.

"Does Pop know about Gene and me?" she demanded.

"To my knowledge he does not." (But perhaps Mike Fry did know.)

"Don't tell him then, please, Mr. Brown. He'd be so mad he'd quit his job. He'd think he couldn't go on working for a woman whose son had—you know the thing I mean?"

"Yes."

"Pop's not young any more. At his age you don't get a job easy. He was outa work a long time before he got this one, and he thinks it's just heaven. I'm not asking any favors for myself. I went into it knowing what I was doing. But Pop—don't tell him, please! I'll tell anything you want if you'll promise."

"I am sorry that I am not able to promise definitely." Westborough frowned at his portion of the overrich salad. "I will, however, do my best to see that the information is withheld from your father."

"Thanks," she said. "A bargain's a bargain. I'll tell you all about it, honest. We had a furnished apartment. I told Pop I was sharing expenses with one of the girls at the store. He only has one night off a week when he can see me so Gene and I were safe from being surprised. Gene paid the rent—that is he gave me the money to pay it. I—well—I loved him. I'm not ashamed of it."

"Why should you be?" Westborough returned. He took the address of the apartment which, he noted, was not particularly close to the abode of the deceased Madame Wu.

"He loved me, too," she went on defiantly. "Gene's wife was one of those goody-goody women. He couldn't stand her."

"Precisely what was his objection?"

"She was always moping around. Like—like a ghost. That's what she was like, he said once, a bloodless ghost. He'd loved her when they were first married, terribly, but she killed it, being so cold and formal and—and distant with him. She didn't love him either. She couldn't love anyone."

"Dear me."

"He tried to stop drinking on her account when they were first married. He drank too much, Gene did. It didn't work. He found out that she didn't— couldn't love him, and it took the heart outa him." She dabbed at her eyes with a napkin. "Gene was always good to me. There wasn't anything in the world I couldn't have had from him."

"Except marriage," Westborough demurred.

"He wanted to marry me. He'd-a married me in a minute if he could. How could he with that mealymouth walking around like a glass saint? She turned all his family against him, even Gene's own mother. That's how cute she was. Sweet. So damn sweet butter wouldn't melt in her mouth, specially when Gene's mother was around. Gee, how I hate that woman!"

"The elder Mrs. Vayne?"

"I didn't mean her, but I do. She was awful mean. Never let him have any money—that is, just in little driblets. Gene's father had played a dirty trick in his will on Gene and his sister."

"Yes?" Westborough prompted.

"Every cent was left to Gene's mother. She was supposed to see Gene and Mrs. Kroll got their shares, but she had the power some way to cut either of them off without a cent if she felt like it. If Gene had even hinted about a divorce he'd-a been out on his ear so fast it woulda made your head spin. Old Lady Vayne thought this Faith woman was some superspecial angel."

"Could not Mr. Vayne have made a frank confession to his wife?" the historian wanted to know.

"To *her!* Fat lotta good it woulda done! Faith knew the side her bread was buttered on, you bet. She was Mrs. Eugene Vayne. She married him for that, and she meant to keep that handle. What difference did it make to her how Gene felt?"

"Then you had no matrimonial hopes whatsoever?"

"You can always hope." Her tears had caused the mascara to run from her lashes in little dark smudges. "Maybe Gene woulda made some money if he hadn't been killed."

"Indeed? By what method?"

"You think I'm kidding, don't you?" she demanded belligerently. "Gene coulda made money, I guess, if he'd put his mind to it."

"I am sure that he could. May I ask the nature of the investment?"

"I don't know."

"You do know something of importance, however, Miss Fry. Will you please explain?"

"It's just something Gene said to me Thursday afternoon."

"Thursday? The day on which Mr. Vayne was killed?"

"Yes."

"Did you see him then?"

"No, not see him. He phoned me at the store."

"He telephoned you from his home?"

"He wasn't a sap. From a pay phone."

"On the Palmas Peninsula pay telephones are scarce," Westborough said severely. "Moreover, Mr. Vayne was playing golf at the Palmas Country Club last Thursday afternoon."

"There's a pay phone at the clubhouse," she said. "Gene had used it before."

"In that event, Miss Fry, I apologize for my doubts." Westborough reflected that Kerry O'Connor had been playing golf with Eugene Vayne that afternoon—and wondered if the fact meant anything. "What was it Mr. Vayne said to you?"

"Let me see if I can remember—oh yes, I know. He said, 'Honey, I've cut myself in on a good deal. If it works out I'll have some money and we can tell my whole damn family to go to hell.' Then he asked me to stay home that night because he'd be over—before nine o'clock he said—to give me the lowdown. But he never showed up; in the morning I read why. They've got Faith in jail for it now, and I hope to God she stays there!"

"Unless I err greatly," Westborough prophesied, "Mrs. Eugene Vayne will be admitted to bail at a habeas corpus hearing to be held before a not altogether unsympathetic magistrate today."

"Does that mean that the old lady's going to get her out?"

"I fear it does."

"Money can do anything," Coral Fry said bitterly.

"It can do a great deal, one must confess. Did you remain at your apartment as Mr. Vayne had instructed you to do?"

"Honest to God I did, Mr. Brown. I was there alone all evening."

II

"Did my note put you to any inconvenience?" Westborough inquired as he stepped inside the hotel room.

"None, Mr. Westborough. I am honored by your visit. I shall ask restaurant to send tea."

The little man took a chair. "I scarcely know how to begin," he said when his host had finished telephoning. "Chuang Tzu has observed that if one allows a beginning it follows that there must have been a time before."

"And time before time which was before beginning," Dr. Liao added, beaming happily.

"Exactly. Rather like one of your Chinese egg puzzles, is it not? Except that one eventually reaches the ultimate ovoid. Whereas, in dealing with infinity—"

"Shall small strive to exhaust great? Short rope cannot reach to bottom of deep well."

Westborough bowed acknowledgment. "You recognize immediately my likeness to the short rope, Doctor Liao. You are an astute philosopher."

"You are a man of enigma," the Chinese returned, smiling.

"Dear me, not at all. I am a man whose life is no more than soot on a kettle."

"I am well frog to which you cannot speak of ocean, summer insect which knows not meaning of ice."

"And I, my dear sir, am a humble soul in quest of information. Which I believe you are able to supply."

The sparring had ended at last. Dr. Liao sat quietly in his chair, his olive face quickly expressionless.

"From English scholar I once learned useful proverb. 'To hold with hare and run with hound.' I am cautious hare. I think, Mr. Westborough, that you are on side of hounds."

"I am on the side of justice," the historian answered.

"Your country has one justice for own sons—different justice for Chinese. Is not it so?"

"In principle, no. Actually—dear me, I confess with shame that racial prejudices are not unknown here. We have sinned in our pride, and so shall we suffer for it in future years."

"We suffer now," said Dr. Liao. "But for different reason. Appeal to arms, we have been taught, is lowest form of virtue."

"As it is."

The Chinese sorrowfully shook his head. "No, my friend, our sages were wrong. We followed false teachings."

"They were noble teachings, and you followed them faithfully."

"Rewards are homes destroyed, men killed, women ravished, children starved and cities occupied. Peking, Tientsin, Shanghai, Nanking, Hankow and Canton in invaders' hands because we have been lovers of virtue."

"Other nations also are suffering for being civilized: the most cultured, enlightened, tolerant, humane and honorable nations of Europe. But moral ideals are difficult to kill. They have survived Goths, Vandals, Attila, Genghis Khan and Tamerlane. Some will probably survive even the present catastrophe."

"Optimism is by no means justified."

"I agree with you," Westborough said sadly. "It is not."

"In harsh school China has learned grave lesson—to fight."

"China has fought heroically."

"She will continue to fight as long as one man is alive to bear arms, one woman to bear children. To iron of Nippon we oppose naked flesh. We die but do not yield. Iron kills but does not conquer."

"You Chinese are indeed a marvelous people!"

"We have many faults, some virtues."

Westborough decided it was time to state the object of his call. "May I tell you a story?" he asked.

"Mind is as mirror which grasps not, refuses nothing."

"We cannot seem to get away from Chuang Tzu today, it would appear. My story is similar to one he has told. The Yellow Emperor lost his magic pearl. Intelligence could not find it for him. Nor Sight. Nor Speech. But the pearl was eventually recovered."

"Sage of Lu, it is reported, could not comprehend profounder wisdom of Librarian of Lo."

"My dear Doctor Liao! Your resemblance to Confucius vastly exceeds mine to Lao Tzu."

Laughter bubbled momentarily within the Oriental's coal-black eyes. "I am inferior man who cannot understand parables," he declared, sobering.

"Instead of the Yellow Emperor shall we speak of another monarch? A Manchu—perhaps the greatest of all who sat upon the dragon throne. There is a tale that in the year 1787 Ch'ien Lung received from Burma a necklace of emerald-green jadeite."

"It is so written in our histories."

"This gift became an heirloom of the imperial family. It was worn, I believe, by the Empress Dowager Tzu Hsi."

"Her fault that today we are invaded," Dr. Liao proclaimed with bitterness. "Old Buddha thought only of herself, not of China."

"With other imperial property the Ch'ien Lung necklace was taken over by the republic when the troops of the Christian General descended upon Peking in October 1924. The whirligig of time brought its revenges. Henry Pu-yi, who had been driven from the Forbidden City, became the Emperor Kang Te under Japanese auspices. Because of fear that the army of Nippon might extend its sway from Manchoukuo to North China in 1933 the imperial treasures were shipped under military guard to a warehouse in the French concession of Shanghai. The later history of the necklace is not so easily ascertained. I have learned, however, that the central government, needing airplanes more than *objets d'art*, sold it to the Jade Merchants' Guild of Peking for a sum approximating one hundred thousand dollars. Furthermore, if my informant is correct, the necklace was transferred from Shanghai to Peking in the early summer of 1937."

Not a muscle of the high-cheekboned Oriental face betrayed that the topic was at all disquieting.

"The Jade Merchants' Guild, needless to say, expected to resell at a handsome profit—perhaps to a wealthy American collector. Before any negotiations could be undertaken, however, war struck Peking with totally unexpected swiftness. Shortly after the historic shots had been fired near the Marco Polo Bridge it became impossible for any private citizen to leave the city since only military trains were permitted to run. The famous necklace was in grave jeopardy. The patriotic gesture of the Jade Merchants' Guild in purchasing the necklace as an aid to Chiang Kai-shek was not an act of which the Nipponese command could be expected to approve. If Peking fell the necklace would be confiscated without compensation of any sort to its new owners. Are my facts accurate, Doctor Liao?"

"Continue, please."

"The necklace, of course, might have been buried. It might have been concealed in some other manner. But the buried may be dug up again; the hidden may be found. Only if it were smuggled from the city—fast being encircled by advancing Japanese—could there be a true hope of its safety. The guild members, meeting in secret session to discuss the problem, decided wisely that a secret is best kept if known to only one man. The jade merchants entrusted the necklace to one of their number, Yee Feh-lu."

Westborough paused. Information was powder in this mental duel; he must not by any means acknowledge that his magazine was wholly exhausted.

"You knew Mr. Yee perhaps?"

"He was intimate friend."

"Mr. Yee is dead." Westborough stated as a fact what he had surmised from the other's employment of the past tense. It was a fairly safe inference. Once a friend, always a friend is the general rule among the Chinese.

"*Ai-ya!* The honorable Yee Feh-lu has ascended the dragon." Emotion surged strongly beneath Dr. Liao's bland face. "Soldier of Nippon broke into shop searching for loot; venerable Yee protested; outcast of dwarf people discharged rifle with fatal results. Yee's oldest son, having no weapon, strangled short-legged one with his hands. Example of Japanese mercy was made of family. House of Yee is no more."

Westborough shuddered.

"What they did to us in Peiping is as nothing to what was done in Nanking," the Chinese continued impassively. "We endure; that is our national virtue."

"Doctor Liao, believe in my sincerity," the historian pleaded. "I will do all in my power to aid a just cause."

"Can there exist understanding between us? We are men of different races."

"We are men," Westborough replied. "That is the main thing. We believe in justice and humanity. We look with horror upon a world ruled by force."

"Heart and mind give opposite counsels. Mind says many times men of my race have been betrayed by men of yours. Mind says Chinese can trust only Chinese. Heart says you are honest, Mr. Westborough. Which is right?"

"Both. Men of my race (to you European and Americans are the same, are they not?) have dealt shamefully with men of yours. That is incontrovertible. The mind is right. But the heart is right also. You may trust me, and I will not betray your confidence."

"That is Chinese reasoning," Dr. Liao declared, chuckling. "I must telephone restaurant and find out why our tea is so long in arriving. Mind works best on a cup of tea, does it not? And perhaps heart does also."

III

"All right, you come in." Wong smiled a cheerful welcome as he opened the vermilion gate. "Missy Faith come home, go topside."

Westborough speculated upon the moot question whether the gateman employed pidgin because he knew no better or merely because he felt it to be a picturesque adjunct to his post. There was no means of ever finding out. The Chinese are a folk of contradictions; leisurely but industrious, stingy yet hospitable, hagglers and spendthrifts. If Wong were able to speak perfect English he would deny the charge for all eternity because a question of face would be involved. Yes, the Chinese are perplexing: rational but illogical, prudent pacifists and reckless warriors.

"Redhead back too," Wong added. "He stay long while now, Missy Vayne say." Westborough thanked his informant and walked toward the paved path by the lotus pond. The garden, drenched in a golden glow from the west, was as lovely as the Jade Emperor's paradise.

He halted to inspect a snail, a mottled brown convolute lump feeding on a leaf. Tomorrow Eiichi's vigilant hand would seize it and consign it to the oblivion to which eaters of gardens may be expected to go. He, Westborough, must do much the same sort of thing tonight. But not to a snail. He plodded slowly toward the guest house, an old, tired man.

Someone was gaily whistling a jig in Kerry O'Connor's room. Westborough took down the Li Po scroll and pushed open the sliding door. The red-haired Irish-American, clad only in trousers and undershirt, was seated on the edge of the bed tying his shoes. His bared arms looked formidably stalwart.

"May I felicitate you upon your release?" Westborough ventured. He was, it must be confessed, uncertain of the reception he would receive from this twentieth-century Cuculain.

"The leprechaun!" Grinning broadly, O'Connor extended his hand. "Bad cess to me for treating you like dirt when you came on an errand of mercy yesterday afternoon. Did I even have the decency to thank you for the cigarettes?"

"Dear me, yes," Westborough replied in embarrassment. "What is the latest news?"

"A mixerum-gatherum, but mostly bad. The coroner's jury found that both deaths were homicides."

"That verdict is scarcely surprising."

"The grand jury," O'Connor continued, "returned an indictment charging Faith with two counts of murder."

"Most unfortunate!"

"It is that. We were lucky to get her out."

"You were indeed. The California penal code, I believe, states that a defendant charged with an offense punishable by death cannot be admitted to bail when the proof of guilt is evident or the presumption thereof great."

"Yes, but the finding of an indictment does not add to the strength of the proof or the presumptions to be drawn therefrom. That's the law, too, according to Mrs. Vayne's attorneys. So we're out of the hoosegow. It took sixty thousand dollars to free the pair of us—black-hearted scoundrels that we are."

"An exceedingly large sum."

"You would be telling me that? My own bond was ten thousand dollars. I might have raised a fifth of it if I had sold everything I had and borrowed everything I could."

"I see," Westborough pondered. "So you also are indebted to Mrs. Vayne for your freedom?"

"And if I am?"

"You have been surrendered into her custody, I presume. On your honor not to leave here until after the trial?"

O'Connor gave a vicious jerk to his shoelace. "It's a better jail than the one where I was."

"A good deal better, but—"

"But what?"

"You have placed yourself under obligation."

"Obligation for what?" the Hibernian snapped.

Looking at the well-knit arm muscles and remembering the exceptionally fiery temper, Westborough concluded that it might be safer not to dwell upon the perils of trifling with the truth under oath. His conscience, however, compelled an attempt at warning.

"You will not be merely a witness but a defendant," he reminded. "Most certainly you will be found guilty of being an accessory if Mrs. Eugene Vayne is convicted of the graver charge."

"She won't be. Hell, there's still some justice left in the world. Isn't there?"

"The county grand jury, however, is evidently convinced of this young woman's guilt."

"Muddleheaded nitwits!" the furious Celt exploded. "Can't see the truth when it's big as a barn door. Dolts! Clodpates! Morons! *Ts'ao ni-ti ma!*" He swore fluently in a mixture of English and Chinese.

"Do you feel better?" Westborough inquired after several seconds had elapsed.

Somewhat sheepishly, the flaming-haired journalist dipped into a drawer for a fresh shirt. "Well, go on," he challenged. "Tell me I'm a great fool."

" 'A great fool never becomes clear-headed.' Chuang Tzu, I believe. A friend has been regaling me with quotations most of the afternoon." Westborough did not think it necessary to add that the friend was Dr. Liao or that the latter had insisted upon driving him back to the Vayne estate after they had finished their conference.

"Devil take the lot of us!" O'Connor exclaimed. "I can't make you out at all. What sort of game are you playing here?"

"I must be changing clothes," the historian said uncomfortably.

"You have an hour and a half to dress for dinner, my slippery little Man of the Hills. Sit down. Let's get the matter straight. Have you taken any of Mrs. Vayne's money?"

"I have accepted a check from her," Westborough was forced to confess.

"That means you ought to be on our side. Are you?"

"I am sorry, but I must go."

"If I could trust you I'd tell you how Faith and I—"

"Please do not tell me," Westborough interrupted hastily. "Dear me, you must not. I am very untrustworthy, I assure you. Most unreliable."

"Leprechaun," O'Connor said genially, "somehow I can't help liking you."

"I cannot accept your liking under false pretenses." Westborough touched the envelope in his breast pocket for reassurance. "You and I are on opposite sides, Mr. O'Connor. Black and white are not more directly antipodal."

IV

Dining that night in the pavilion of pale yellow satin walls and gigantic moon window Westborough sensed the almost universal condemnation of those seated at the table. He accepted it as just, realizing that to nearly all he was only a tactless guest inconsiderately prolonging a visit during a trying period. Looking upon his conduct through the eyes of his fellow diners, the courteous little savant felt himself to be truly a boor, a Boeotian. The worst of that wretched meal, the unhappy sleuth mused, was the appearance of the released prisoner.

Faith Vayne bore not the slightest semblance to the woman he knew her to be. (He remembered the apt metaphor of Perseus: "The cunning fox lurking beneath the specious face.") She seemed a lady to the manner born. She wore her simple black gown with gentle dignity. She seldom spoke unless directly addressed. She made no effort to charm, which would have been effrontery. She was not tearful, which would have been hypocrisy. Her deportment was everything that it should be, nothing that it should not. Though she resembled Messalina she persisted in looking like Saint Elizabeth. It was most unfair.

He steeled himself against the treachery of pity. He must think of others—those helpless others so cruelly wronged. Justice was greater than mercy. The snail had feasted upon the leaf too long. The gluttonous gastropod richly deserved to be plucked off and trampled underfoot.

"I must see you alone," he whispered as they were quitting the table for the living pavilion. "A matter of extreme urgency. Will you come to the tea pavilion as soon as you can leave?"

Her face was pale. Her lips barely moved as they formed an affirmative answer. Westborough did not need to exert his powers of invention in formulating an excuse for not partaking of after-dinner coffee; Jocasta Vayne was giving him virtually a free hand. Upon reaching the tea pavilion he first saw that each bamboo shade was unrolled to the bottom. He moved

two chairs to the little lacquered table and shifted the position of a floor
lamp so that the light was shining directly on the seat of the largest chair.
These tasks accomplished, he had nothing to do but wait. She did not keep
him waiting long.

He heard the sound of light footsteps; then she stood shyly in the entrance. Westborough closed the door. "Will you please be seated there?" he
requested.

Obediently she crossed to the chair by the floor lamp. He thought of a
lily beaten to the earth by a storm, lifting its head sedately at the return of
the sun. But there was war between them. The septuagenarian knight girded
on cuisses and breastplate.

"It is kind of you to humor an old man's whim."

Soothing words he must find. Gloss and tinsel, paste and brummagem.
All tactics were permissible. All ends to victory justified.

"What did you wish to see me about, Mr. Westborough?"

"Your mother-in-law has employed me to discover evidence to prove
your innocence."

Let her be deceived. Let her be gulled, cozened, hoodwinked. She deserved no compassion, this woman of sham and lies.

"But, Mr. Westborough! I thought that you wrote books on Roman history."

"That is my profession, yes. However, I sometimes take a hand in matters of this nature."

"Oh." They regarded each other for a wordless instant—aging Claudius
and reincarnated Messalina. "Why is everyone against us?" she asked.

"Is everyone?"

"Those men on the grand jury were. I told them the truth—Kerry told
them the truth. They wouldn't accept it. Why are people so anxious to
believe the worst? Why are they so vindictive toward us?"

The specious face! The cunning fox!

"You loved your husband greatly, did you not?"

She shook her head. "I tried to be a good wife to Gene, but I didn't love
him."

Honesty was the last artifice he had expected her to use. She was as wily
as she was destitute of scruples. With a few simple words she had thrown
his plan of strategy agley.

"You married him for love, however?"

"No, not even that. Because I needed an object in life."

"An object? I must ask you to explain, Mrs. Vayne."

"China did something to me," she informed him, nervously twisting her
hands. "I couldn't slip back into the old routine again. I wanted to do something more worthwhile than selling jade to rich, careless women. To save a
man from himself *is* worthwhile."

"You married him to reform him?"

"To help him," she corrected. "I thought that I could. I failed but I did
my best. Is it wrong to marry a man for such a reason?"

He tossed the ball directly back to her. "You know the answer to that."

"It was wrong," she said faintly. "He didn't need me as I thought. He didn't want me as he made me believe."

"He did," Westborough contradicted, seeing no reason to be lenient. "But he didn't want what you gave him. He wanted a mate, not a Saint Elizabeth. He wanted a woman and embraced a bloodless ghost."

"Oh!" she moaned. "That's exactly what he called me—a bloodless ghost."

"You destroyed where you could have saved. In the end he turned on you—a savage, revolting against the cheat. He could not hurt you—"

"He did!"

"No, he could not touch you. He had only mud to throw, and you throve on martyrdom. The more you were persecuted the higher you rose in the esteem of his family."

He wanted her to wither him with the fury of a termagant—blast him with lightning rage. She did not. Her head remained as graciously poised as ever though her sensitive mouth quivered. "Perhaps I deserved that," she said. Westborough coughed, beaten and ashamed.

Ashamed in spite of all that he knew about her! He endeavored to withdraw his shattered forces.

"Dear me, I am sorry. It is barbarous to say such things."

"Perhaps they were true, Mr. Westborough. I never thought of it that way before."

Ornament of a meek and quiet spirit ..." How could one fight against that? He tried a flank attack.

"You knew in Peking, I believe, the jade merchant, Yee Fehlu?"

"Yes, I knew him very well."

"I learned this afternoon that Mr. Yee is dead."

"Dead! Oh, I am sorry! That dear old man."

"He was killed by a Japanese soldier who broke into his shop."

Her deep blue eyes welled mistily with tears. "Life is so cruel!" she sighed. "Yee was honest and upright. Good. As the Chinese understand goodness. I do not believe that he had ever caused another to lose face or broken anyone's rice bowl. He liked me. We became close friends. Can you tell me why such things are permitted to happen?"

"Because we are living in the age of the New Jungle. Tooth and claw have returned as bombing plane and tank. Treachery masquerades under the banner of friendship. Honor is a handicap in the battle for survival, a luxury to be uprooted."

"You frighten me."

"You should be frightened, Mrs. Vayne. Yee's secret did not die with him."

"What secret? I don't understand you, Mr. Westborough."

"Did you ever hear of the Ch'ien Lung necklace?"

"Yes, of course. It is very famous."

"Did you ever see it?"

"No, only a colored plate of it once in a book on Chinese jades."

"You never saw the actual necklace?"

"How could I?"

"Where was it when you were in China, Mrs. Vayne?"

"I don't know. Shanghai, I suppose."

"It was in Peiping," Westborough said severely. "The Jade Merchants' Guild had purchased it from the central government and brought it back to Peiping."

"In time of war?"

"Did you know that war was coming before the Lukouchiao clash on the night of July seventh?"

"No, I don't think anyone did—not even the Japanese. But what does all this have to do with Yee?"

He wondered why so artful a woman had failed to realize that she was overdoing her pretense.

"Your late friend Yee Feh-lu was a virtuous man, as you have said, an upright man who had never broken another's rice bowl. Because this was true the guild entrusted the necklace to his sole care, exacting no other pledge than his promise to see that it was smuggled safely from Peiping. Acting with typical Chinese caution, Yee confided his plan to only one other person, and her cooperation was indispensable. He trusted a woman not of his race."

"Yes?" she breathed.

"He called at her hotel in the early evening of July 27, 1937—that, Mrs. Vayne, was the night you departed from Peiping, was it not?"

"I don't remember the exact date."

"It was the same night. The military situation was extremely critical. Peiping was almost entirely cut off from the outside world. The only possible way of leaving the city then was by the special train on which you rode."

"Oh."

"This young woman, as an American, a privileged person shielded by the powerful aegis of the United States government, could travel unmolested by the Japanese. Yee was, perhaps, a trifle credulous. But he had come to know her well during her stay in Peiping, and her gentle manner had endeared her to his Chinese heart. He had not the slightest doubt of her honesty and good intent. Yee is scarcely to be blamed. She has deceived others since of her own nationality who have known her more intimately than the Chinese jade merchant."

"Are you saying, Mr. Westborough, that *I* was that woman?"

"Yes," he said sternly. "Her name was Faith Kingston."

"It isn't true. Yee never came to my hotel in all the time I was in Peiping."

The woman's shamelessness was as inordinate as Hitler's ambitions. Immediately Westborough produced the document which had been entrusted to him that afternoon.

"Here is the receipt you signed."

Startled, she glanced over the columns of ornate Chinese characters. "I signed this? Why, my name *is* here, my Chinese name. But this is—"

"You read Chinese, do you not, Mrs. Vayne? Translate this, please."

" 'I this day receive from Yee Feh-lu the celebrated chain of jade a king of Burma presented to the Emperor Ch'ien Lung. I promise faithfully to deliver it to the merchant Li Feng-chou, Los Angeles, United States.' That's Mr. Lee. 'If I betray this sacred trust may I have no sons. May the man I marry learn to hate me.' He did." She choked. " 'May the spirits of my ancestors revile me.' "

"Is that all?"

"Except my name."

"Which is in English as well as Chinese. The English signature of Faith Kingston is in your hand."

"It—it looks like my writing."

"It is yours."

"It can't be. I didn't sign it."

"Prevarication is useless. The signature can be proved by a handwriting expert, I feel sure. If necessary it will be proved. Why persist in so stupid a denial? Yee Feh-lu called when you were packing to leave Peiping and surrendered the Ch'ien Lung necklace into your care."

"No, it didn't happen. It wasn't real."

"It did happen, and this paper is the proof of it." He retrieved it hurriedly before she could think to destroy it.

"It wasn't real," she kept on saying. "I know it wasn't. It was only one of the things Madame Wu made me see in the crystal. A sort of dream."

"Dream!" Westborough echoed. "Dear, dear me!" A rocket burst within his brain, and he saw with amazing clarity. "Dreams and crystal visions are only memories, albeit often distorted ones."

He was sick with shame for having been so long blind. The phenomenon was weird but scientifically possible. His mind, it seemed, had been willfully closed to the truth.

"We do not, cannot dream of things totally unfamiliar to us."

"I don't know what you mean," she said.

"Mrs. Vayne, did you not tell me that you were escorted from Tientsin on the morning of July thirtieth? The morning after the Japanese had bombed the native city?"

"Yes. Everyone was talking about it."

"You had spent the previous night—the night of July twenty-ninth—in Tientsin?"

"Yes."

"And you did not see the bombing yourself?"

"No-o."

"How did you avoid viewing the horrible spectacle?"

"I don't know," she cried. "I was there. I had to be. I—the train probably didn't reach Tientsin until the bombing was over."

"There was fighting in the vicinity of the railway station all day. No train could have entered the city on July twenty-ninth."

"But I—I did spend that night at the American consulate. How can I possibly be mistaken?"

"Did the special train on which you left Peiping run on schedule past the junction of Langfang?"

"Why—uh—yes."

"I am sorry, but it did not. It was stopped at Langfang by Japanese soldiers. Explaining that an emergency had arisen and that the railroad must be kept free for troop trains, they forced it to a siding. It was held there until noon of the next day, July twenty-eighth. Will you please tell me what happened to your train afterward?"

"I—I can't remember."

"You should be able to remember if you rode on it. For reasons known only to the Japanese military it was switched to another siding at a village on the Pei River about fifteen miles beyond Langfang. After it had been there two or three hours Chinese soldiers surprised the Japanese garrison and blew up the bridge over the Pei Ho. Thus your train was delayed for a very long time indeed. It did not reach its destination until July thirty-first—a whole day after you had left."

"But—but," she faltered. "How *did* I get to Tientsin?"

"A most relevant question. Mrs. Vayne, how did you?"

V

Minutes passed before she lifted her bewildered face. "I thought that I came on the train," she said.

"You *thought!* Exactly! Do you have any *memory* of the journey?"

"No-o," she admitted tremulously. "You guessed, didn't you? I—I never told anyone."

"Has it worried you a great deal?"

She lowered her eyes. "Yes. Horribly."

"Do you recall boarding the train?"

"Not actually. But I know I did board it."

"Do you remember going to the station?"

"No."

"When was your last memory before the hiatus?"

"The afternoon of that day."

"The day you were to depart from Peiping?"

"Yes. I was all ready to leave except for a little packing I had to finish."

"What is the next thing you remember?"

"Waking up in a strange bed in a strange room."

"Tell me about it, please."

"Cots were all around me … I thought for a moment I was in a hospital. But the woman in the next bed said it was the American consulate. I asked, 'Peiping?' and she answered, 'No, Tientsin,' thinking, I suppose, that I was dazed by sleep. Nobody paid much attention to me; they were all too excited over the bombing. I wondered if I could have been in an accident and been carried there unconscious. I should have asked someone, I know, but I didn't. When I found my suitcase I remembered I had been on the train."

"You did not *remember*," he corrected. "You rationalized. Your mind provided a plausible, though specious, explanation to fill up the long blank space. Doubtless the realization of the amnesia was extremely unsettling, was it not?"

"Oh yes. Terrifying."

"Therefore, as human beings very often do, you believed as you wanted to believe. To think that you had arrived by the train on which you had planned to arrive minimized the horror of an extended lapse in consciousness so your mind readily accepted the fiction. Because you were hustled away from Tientsin before you had a chance to be contradicted the invention was allowed to take the place in your memory of an actual fact."

"What causes amnesia?" she asked.

"Many things may."

"Could it be because"—she balked at saying it—"because I'm not well mentally?"

"Whatever made you think of that?"

"When I reached Shanghai I looked up amnesia in a dictionary; there was something in the definition about brain injury. That—that frightened me. I'm a coward, I guess. I was ashamed to tell anyone."

"Quite understandable. In fact, a natural attitude. According to an eminent authority on the subject, suspected mental abnormalities are in general concealed or repudiated."

"I was afraid to have children," she confessed, white lipped. "Gene couldn't understand. He wanted a son. When I didn't he turned on me. I—I didn't have the right to marry him."

"On the contrary. Pray set your mind at rest, my dear."

"Could I have taken that necklace from Yee—the Ch'ien Lung necklace I would have given almost anything just to see—could I have signed that paper, as you said I did, and not known one thing about it afterward?"

"Yes."

"It—it doesn't seem possible."

"Many equally as unbelievable cases have been noted in the annals of medical psychology."

She smiled fleetingly. "So I'm not the only freak?"

"You are not a freak at all, Mrs. Vayne. Dear me, no! There might be a variety of wholly external causes. Shock, perhaps—physical or emotional. It is, however, rather idle speculation. The particular cause obviously lies buried in the vanished part of your life."

"Yes, I can see that," she declared. "It has blotted out its own memory."

"But not only its own. The memory destruction was manifestly not confined to the shock itself or even to the period following it, which evidently lasted until you awoke in Tientsin. There was also a backward-working effect. Retroactive amnesia is the technical term. Everything that transpired between the afternoon of July twenty-seventh and the morning of July thirtieth was obliterated from your consciousness. But nothing else. Examples of this peculiar type of selectivity are not at all uncommon. Ribot, I believe, made the observation that in memory disturbances the effect begins with the recall of the most recent experiences, spreading progressively to the older and hence more perfectly established memories. I am explaining this very poorly, I realize. You will find the subject discussed in any standard work on abnormal psychology."

"But if I did take that necklace from Yee—took it and lost it? Oh," she cried, "how much harm have I done?"

"You are scarcely to be blamed. Moreover, perhaps the harm may be undone. We must revive your lost past."

"How?" she questioned anxiously.

"You told me once of a dream you had—a recurrent dream. Will you please describe it to me?"

She did so.

"The entire incident," he pondered, "may be an actual occurrence—unrecognized as a memory, however, because it is divorced or dissociated from the elements of recognition and localization in the past. If we could restore either of these—"

"Then I would remember again?"

"In all probability. Let us attempt a fusion with historical events. Chinese soldiers surprised a Japanese garrison on the Pei Ho and dynamited the bridge they guarded. Could that have been *your* bridge, Mrs. Vayne?"

"The dream always ends in a sort of explosion," she said.

"Excellent! The dream explosion is probably the memory of the actual blast. We are making progress. We know from your 'dream' that you were on a train—the special Peiping-Tientsin train was the only one you could possibly have taken. The bridge episode enables us to locate the point at which you became separated from your fellow travelers. Not from all of them, however. You had a companion in the adventure whom you later identified as Mr. O'Connor."

"Yes," she confirmed.

"You failed to recognize him the other day. Obviously you had not known him long since memories prior to July twenty-seventh were not affected. It is a reasonable assumption that you met on the train. Perhaps you rode in the same compartment."

"We can ask him," she suggested practically.

"I have already done so, but it was a most lamentable failure. He vehemently denied any previous acquaintance with you."

Her mouth puckered questioningly. "But he must have known me. Otherwise—"

"Otherwise his whole behavior becomes inexplicable," Westborough finished. "Quite, I agree, but Mr. O'Connor is a gentleman who prefers to keep his own counsels. Let us not disturb him for a time. We now have you and him cut off from your train but on the Tientsin side of the wrecked bridge. An interesting situation for romance."

He saw that she was blushing furiously. "I was referring to romance merely in the sense of a fictitious tale of adventure—nothing personal, I assure you. The distance to the city could hardly be much over twenty miles. You might walk, perhaps, but undoubtedly your feet would have been sore or swollen afterward. Did you note such a condition when you woke in Tientsin?"

"No, nothing like it."

"Ergo, you did not walk. Though, I believe, a motor highway was not far away a pickup from a car was not at all likely. All motorized vehicles allowed to run on that day would be loaded with Japanese troops. Certainly you did not fly. There remains, however, the river. A small boat perhaps?"

Her eyes gleamed eagerly. "Oh yes, we might have hired one."

"Did you?"

She became immediately gloomy. "I haven't the least idea. It's maddening!"

"A logical reconstruction is not enough, it would appear." Westborough grew pensive.

"How do you know," she asked, "that I *can* remember? Or do you know?"

"If the lost were beyond possibility of recall, Mrs. Vayne, you would not have had your recurrent dream. Nor would Madame Wu have been able to conjure the fragments of the past with her crystal. Dear me, why do we not try the crystal again. Are you willing to submit to it?"

"Of course, anything. But there isn't one here."

"True. A ball of clear glass should do quite as well as the quartz, but we do not seem to have that either. Most unfortunate. H'm, I remember now that results have been obtained merely with a tumbler of water. That we do have, I hope."

She found glasses in the tea cabinet and filled one with water from the brass kettle.

"Sit in a comfortable, relaxed position," he directed as she fastened her gaze on the glass. "You must not try too hard. Try not to think of anything. Your mind must be still: as the Chinese say, a mirror reflecting—"

"Witch doctoring, is it?" Kerry O'Connor demanded scornfully from the pavilion door.

VI

The historian ventured a mild reprimand. "You are interrupting an experiment, Mr. O'Connor."

"'Tis more than interrupting I'll be doing."

Noting again the young man's tendency to revert in moments of excitement to the lilt of his Irish forebears, the elderly savant reflected briefly upon the permanence of the mind's earliest impressions.

"Kerry," Faith Vayne remonstrated. "Don't be angry with him, please."

"And why should I not be angry with the spalpeen?"

"But, Kerry! He's only trying to help me to remember."

"Playing with your mind, is he? Your poor bruised mind? He will not. I am taking you out of here."

"You labor under a misapprehension," Westborough informed the wrathful descendant of Eire. "Mrs. Vayne is not insane."

O'Connor immediately knotted his right fist. "And who would be saying she is?"

"Try to be more reasonable," the little man urged. "You admire the Chinese, I believe. They are always reasonable. We shall not accomplish anything if we waste our time in fruitless quarreling."

"Trust him, Kerry," she pleaded. "He wants to help us and he is wise. Mr. Westborough is one of the wisest men I have ever met."

"Leprechaun," O'Connor muttered, seating himself. "You have another chance."

"Thank you. I shall endeavor to deserve it. I understand why you lied to me yesterday, Mr. O'Connor."

"Do you now?"

"You did meet Faith Kingston on the Peiping-Tientsin train. You knew, however, she would deny any previous acquaintance with you so you falsified in order that your account might conform to hers."

O'Connor looked moodily at the golden dragon which writhed over the lacquered door of the tea cabinet. "She was in a tight spot," he said finally.

"You believed, did you not, that her mind had been affected?"

"And if I did?"

"You did not consider that insanity might possibly make an excellent defense?"

"I didn't want a gang of dirty alienists prying at her mind like an oyster," O'Connor proclaimed irately. "We already had a defense—the best there is. The simple truth."

"I believe it *is* the truth, Mr. O'Connor."

"That's the most sensible thing you've said to me."

"I own that I have been extremely confused. Like Chuang Tzu I scarcely know whether I am a man dreaming I was a butterfly or a butterfly now dreaming I am a man. What actually occurred in North China, Mr. O'Connor—"

"Make it Kerry."

"Thank you. I am pleased to have attained the distinction of being numbered among your friends. After you and Miss Kingston had been isolated by the destruction of the bridge you found a boat, I presume?"

"Right. We hailed a coolie with a sampan. A little flat-bottomed skiff with painted eyes on the bow, propelled by a single big oar at the stern. The owner was too poor to rig up a sail. We haggled with him for half an hour over the price of a row to Tientsin. He wanted to ferry us across the river and let it go at that, but with the bridge out what was the use of returning to the train? I knew it would be held up for two or three days, and I thought we might be able to make Tientsin late that night. The distance wasn't impossible. But we had bad luck. He turned into a little creek to ditch the Jap river patrol—hid the sampan under the overhanging branches of a willow. Don't you recall any of this, Faith?"

"It all seems totally unfamiliar," she confessed shamefacedly.

"That is only natural," Westborough asserted sympathetically. "You are not yet able to synthesize these events with your own recollections. I suggest, Kerry, that when you resume your narrative you include all the details you are able to recall, no matter how inconsequential they may seem. Mrs. Vayne's lost memories have not been obliterated, but they are unavailable to her. They are, as it were, blockaded behind a door. Any trifling little happening may prove to be the key. Do you understand?"

"I'll tell what I can," O'Connor answered a trifle shortly. "We didn't have any baggage with us except Faith's suitcase. All my stuff had been left on the train, but Faith wouldn't leave her jade—even for a minute—so I offered to carry it for her. I was the one, you see, who'd suggested that we stretch our legs a bit. Bright idea, I don't think, but the village looked peaceful enough, and the train seemed to be rooted there forever. We hadn't intended to go far, but we ran into the bridge before we knew it. After that—well, you must know what happened at the bridge."

"Yes," Westborough said. "Pray continue at the point where you had turned into the creek."

"The Japanese patrol boat didn't chase us, but a squad of ragged soldiers popped up and commandeered the sampan pusher. The services of all loyal Chinese, I gathered from their clatter, were being requisitioned for dirty work along the highway in order to slow up the Japanese motor advance. Faith settled things with our boatman. She was better at handling the natives than I was, knew more of their language and had more patience. He promised to be back at dawn (if the Japanese sharpshooters didn't get him) but, in case we might be tempted to steal his property in the interim, he carted the oar away with him. I was pretty mad. I offered to buy the boat but he wouldn't listen. After crowd had gone I wanted to look for a pole or something, but Faith wouldn't hear of it. She insisted that she'd rather be anchored under the willow forever than break a poor coolie's rice bowl. She was right of course." There was distinct admiration in the tall young man's voice. "I admitted it after I'd had time to cool off.

"The sampan wasn't very big. It wasn't comfortable to sit in, but it was drier than the fields. The sun went down. Crickets began to chirp, and we saw a fox sneaking off through the grass. Some imp or goblin in disguise. The Chinese have a lot of eerie beliefs about fox spirits. We talked. Lord, how we talked that night! Faith was sweet. Most women would have been plenty sore at a fellow who got them into such a mess, but she wasn't. She kept telling me it wasn't my fault. But it was, and we both knew it.

"The stars came out. Bats fluttered around in the darkness, and an owl hooted. Little ghostly lights flitted over the ground, will-o'-the-wisps or maybe the evil souls the Chinese say are about. Anything seems possible when you're spending a night out in the open in China. Faith fell asleep with her head on my shoulder. Hell, she had to put it somewhere! Now and then we heard firing—scattered and far away. I held her in my arms until daybreak. I—Oh, what the devil! I had to keep her from getting a chill, didn't I? It didn't mean anything. Just after dawn the boatman came back, gay as a lark. He and his friends had been playing a little game with the black dwarfs.

"He told us gleefully that they had been busy all night digging trenches across the highway to force the Jap trucks to stop. Whenever one did soldiers crouching in the kaoliang raked it with rifle fire. They had a swell party. Thousands of the monkey people had been killed, he insisted, probably a slight exaggeration. I couldn't share his enthusiasm about how soon all the short-legged ones were going to be driven back to the islands. The Japs have one thing in common with the British: they don't quit when the going gets tough. And they have one thing in common with the Jerries: there are no tactics too dirty for them to use. I scented trouble in the air, but I couldn't foresee what was going to happen to Tientsin. Nobody could.

"It wasn't very long after we had started sculling down the river that we began to hear shooting. Steady firing—not intermittent bursts like those we'd heard during the night. It kept growing louder and louder until finally I had to realize that we were headed right into a major battle. Sweet prospect! But I couldn't think of anything else to do except to go on.

"Know anything about the layout of Tientsin? It's not a walled city like Peking—the wall was torn down years ago as a punishment for the Boxers. (Lord, the things that poor China has had to take from the world on account of that bunch of wild-eyed fanatics!) There are British, French, Japanese, Belgian, Russian and Italian concessions; the first three are across the Hai River from the East Station where the bulk of the fighting was going on. The American consulate is in the British concession near the river, but the United States Fifteenth Infantry barracks were in the Chinese quarter. Later you'll see how important that last fact became to us.

"Fortunately I knew the native city fairly well. Tientsin had been my stamping ground for several months, and I hadn't confined my explorations to the British and French concessions, thank God! One of the things that saved us was that I carried the lay of the land in my head. No stranger could have ever gotten through that jumble of narrow walled streets and crooked rivers that make up the Chinese city. But I'm getting ahead of myself.

"We saw a sign for a teahouse when we came to the city. There was a landing pier and a little rickety flight of stairs leading up from the river. I didn't like the look of things ahead, I'll confess, and we were hungry. It sounds silly to mention it now, but we hadn't eaten for twenty-four hours. The teahouse looked like a good bet for both food and tidings.

"I told the boatman to wait for us at the pier. There weren't many customers inside the teahouse, and the proprietor acted plenty scared. But he brought us tea, steamed dumplings and news. The latter wasn't good. He said we couldn't go much further down the river and we couldn't get into any of the foreign concessions, which were all blocked off with barbed wire and sandbags. Not very cheerful! It looked like our only chance was to get to the Fifteenth Infantry barracks. The teahouse owner wasn't encouraging over that either. He'd heard it on the grapevine that half of the American soldiers were in summer camp and the rest were helping to guard the British concession. All the while we were talking to him Jap trench mortars were roaring like mad bulls. The planes hadn't taken off yet though.

"We gulped down the tea and bolted our dumplings and ran down the rickety stairs to the river. The boatman was gone—panic-stricken, I suppose. We never saw him again. There wasn't anything to do but walk. Men and women and little Chinese kids were milling in the narrow, dusty streets like a flock of frightened sheep who sensed that the wolf was out for a kill. Scuttling for safety, poor devils, as if there was any of *that* being handed out.

"Hell, this little affair in Tientsin doesn't seem like much after what's happened since. Put it down, however, that it was the beginning of a glorious new era. On July 29, 1937, the world received an actual demonstration of what modern bombing planes could do to civilians, and it's a lesson that's been well taken to heart. When it's carried to the ultimate conclusion—But we'll skip that.

"Faith's jade-loaded suitcase (you can be sure she had insisted on taking it into the teahouse with us) came in handy as a battering ram. By swinging it ahead of me, I managed to force a path through the crowd. Faith stayed just in back of me, with both arms locked around my waist. It was the only way we could have kept together. We hadn't gone very far when the first squadron of planes was in the air.

"I can't describe the hell they made. Words don't seem to fit: infernal regions, abode of the damned, place of torment ... plain, simple hell comes the closest. Hell suggests fire, sulphur, brimstone, the inside of a volcano scorching and boiling—well, it was almost like that! The racket alone was enough to drive you crazy, and that was the least part of it. Some bombs were incendiary, and when fires started there wasn't anyone to put them out. Long columns of flame leaped up in a dozen places. They bombed a girls' school and the youngsters came out yelling. Smoke was hazy in the air like China's funeral pall.

"People rushed from burning houses, dazed by what had happened or else screeching like animals. Men lay dead, dying, in the streets, and others walked on them, too panicky to know or care. Flimsy little Chinese houses crumpled into splinters. I can't begin to tell you a tenth of it—wounded women, screaming children ... It's only another set of statistics when you read that so many hundreds or thousands of noncombatants were killed. You don't know what it means. You can't know unless you see them killed before your eyes. Unless you see them writhing in torment. Unless you smell blood and burning hair—"

"Stop!" she begged. "Please."

"Sorry, mavourneen," he apologized. "I was only obeying instructions to shoot the works."

"It's too awful. I can't stand it."

"You're lucky you've forgotten. I wish I could. Those devils in the air came on and on like ocean waves. As soon as one squadron had dropped its load and headed back another was right on deck to massacre in wholesale for dear old Nippon. Banzai!"

"Yellow-winged planes!" she said with a shudder.

"Faith!" he cried. "You're remembering."

"Yes. I can see them swooping down above our heads. Oh, horrible!"

"I believe we need search no longer for the cause of amnesia," Westborough asserted. "To a woman's delicately organized nervous system such an intense emotional shock might—"

"'Tis shock it was!" O'Connor ejaculated. "She was shell-shocked and I never knew it. Faith, you were in a queer state the latter part of the time."

"Was I?" she asked. "How?"

"You didn't seem to be feeling or seeing anything. Almost a blank look on your face. But you did everything I told you to do, and you answered sensibly when I asked you questions, so I thought you were all right. But I should have known. You weren't yourself at all. Queer!"

"The shock," Westborough explained, "doubtless resulted in a temporary dissociated mental state in which Miss Kingston remained capable of automatic responses. The condition is akin to somnambulism and is, like the latter, associated with amnesia upon recovery of full consciousness. As so frequently happens in such cases of dissociation the amnesia extended backward, thus erasing from her mind all the events of the harrowing journey. Most understandable."

"I'll cut the rest of it short," O'Connor said, continuing. "We reached the barracks, Lord knows how. A sentry squinted at our passports and let us inside. Then we played into luck. A detachment of troops was just about to march out to relieve the forces in the British concession, and so we had a military escort all the way to the American consulate. They had room for her there; they had put up extra cots all over the place to take care of refugees. I left her, knowing she was in practically the safest place in Tientsin and having a man-sized job on my hands.

"I was a newspaperman in those days, and I'd stumbled into a whale of a story. It took a long time to get the facts together and still longer to get a wire. What with one thing and another, including a little sleep on the floor of the telegraph office, it was noon the next day before I could get back to the consulate to ask about Faith. Then I learned that she had been included in a party of women they had sent down the river to a Dutch steamer at Tangku. She hadn't left any word for me—oral or otherwise. And not so much as a single scrap of writing ever came to me afterward though I knew she knew the name of the paper I worked for." He grinned self-consciously.

"I couldn't help believing that something on the order of a dirty trick had been played on me."

Westborough had a great deal to say.

"I believe that I can explain the strange effect you had upon Mrs. Vayne, Kerry, when she saw you again at the jade exhibit. Doctor William McDougall in his *Outline of Abnormal Psychology* discusses the concept of redintegrative mechanism whereby a partial stimulus may reinstate the reaction previously made to the complete whole. He cites as an example a child frightened by a large, black, growling and moving quadruped. On a later occasion the growl alone is sufficient to provoke the same fright reaction. You, Kerry, were that growl—a partial stimulus. Though Mrs. Vayne did not consciously recognize you your presence sufficed to return her for a short while to the dissociated mental state in which she had last beheld you. When she recovered she was naturally baffled. She even conjectured that she had been hypnotized, but it was merely ..." His voice trailed away, unheard.

"Kerry, I forgot!" A hand fluttered despairingly to Faith's slim white throat. "I—I loved you, dear. I promised to marry you. Oh, my darling, what have I done to you?"

PART TEN: THE THREADS UNRAVEL

WESTBOROUGH was closeted for an hour on Sunday morning with a member of the Vayne household, shortly after which he departed from the guest house. He spent the next two days at the home of his former hosts, the Launays, who, far from reproaching him for desertion, received him with unmerited cordiality. Except for certain telephone conversations the Vayne case appeared to have entirely slipped his mind. On Tuesday afternoon, however, he was admitted again through the vermilion gate and took the zigzag path among the fuchsias and bamboo grove to the crest of the hill. In the living pavilion a moderately large circle of his acquaintances had already assembled.

Sipping a cup of Jocasta Vayne's incomparable Darjeeling, he took a mental roll call: Mrs. Nicholas Vayne, here; Mrs. Eugene Vayne, here; Mrs. Lydia Kroll, here; Mr. Jasper Kroll, here; Mr. Jethro Coggin, here; Mr. Kerry O'Connor, here; Dr. Liao Po-ching, here; Mr. F. C. Lee, here. All present or accounted for. Good. Another extremely important personage was also in sight of the onyx top of the low oval table: the Jade Maiden, P'i-hsia Yüan-chün, whose names are the Green Shiver, the Heavenly Nurse, the daughter of T'ai Shan, Lady of the Blue Sky and Princess of the Purple and Azure Clouds that Herald the Dawn. Most excellent. The savant surrendered his cup and saucer to the care of number-one boy, Wing.

"An unbelievably strange tale has been brought to my attention. I am sure that all of you will be interested because so many of you are concerned." It was surprising how quickly the tea chatter subsided.

Equally surprising was the attentiveness with which Westborough's lengthy monologue was followed. He talked for nearly half an hour with almost no interruptions.

"My story begins—dear me, just where shall I begin? With the royal gift of a Burmese king to the Manchu emperor, Ch'ien Lung?" He glanced at the shriveled face of the venerable Lee. "With the purchase of that imperial heirloom by the Jade Merchants' Guild of Peking?" He regarded the placidly smooth countenance of Dr. Liao. "No, I think not. I think I shall commence with an American lady who had the ill luck to be in China at the beginning of the Sino-Japanese conflict." His eyes rested momentarily upon the pale, anxious face of Faith Vayne. "As she was packing to leave Peiping there called at her hotel a jade merchant named Yee Feh-lu. There was a warm friendship between the old Chinese and the young American—one of those rare friendships between Oriental and Occidental which can occur only when there has been established a basis of mutual confidence and respect. Mr. Yee brought with him that statuette." Westborough's gaze turned toward the frowning little goddess on her limpid gray pedestal.

"He offered it to her at a remarkably low price. She had some funds left from the sum entrusted to her for jade purchases and could not refuse the exceptional bargain. Yee's bill of sale remained in her possession as evidence of the transaction, which, I may say, was purely incidental to the main object of his call. He asked her—as a favor from one friend to another—to smuggle an almost priceless object through the Japanese lines then so fast closing around Peiping.

"Miss Kingston accepted the grave risk without an instant's hesitation. She agreed to deliver the historic Ch'ien Lung necklace to a gentleman of Los Angeles: Mr. Li Feng-chou or—Americanized—F. C. Lee, and instruct him verbally to sell the necklace on behalf of its Peking owners, holding the sum in trust for them until conditions in North China became settled. Needless to say, she did not also promise to smuggle the necklace through the United States customs although she is—technically at least—guilty of the offense. However, I do not believe that she will be penalized when the circumstances are fully explained. For Faith Kingston experienced the misfortune of losing some sixty-five hours from her memory. When she departed from Tientsin she had not the slightest idea that she was carrying with her the world's most valuable jewel-jade.

"Some of you know, others may have guessed, the manner in which the smuggling was accomplished. The fantastic story of the suicidal ancestor fabricated by Doctor Liao's ingenious imagination has elements of truth. The figure was once the property of a Taoist pope and may, for want of a better term, be designated as a ghost bottle. I might mention the Arabian Nights tale of genii imprisoned in sealed jars. Chinese Taoists have much the same curious belief. They hold that an evil and malignant spirit may be driven by incantations to take refuge within a bottle, from which it cannot escape to plague humanity further unless someone is so stupid or ill-advised as to remove the cork. Such a ghost bottle de luxe was our little Jade

Lady. I shall explain shortly the simple method by which her concealed mechanism is worked.

"Only two persons—Faith Kingston and Yee Feh-lu—were aware that the Ch'ien Lung necklace, carefully packed with cotton to prevent rattling, had been stowed within the hollow interior of the statuette. Miss Kingston became an amnesia victim, and Mr. Yee lost his life, an undeserving victim of war and aggression. He had, however, taken the precaution of concealing Miss Kingston's signed receipt and his own written explanation of the circumstances in a dragon vase of rare, bright yellow jade. Just before the fall of Peiping, as an additional safeguard against an expected Japanese search of his shop, he sent the yellow vase to the home of an intimate friend, to wit, Doctor Po-ching. Foresighted though Yee was, however, he had failed to anticipate his early death. Doctor Liao was told nothing. Only through a lucky accident several months later did he discover the carved dragon's removable head. The time has now come to tell of the part in this complex drama played by a distinguished scholar. His was a role of patriotism.

"After the merchant Yee's tragic death the guild had become, if not reconciled, at least acceptant of the total loss of the necklace. Visiting the members separately, Doctor Liao secured from each a conditional agreement to relinquish his share in favor of the Chinese central government in the event that the necklace could be recovered. Shortly afterward he left Peking. Undergoing almost incredible hardships for a man of his years, he journeyed a thousand miles up the Yangtze River to remote Chungking, the new capital of the central government. Upon hearing his story the government dispatched him to the United States, ostensibly (since he spoke excellent English) on a lecture tour to win American sentiment for the Chinese cause. This mission he has fulfilled with diligence and competence. He had, however, another, more ulterior assignment; namely, to gain legal possession of the lost Ch'ien Lung necklace and convert it into cash for the central government's war chest. And in this he encountered many difficulties.

"Some were of his own making. He will forgive me, I am sure, for saying this. Doctor Liao is scarcely to be blamed for preferring the indirect to the direct approach. Mr. Lee informed him that he had never received the necklace from Miss Kingston; it is small wonder that the visiting ambassador jumped to the conclusion that his dead friend had been betrayed by a thief. The thief, moreover, had been clever enough to marry into a wealthy family and was now under the powerful protection of Mr. Lee's best customer. Dear, dear me! Caution was certainly necessary. For all that either of these Chinese gentlemen knew to the contrary Mrs. Nicholas Vayne herself might be implicated in the crime.

"But although forced to be canny Doctor Liao was not inactive. Mrs. Vayne's recent jade exhibit gave him the opportunity to learn that she did not openly admit ownership of the Ch'ien Lung necklace. Whether or not it was in her secret possession was more difficult to ascertain. Reasoning that the necklace might still be concealed within the jade goddess, he made an ingenious attempt to secure permission to examine the statuette in private. But the container had already been stolen. Before relating Doctor Liao's next move I must refer to the culpability of the late Eugene Vayne.

"I grieve to say in the presence of his wife, mother and sister that Mr. Vayne's conduct was not honorable. Having discovered the presence of the necklace, he stole the statuette and hid it at the bottom of the lotus pond. Such was the state of affairs on last Wednesday afternoon when Doctor Liao came here for tea. And now the complications grow additionally complicated by a new actress: the unfortunate Chinese lady, Madame Wu.

"Informed by Mrs. Kroll that Madame Wu had been invited to the house on Thursday morning to recover the lost statuette by 'psychic' means, Doctor Liao lost no time in turning the knowledge to account. He made an appointment with Madame Wu for Wednesday night and laid all of his cards upon the table. It is no exaggeration of fact to call Madame Wu a charlatan, but, impostor or not, she was also a patriotic Chinese and wholly sympathetic. She pledged Doctor Liao her unstinting cooperation and served him faithfully to her death, poor lady! May I add that she accomplished much?

"Whether by psychic means or not she found out Eugene Vayne's secret. More: she persuaded him to take her into partnership with him and even induced him to bring her the necklace that night. This, by the way, is the true explanation of Mr. Vayne's presence in her apartment on the evening of the tragedy.

"Mr. Vayne, however, was not able to bring the necklace. He was frustrated in his endeavor to recover the Jade Lady from the lotus pond. Empty-handed, he kept his appointment with Madame Wu. That remarkable lady then made a remarkable effort to secure the statuette through Mr. Vayne's wife. Dear me! I have talked myself hoarse, and you have all listened in the kindest possible manner. It is high time your patience is rewarded. You are all anxious, I am sure, to know what actually did become of the historic jade chain. If you will bear with me only a few seconds longer—"

As he walked over to the statuette on the low oval table Westborough removed from his coat lapel an ordinary straight pin. "Note carefully," he said, "the carving of the Taoist symbol of the Hare-in-the-Moon." He inserted the pin into a tiny, almost invisible hole in the eye of the hare. Upon release of the trigger holding the concealed spring a circular plug of jade was expelled outward.

Westborough's index and second fingers explored the opening. "The most famous jade in the world," he declared, drawing out an object of glowing emerald green. "Once the property of Ch'ien Lung." The beads filtered slowly through his fingers into another man's cupped palms. "No one will question your right to these as the agent of the Chinese central government."

"My friend"—Dr. Liao was beaming joyfully—"unworthy self is duly grateful."

II

The hour was late. Orion and the Pleiades had set long ago. Bright Sirius was gone, too, and ruddy Aldebaran; blazing Arcturus had progressed appreciably in his fourteen-hour stride across the sky. But the moon had not yet risen. Only the minikin sparkles from inconceivably distant suns leavened the night. The two human beings seated at the base of the great wall were grateful for darkness. It masked their presence, wrapped them from view in coats of invisible black. Darkness was necessary to them.

They were patient men. Since dusk they had kept their lonely vigil, conversing rarely and only in hurried whispers. Silence was also necessary to them. A breeze, touching them with its chilly finger, brought to their nostrils the scent of brine. So close was the sea that its rhythmic beating was never absent—a vast pulsating heart, ebbing and flowing, advancing and retreating, systolic and diastolic. They listened intently for another sound.

A faintly audible creak reached their ears. Quietly rising, they flattened like shadows close to the wall. The slight squeak was the noise for which they had so long waited. They turned their gaze upon the slowly swinging leaf of a ponderous gate. Their eyes with the marvelous facility of those organs had adapted themselves to the scattered trickles of starlight. They knew, by intuition as much as by sight perhaps, that a figure was emerging.

It carried a flashlight. As the direction was shifted they were permitted a brief glimpse of the phantomlike form. Dimly they perceived a woman of medium height, mantled in a long cape. Her head, they saw, was shrouded by a sort of wimple. From her almost soundless motion they drew the conclusion that she was wearing rubber-soled shoes. The beam of light focused upon the highway in front of them. Each man ceased breathing as she glided past.

They did not follow, content for the moment merely that they had not been seen. A few seconds went by, and the gate opened again. This time it was a tall, broad-shouldered male who came out. They hastened to accost him.

"Good boys!" he exclaimed in a young man's rich baritone. "Right on the job, I see. Which way?"

"To the right," one of the watchers replied softly. Groping their way along the black road, they ascended a slight rise and found the woman had just left the highway.

She had taken to the rolling wastes. They stumbled through clumps of sage and creosote, trailing the will-o'-the-wisp in her hand. Continually they lost ground. She had light, and they had not. She might make noise, but they dared make none. For these reasons she could go much faster. Duller and duller glowed the distant beam. Soon, perhaps, it might become altogether invisible. A grave disaster!

None of the pursuers had been sufficiently farsighted to foresee such a calamity. Now all realized that if the speck of light were lost in that wide tract of wilderness they had only an infinitesimal chance of ever stumbling upon their quarry again. If only the moon would rise! But the moon was not due for an hour.

"We have felled tree," whispered one of the three. "But we may fail to catch blackbird."

"The blackbird will be caught," the youngest man promised grimly. "Look, fellows! It's stopped now. All we have to do is close in."

All!

It was true, however, that the woman seemed to have halted. Exultantly they stalked her. Taking advantage of the cover afforded by the creosote, they flitted from bush to bush. Painfully slow work! They must move silently, a difficult feat when they could see so little. But foot by foot they drew closer to the wavering glimmer. At last they were able to see the woman herself. She was standing on a slope a little above them, shifting the beam over an enormous nest of cactus. The youngest man, gripping each of his companions by the shoulder, drew their heads toward his in a sort of football huddle.

"Close in from different sides. You take the right flank, you the left, and I'll take the center. Okay?"

The other two bobbed their heads in wordless agreement. Each was over twice the age of their young accomplice, but neither thought of questioning his capacity for leadership. They were scholars; he was a man of action. Unconsciously they realized that his judgment was now the best.

"Rush when I signal," he whispered tersely. "Not too much of a hurry. Wait till it's actually—"

It wasn't necessary that the sentence be finished. They scattered to their separate posts and began to climb the hill. Presently all were so close that it was not safe to go farther. Sulking behind the pungent greasewood, they waited silently for the woman to do the thing she had come to do.

Her flashlight swayed unsteadily over the prickly cactus. Plainly something was causing her anxiety. The watchers could not see her face, only the white wimple. Finally she found a spot in the clump that seemed pleasing to her. As she knelt on the ground her hooded head made her look like a nun in prayer.

She laid the flashlight down, blocking it with a clod of dirt to keep it from rolling, and put on a pair of leather gauntlets. Into the heart of the cactus her arms darted like striking snakes. When she withdrew them it became evident she was holding something. ...

Kerry O'Connor yelled, "Okay, fellows!" Hearing their friend's ringing voice, Westborough and Dr. Liao also sprang forward. The woman dropped her booty, but she did not run. She whipped off her right gauntlet and in a virtually continuous movement plunged her hand within her cloak. As O'Connor ran toward her she leveled a revolver and pulled the trigger. O'Connor was not five feet away. A miss was impossible, but the young Irish-American did not fall.

The hammer clicked harmlessly upon an empty chamber. She pulled the trigger again, and O'Connor wrenched the gun from her hand.

"A wolf in sheep's clothing." He laughed, tearing off the improvised wimple. "You're caught with the goods, Jasper Kroll."

ADDENDUM

Letter from Theocritus Lucius Westborough
to Captain M. P. Collins

MY DEAR CAPTAIN:

Mr. O'Connor has kindly volunteered to take my dictation on the typewriter while we are waiting for your men to call for the prisoner. I will, of course, be glad to come to your office to discuss matters in person, but there are excellent reasons for setting down my conclusions in the permanent medium of black and white.

First allow me to call your attention to 108 jade beads collectively known to history as the Ch'ien Lung necklace and to a curious case of retroactive amnesia. ...

(Several paragraphs which would be repetitious to the reader have been omitted. C.B.C.)

And so I was forced to turn away from Mrs. Eugene Vayne and search elsewhere for a suspect. The murderer was also the thief, I reasoned, or there could be no adequate motive for the double killing. And it was evident that the thief must possess three indispensable qualifications:

(1) A knowledge of jade to enable him or her to recognize the great value of this matchless object.

(2) An opportunity to learn of the presence of the necklace in the hollow interior of the jade goddess.

(3) A residence on the Vayne estate.

Mr. Kroll fulfills the three conditions. (1) He had delved deeply into the fascinating subject of jade and has stored his mind (if you will pardon the misquotation) with many quaint and curious items of forgotten lore.

(2) Mr. Kroll assisted in arranging the pieces of the Vayne collection which were photographed for publicity to herald Mrs. Vayne's ill-starred jade exhibit. The Green Shiver was among the pieces then photographed as is proved by the print I am sending to you with this letter. It is possible he discovered at that time the tiny hole in the eye of the Taoist hare. Probing with idle curiosity, he might accidentally have learned how the plug in the statuette's base is forced open. Though he could hardly have made then a detailed examination of the necklace unknown to the others in the room he might easily have seen enough to intrigue his interest and determine him to make a future secret inspection.

(3) It is self-evident that Mr. Kroll fulfills the third condition.

Upon examining his qualifications for the role of murderer, however, I found him sadly lacking in opportunity to commit the crime. Moreover, I encountered another difficulty. It did not seem possible that he could be the "prowler" who had so agitated the unfortunate little Pekingese. Mr. Kroll, I could testify from firsthand knowledge, had been in his bed at the time the dog was barking. Could I be doing him a grave injustice?

I examined in detail all remaining possibilities. These, needless to say, were limited to the persons meeting the third theft condition, i.e., residence on the grounds. At first Mr. Coggin seemed a likely candidate. His knowledge of jade is probably equal to Mr. Kroll's, and he had even better opportunity than the latter to learn the secret of the Ch'ien Lung chain. But, and this was a grave objection, *Mr. Coggin fulfilled the second condition too well*.

My theory necessitated that the thief should have access to the Taoist goddess *only* while Mrs. Vayne's collection was on display in the living pavilion: to be more specific, only during the night of Monday last week. Mr. Coggin, carrying on his person a key to the locker in which the jade was stored, could have removed the necklace at any other convenient time and would have undoubtedly done so. I removed him from the list of suspects.

Mrs. Nicholas Vayne, even if capable of filicide (which I could not for a moment believe), might be spared the taint of theft on the self-same grounds which had eliminated Mr. Coggin. Mrs. Eugene Vayne, who conforms to the three conditions, had already been weighed in the balance and found not wanting. Mrs. Kroll does not meet the requirements of condition one.

Nor, obviously, does Mr. Fry, the chauffeur. The other servants, however, are in a different category. Oriental reticence being what it is, I could not feel justified in casting out any of the four on account of lack of knowledge. If any were eliminated it must be from the opportunity condition.

First the gardener. In order to prevent possible racial friction Mr. Kawabe had been given strict orders to keep away from the compound. I questioned the house servants who, as Chinese, had no particular love for him. It was

generally conceded, however, that Mr. Kaw
injunction and had entered none of the buildin
outbreak of the Sino-Japanese war. I scratched h

The Chinese trio was more difficult. It seemed
Wong, who rarely left the gatehouse, and Weng, who
in the kitchen when on duty. Number-one boy Wing, th
ignored. As well as Mr. Coggin or Mr. Kroll he fulfills th
ditions and, unlike Mr. Coggin, he had access to the jade
during the required night. Wing, I must frankly confess, pu
some little time.

However, I had already determined that thief and murderer must
tical. Could Wing have committed the two killings of last Thursday ev
You yourself, Captain, have demonstrated that he could not. Allow m
review your own reasoning. Wing, according to Mrs. Eugene Vayne, wa
on the grounds at the time she left with Mr. O'Connor, and the latter's car
was the last vehicle there. Unless miraculously transported through the air
by jinn it was not physically possible for Wing to have arrived at Madame
Wu's apartment in advance of Mrs. Vayne and Mr. O'Connor.

With all other suspects eliminated, necessity compelled my ultimate return to Mr. Kroll.

Considering first the important question of motive, I endeavored to put
myself in his place. If I were Mr. Kroll I should not have married Mrs.
Kroll except for money. (I regret exceedingly that it is necessary to speak
slightingly of that poor woman; for her serious misfortunes I am deeply
sorry.) I would soon learn that my wife had no money of her own and
would have none until after her mother's death. It seems a long time to
wait. Jocasta Vayne is only fifty-eight and in perfect health. Instead of
gaining a fortune I have merely imprisoned myself within a gilded cage.
My wife, a devoted but foolish woman, bores me with silly chatter, but I
must smile and pretend interest because I am here only under her suffer-
ance. My wealthy mother-in-law is an avowed enemy. Scarcely a day passes
in which I am not wounded by her caustic tongue. She refuses to allow us
a sum sufficient to maintain a separate establishment; it seems she takes
almost a sadistic delight in having me under her thumb to torture. But what
can I do about it?

Shall I leave? Shall I, with poor qualifications, enter the grim struggle
for living in an unsympathetic business world? Shall I renounce all the
little luxuries which make life worth living? No. On the whole it is prefer-
able to be a kept dilettante. I hide my shame beneath a sedulous pretense of
absorption in the occult. This serves the dual purpose of annoying my
mother-in-law and keeping my silly wife amused. (Extra-dimensional beings must have been a godsend to the man.) But despite this relief I am
becoming increasingly—there is an expressive slang phrase—fed up. Under such conditions I perceive an opportunity to make money, so much
money that I can, whenever I wish, part company with my sharp-tongued
mother-in-law and vapid spouse. Shall I hesitate because it involves an

ient I beg of you to realize that
thing more serious than remov-
keting it clandestinely. The at-
hich put more and still more
n to kill. But murder was far
o.

ad for suspecting Mr. Kroll,
lized at once that while my
e else. More than abstract
and force a thief to dis-
nvince you and a skepti-
where was it possible to secure
y? Only from Mr. Kroll himself.

the necklace, I reflected, he obviously would not carry it
his person for any length of time. Nor could he risk concealing it in
his own pavilion. That pavilion was also Mrs. Kroll's, and what married
man is ever able to hide successfully an object in the home from his wife?
Moreover, the pavilion was tidied daily by the lynx-eyed Wing—another
source of danger. Mr. Kroll, being far from a fool, would undoubtedly se-
crete the necklace elsewhere.

Within the grounds? Exceedingly dangerous. The finding of the Jade
Lady in the lotus pond had doubtless taught our culprit the folly of trusting
to a cache inside the walls. Nor was this necessary. Emerging from the
vermilion gate, Mr. Kroll had only to take a brief walk to reach a large area
of seldom-visited wasteland where a few handfuls of dirt scooped over his
stolen treasure would preserve it indefinitely from discovery.

It was, decidedly, a needle-and-haystack problem. A million Ch'ien Lung
necklaces might have been safely buried in the hilly, semidesert acres across
the road from the Vayne estate. Dr. Liao and I had no hope of ever locating
the needle unless the thief could be induced to betray himself.

A few words will acquaint you with the details of our plan. On Sunday,
the morning following the startling disclosures made to me by Mrs. Eugene Vayne and Mr. O'Connor, I requested a private interview with Mrs.
Nicholas Vayne. Without her permission the scheme would have been impossible, but she cooperated with us to the fullest extent. Shortly after concluding our conversation I packed my things and departed: partly because
my business could be better conducted from a distant headquarters and
partly to make the criminal believe I had abandoned the chase. Mr. Kroll, I
must mention, had suspected my ulterior aims from the first day of my
visit. I am not sure just why. Possibly my name had lodged in his remarkable memory in connection with some previous case. I trust you will pardon the digression. The fact that Mr. Kroll did suspect me assumes major
significance in this bizarre and baffling affair.

Let us, however, return to our muttons. Upon my return to the Launay
home I abused once more John and Adrienne's gracious hospitality by ex-

tended telephonic communications. First I called Dr. Liao and outlined the situation; he got immediately in touch with Mr. Lee, whose sagacity and business knowledge were to prove invaluable to us. I was extremely doubtful, it must be confessed, if an imitation of the necklace could be produced, but Mr. Lee, it turned out, sells the products of a Chinese artist who is able to achieve miracles of craftsmanship with silver wire and stained glass from old church windows. Luckily a pattern was at hand. A colored plate of the necklace appears in one of the standard works on Chinese jade, and the volume was in Mr. Lee's large library. When the task had been completed Mr. Lee dispatched his son to the Vayne estate. Needless to say, young Charles Lee had instructions to deliver his package only to Mrs. Nicholas Vayne in person. She received the spurious necklace secretly and in secrecy packed it within her then empty statuette. We had—to use Dr. Liao's picturesque proverb—felled a tree to catch a blackbird, but the results were all that I had anticipated. Mr. Kroll, losing for once his habitual pose, appeared utterly flabbergasted upon beholding our replica. Nor was it possible for him to detect the fraud. The artist had copied the design and dimensions of the original with the most meticulous care. True the beads were only bits of green stained glass, but they might have deceived even an expert were he forced to rely upon sight alone. We encroach here upon a paradox of the jade trade. The more valuable a piece of imperial green jadeite, the more closely does it resemble flawless glass of the same color. One familiar with the stone may of course always recognize it by the characteristic "feel" or texture, but Mr. Kroll, you may be sure, was not given the opportunity to employ his sense of touch. He saw Mr. Lee, perhaps the foremost authority in Los Angeles on jade, examine the necklace and pronounce it genuine. Had the object believed to have been so safely buried been found? What else was the victim of the hoax to think?

When I saw Mr. Kroll's face I felt sure that he would enjoy no peace of mind until he revisited his hiding place. I concluded also that it was extremely likely the attempt would be made this very night.

It now became necessary for Dr. Liao and me to secure an assistant inside the grounds. I could not return to the guest house myself without warning Mr. Kroll that my interest in the case persisted, and Mrs. Nicholas Vayne, who had already been of such enormous service to us, could hardly be asked to undertake the rough work of shadowing. Though it was unlikely Mr. Kroll had an accomplice that possibility nevertheless existed. Therefore it appeared wisest to confide our plot to only one other person.

I selected Mr. Kerry O'Connor for two excellent reasons: he had a huge personal stake in the taking of the criminal and would, moreover, impart to our enterprise a certain rugged character which it had hitherto lacked. Dr. Liao is only ten years my junior, and both of us have led sedentary lives. Frankly I was not at all sure that we would not prove—to employ theatrical argot—"flops" at effecting the capture. Mr. Kroll is considerably younger than either of us, and I knew him to be cunning and dangerous. With Mr. O'Connor's aid, however, success was assured.

I should like at this point to acknowledge our indebtedness to this brave and resourceful young man (Applesauce—Kerry O'Connor). He it was who removed the shells from Mr. Coggin's revolver—fortunately the only firearm on the grounds—lest our cornered fox try to repeat his previous exploit. The precaution was fully justified. Mr. Kroll fired point-blank at Mr. O'Connor and would undoubtedly have also endeavored to kill both Dr. Liao and myself. But "every man is the architect of his own fortune." For us the ancient Latin adage held good.

I regret to report that we were able to obtain little information from our captive. Though taken with the genuine necklace actually in his hands Mr. Kroll persistently denied that he had anything to do with the murders. This steadfastness, I must say, I had not in the least expected of him. The prisoner is at present confined above the garage where, under the joint guardianship of Mr. Fry and Mr. Kawabe, his chance of escape is almost negligible. With your great experience in such matters you will probably be more successful than we in inducing him to confess. If he should still prove recalcitrant when you talk to him, however, you may find a chronological reconstruction of events helpful. I am taking the liberty of preparing one— largely a tissue of guesswork, I confess, but it holds together. "Things which will stick require no glue." (I trust you will pardon the quotation from a favorite Oriental philosopher.)

Let us begin with the night following the jade exhibition. Mrs. Kroll, a sufferer from insomnia, is in the habit of drinking a glass of warm milk immediately before retiring. It would be a simple matter for her husband, who usually prepares this beverage, to administer a soporific. A bottle of sleeping tablets which was found in the Krolls's bathroom provides confirmation of this hypothesis. Leaving his wife in drugged slumber, Mr. Kroll went stealthily to the living pavilion for a second and more detailed examination of the hollow jade statuette.

How much he actually knew at this time is open to conjecture. I have reason to believe that he had eavesdropped on a conversation between Mr. O'Connor and Mrs. Eugene Vayne earlier in the day. Did he guess that she had experienced the amnesia? Possibly—Mr. Kroll is astute. This much is certain: when he had reopened the statuette and had the necklace for the first time actually in his hands he at once recognized its monetary value.

And at this point Mr. Vayne, rousing from drunken slumber on the living-pavilion sofa, dealt himself a hand in the game.

The two men greatly disliked each other, a dislike founded upon mutual and reciprocal contempt. It is fairly easy to synthesize the scene occurring between them. Mr. Kroll could have quieted his brother-in-law only by a promise of an equal share in the proceeds. Mr. Vayne was readily tempted. He was not a strong moral character, alas, and he was in urgent need of money for a personal reason which I prefer to discuss with you in private. But the two partners could never trust each other. Tiger and deer do not stroll together as the Chinese maxim goes. Mr. Vayne, doubtless befuddled by alcohol, refused to allow Mr. Kroll to take away the necklace. Physi-

cally he was the more powerful man and, moreover, Mr. Kroll would recognize the dangers of noise. They compromised. The necklace was restored
to the statuette which Mr. Vayne, since he could only have watched Mr.
Kroll from across the room, probably did not know how to open. Mr. Kroll
then withdrew from the field, leaving his brother-in-law in temporary possession of the trophy. What Mr. Vayne did then we already know. To steal
the statuette was a blunder, a stupid mistake of which Mr. Kroll could not
conceivably have been guilty. It would have been vastly safer and entirely
adequate merely to have removed the treasure. But the late Eugene Vayne
was not a clear thinker.

Shortly after discovery of the theft Mrs. Vayne invited me to undertake
the unpleasant task of spying upon Mr. O'Connor. I accepted—but not to
prove this fine young man's guilt. I suspected Mrs. Vayne's sincerity, fear-
ing that she had a secret motive for wishing him harm and that he was to
be—"framed" is the proper term, I believe. Dear, dear me! I was never
more mistaken. I apologize for intruding personal matters of little consequence. It is only material that from the beginning Mr. O'Connor's and my
roles of simple guests were mistrusted by Mr. Kroll.

He is shrewd enough to have drawn the true conclusion why we were
allotted the adjacent rooms in the guest house. It is understandable why he
should fear that my thoughts might possibly wander away from Mr.
O'Connor and why he should take some little risk to fix them more solidly
there. I enclose the threatening note written upon Mr. O'Connor's portable
typewriter. Should there be latent fingerprints on it other than my own they
will be of the utmost importance. For it was while clandestinely entering
Mr. O'Connor's room for the unworthy purpose of increasing my suspicions of him that Mr. Kroll discovered the other's revolver. And thus the
means of killing lay readily to his hand.

May I now discuss Madame Wu's part in the complicated imbroglio? ...

(Information already known to the reader has been purposely omitted.
C.B.C.)

It is, I think, significant that of all the people involved only the Krolls
appear to have been previously acquainted with her. I suggest a possible
line of inquiry. Might not Jasper Kroll have augmented his income with
commissions for referring friends to the deceased seer? Can not her success with such clients be attributed to confidential reports which he was
able to furnish her? I do not know, but it would be interesting to find out.
Unless we concede her alleged powers of psychic perception to be genuine
some such background of relationship is necessary to account for the celer-
ity with which she discovered his complicity in the theft.

How, you may ask, am I so certain that she did discover it? For two
reasons; namely, Mr. Kroll was previously known to her, and she specified
that he should be the second person to see her privately on that eventful
forenoon. I was the first and, I might say, the only other person to be so
honored by such specific request. All of the others she was content to take
in any order they chose to come to her—patently she had less interest in

them. (I do not believe she had any particular interest in me either, but it would have been too obvious to have asked for Mr. Kroll first.) Though we float on the waters of doubt concerning what actually was said at their interview it is not impossible to speculate. I submit the following, admittedly sketchy suggestion:

Mr. Kroll was taxed with the crime. He denied it. Madame Wu, whose perceptions were phenomenally quick, recognized the lie immediately. She tried to coax him into taking her into partnership, offering, perhaps, to find a purchaser for the necklace. (Her true object, to secure it for Dr. Liao, she would naturally not mention.) Cajolery failed without doubt. Saddled already with one unwanted partner, Mr. Kroll could scarcely be anxious for another. Madame Wu then changed tactics. I am convinced that she threatened to make occult revelations to Mrs. Kroll.

Please allow me to explain before condemning this as too absurd. Remember that Mrs. Kroll believed implicitly in the powers of her psychic counselor. Any charge, true or false, even a charge against her husband, was likely to be accepted if it came from this pythoness. Since his Lydia was still necessary as a source of income Mr. Kroll would not dare to take the risk. He would be forced to confess that the statuette containing the necklace had been stolen and hidden by Mr. Vayne. After agreeing to work together to secure it they made an appointment to meet again that evening.

Mr. Vayne was doubtless much easier for Madame Wu to deal with. He would be as putty in the Chinese girl's dexterous hands. Let us conjecture that she told him it was necessary to have a safe person to handle the sale of the necklace—he could scarcely question the validity of such an argument. No matter what she said, however, we knew that he did promise to bring the statuette to her apartment that evening. I think that he left the tea pavilion feeling that the money for his share of the necklace was as good as in his hands. This is not pure speculation either. Allow me to quote Mr. Vayne's own words to a close friend. He said over the telephone that same afternoon: "I've cut myself in on a good deal. If it works out I'll have some money and we can tell my whole damn family to go to hell." Under the circumstances these two sentences are vastly illuminating.

We are, however, primarily interested in Mr. Kroll. Consider his position after Madame Wu had vanquished him in their verbal duel. First, his dreams of independent affluence have definitely vanished. What might have been enough for him to live upon in comfort would not be enough when reduced by two-thirds. Second, two persons have damaging holds upon him. As we have seen Madame Wu has already demonstrated what she can do, and the dipsomaniacal Eugene may easily babble the secret the next time he becomes inebriated. Fear and avarice united, urging Mr. Kroll to kill both. Purloining Mr. O'Connor's revolver before luncheon last Thursday, he went to the Chinese lady's apartment that night with intentions of murder definitely in mind.

(Thursday, by the way, was a very good time since it was the day for Madame Wu's maid's afternoon and evening off. Did Mr. Kroll know in advance that Miss Pearl Blossom would be absent? Or had he planned to kill the maid too? Either is possible.)

It is now that both Mr. Kroll and Madame Wu receive a serious setback. Mr. Vayne was prevented from bringing the statuette. Madame Wu immediately telephoned to Mrs. Vayne. (May I inquire if your men have been successful as yet in confirming that call?) I feel certain Mr. Kroll recognized that Madame Wu's ingenious scheme was foredoomed to failure. Faith Vayne is an exceptionally conscientious young woman. It was most unlikely that she would take the Jade Lady from the grounds without her mother-in-law's permission. And the permission could not be secured on that evening since Mrs. Nicholas Vayne was away from home. (Eugene Vayne was able to furnish the latter information.)

Under such conditions why did Mr. Kroll delay his crime so long? Why did he wait until Mrs. Eugene Vayne had arrived in the building before shooting? Alternative theories are possible. One is that Mr. Kroll waited deliberately in order to implicate Mrs. Vayne as she was implicated. I find this a little difficult to accept. Mrs. Vayne had never done any harm to Mr. Kroll. As far as I could tell during my several days as a member of the household they were excellent friends. I think that there exists a simpler, more natural reason. Mr. Kroll procrastinated because of fear.

One cannot murder as nonchalantly as one orders an ice-cream soda. Unless one is a gangster or a soldier (and even then, perhaps) one must work oneself up to a high emotional pitch. Not until Mrs. Vayne was actually in the downstairs vestibule, not until he realized that in one or two minutes she would be at the door and his opportunity wrenched from him forever, did Mr. Kroll become sufficiently desperate to perform his terrible deed.

When he did start, however, he went into action quickly. I trace his movements for you to accord with what is already known about the crime. He turned the knob controlling the volume of the radio, perhaps using his handkerchief to avoid fingerprints. Doubtless this method of concealing the noise of the shots had been in his mind ever since he had entered the apartment. Madame Wu, who had stepped from the intercommunicating telephone to open the door to the outer hall, would turn in surprise at the sudden racket. Mr. Kroll fired and missed, fired a second time with better luck and wheeled to confront Mr. Vayne, who had just risen from the divan and was striding toward him. He fired and Mr. Vayne fell; to make certain, however, the murderer ran forward and put the second shot in Mr. Vayne's brain at close range. Rushing abruptly into the reception room, he performed the same office for Madame Wu. He would not have had time to notice that she had managed to open slightly the door to the outer hall. Darting into the study, Mr. Kroll hurriedly wiped the weapon with his handkerchief and tossed it into the living room near Mr. Vayne's body. He had gone into the study, I believe, closing both its living-room and reception-room doors behind him, before Mr. O'Connor entered the apartment.

Mr. O'Connor, who might perhaps have captured the murderer by prompt action, stood momentarily astounded by the dreadful sight. Anyone else would have done the same. While the radio was being turned off Mr. Kroll seized the appointment book from the study desk and went on into the dining room. Crouching under the dining-room table, he hastily tore out the leaf for that day, thus removing the only evidence of his visit.

Before Mr. O'Connor was able to search the apartment Mr. Kroll had had time to run through the pantry into the kitchen and open the fire-escape window. Before Mr. O'Connor found the fire escape Mr. Kroll had descended to the yard below where he could not be observed in the darkness. Emerging through the gate on the north, he raced down the walk between the two buildings to his car. All of this is fairly easy to reconstruct, given a floor plan of the apartment and knowing what we do of Mr. O'Connor's and Mrs. Vayne's movements, but now we come to one of the most puzzling developments in the history of this terrible affair.

We know from Mrs. Vayne's testimony that the murders must take place within a few seconds of eight o'clock. We also know from Dr. Liao's statement that Mr. Kroll was dining with him at the same hour. The distance between Madame Wu's apartment and Dr. Liao's hotel is sufficient to necessitate a traveling time of from twenty minutes to half an hour. Are we, then, to be compelled to accept Mr. Kroll's alibi and abandon our case against him? I think not.

Dr. Liao's sincerity is not open to question, but how does Dr. Liao know? Merely because Mr. Kroll came a few minutes in advance of the Chinese dinner, which had been ordered for eight o'clock. It does not follow from this, however, that either Mr. Kroll or the dinner arrived at the scheduled time.

Punctuality is not a Chinese virtue, and the restaurant which Dr. Liao patronizes is a characteristic offender in this regard. I can testify to this from personal experience. On Saturday afternoon when I called to confer with Dr. Liao he hospitably ordered tea. It was necessary for him to telephone twice before it finally reached us. The dinner could easily have been even later than Mr. Kroll.

I hear a protest from you. The waiter, the cook and the restaurant proprietor swore in unison that Dr. Liao's dinner was delivered to him at eight by their electric clock. True. They did so swear. Three men, you reason, cannot be either wrong or lying. But chance played directly into Mr. Kroll's hands in a most remarkable way.

It would be unkind and untrue to say that the Chinese are habitual falsifiers. They are not. Speaking generally, however, it is safe to say that they do have a more flexible conception of the truth than we of the Occident. To a Chinese a lie is no lie when it is told for the purpose of preserving face.

The cook could not admit that he had been half an hour or so late in preparing the dinner of a distinguished gentleman from Peking without grievous loss of face. The waiter who served the distinguished gentleman and his guest could not admit that the dinner was late without causing the cook to lose face—a barbarism. The proprietor, likewise, could not make the admission without loss of face to his restaurant—most deplorable. Thus they unanimously insisted the dinner had arrived on the hour at which it had been ordered. And thus Mr. Kroll, through circumstances which he could not possibly have foreseen, was presented with a superficially perfect alibi. He does not deserve such good fortune.

We may now skip to the early hours of Friday morning. Mr. Kroll, learning, no doubt, from the man he murdered that the jade statuette had been carried to the living pavilion, realized it would shortly be restored to the lockers. Either he must make a bold attempt to secure its treasure during the hours of darkness or lose the fruits of his horrible crime. Again the unsuspecting Mrs. Kroll was drugged with a tablet. As her scoundrelly husband started to leave their pavilion he passed by the basket of the little dog, who raised his head with a growl.

The animal could not have been greatly excited by the familiar footsteps. Goblin, I believe, was merely registering a protest against the unconventional departure. Mr. Kroll might safely have ignored the slight noise. Doubtless he had ignored it when he had left the pavilion in the same manner on the preceding Monday night. But we must bear in mind his mental condition has altered greatly since then. He is now in a state of extreme nervous tension—the only possible state he could be under the circumstances. Jumpy and on edge, he responds almost instinctively to the stimulus of danger.

He stoops toward the basket, speaking soothing words while his hands encircle the Peke's hairy throat. His fingers tighten upon the canine windpipe, choking first the breath, then the life, from his helpless victim. Mr. Kroll's third murder! Carrying the tiny corpse outside, he quietly unbars the gate in the stairway court and throws the dead dog in the bushes.

Now he goes to the living pavilion to reap the reward of his perils. First to locate the statuette. He cannot see it. Is he going to experience another failure? No, it is here on the floor behind the screen. He breathes freely again. Thrusting a pin into the hole in the hare's eye, he releases the concealed spring for the third time. The jade plug pops forth—it is not necessary to detail the mechanics of the ingenious contrivance—and Mr. Kroll reaches into the opening for the second time to take out the hundred-thousand-dollar contents. Is it possible that in spite of all his efforts some other person has beaten him to it? Can he have lost? No, he has won. He holds in his shaking hands the world's most costly imperial green jewel-jade. Victory!

You have the right to voice objection, reminding me that Mrs. Kroll (who could not have been deeply under the drug's influence) was aroused by the barking dog. True. And Mrs. Kroll did not wake up until *after* her husband had returned to his bed. Also true. To these arguments I can only counter with questions. Are you sure it was *Goblin* who was barking then? Was Mrs. Kroll, stirring confusedly from her drugged slumber, able to distinguish clearly whether the alarm came from outside or *inside* the pavilion? Did any of us hear a *dog* at all?

We heard something which closely resembled a dog's yelps, to be sure, but the human throat is capable of almost unbelievable feats—witness Charlie McCarthy. I was once acquainted with a man able to imitate the howl of a timber wolf with startling fidelity. May not Mr. Kroll possess a similar accomplishment? We could not persuade him to admit it, I own.

A few words more. For reasons previously outlined Mr. Kroll, instead of carrying the necklace back to his own pavilion, concealed it under the concave base of a large bronze floor lamp. While we were all beating the grounds in search of a nonexistent prowler he became apprehensive concerning the security of this temporary hiding place. Tiptoeing up the steps in the darkness, he reentered the compound, unseen, to discover with horror that I was in the very act of lifting the lamp. Immediately he opened fire with the first object on which he could lay his hand; to wit, the jade buffalo. I do not know where he put the necklace just after he laid me *hors de combat*, but the question is unimportant. We do know that he seized the earliest opportunity to plant his booty outside the grounds.

I must pause at this point to pay tribute to his choice of burial ground. Mr. Kroll could hardly have selected a more superb site. Few people in this world are either born with or acquire a love of digging in a cactus bed. The necklace would have been safe there forever had not Mr. Kroll himself been tricked into divulging its whereabouts. That, however, has been amply covered.

This concludes my history of Ch'ien Lung's chain—and the chain of crimes which wove itself about the inanimate jade. In my reconstruction I have not overlooked any of the known facts. I confess having liberally supplemented them with imagination; that is a historian's special prerogative, is it not?

I own that I may have made minor errors in interpretation. The case is the oddest, most complicated and most baffling with which I have ever been associated. But I consider, and I am sure you will also, that the major premise of Mr. Kroll's guilt has been fully established.

In closing let me add my hope that when you have presented this latest development to the district attorney he will see the simple justice of nol-prossing the actions against Faith Vayne and Kerry O'Connor. These likeable and wholly innocent young people have already endured far too much undeserved suffering. I pray with all my heart that they may be spared the ordeal of undergoing criminal trial.

Your obedient servant,
(*Signed*) *Theocritus L. Westborough*

If you enjoyed *Green Shiver* be sure to ask your bookseller for *Murder Gone Minoan* (0-915230-60-7, $14.95). For more information on The Rue Morgue Press please turn the page.

About the Rue Morgue Press

"Rue Morgue Press is the old-mystery lover's best friend, reprinting high quality books from the 1930s and '40s."
—*Ellery Queen's Mystery Magazine*

Since 1997, the Rue Morgue Press has reprinted scores of traditional mysteries, the kind of books that were the hallmark of the Golden Age of detective fiction. Authors reprinted or to be reprinted by the Rue Morgue include Dorothy Bowers, Pamela Branch, Joanna Cannan, Glyn Carr, Torrey Chanslor, Clyde B. Clason, Joan Coggin, Manning Coles, Lucy Cores, Frances Crane, Norbert Davis, Elizabeth Dean, Constance & Gwenyth Little, Marlys Millhiser, James Norman, Stuart Palmer, Craig Rice, Kelley Roos, Charlotte Murray Russell, Maureen Sarsfield, Margaret Scherf and Juanita Sheridan.

To suggest titles or to receive a catalog of Rue Morgue Press books write P.O. Box 4119, Boulder, CO 80306, telephone 800-699-6214, or check out our website, www.ruemorguepress.com, which lists complete descriptions of all of our titles, along with lengthy biographies of our writers.